序　言

　　閱讀測驗是學測、指考，以及學校月期考都會考的題型，而且配分通常都很重，少則十分，多則三、四十分都有可能。這麼重要的題型，要參加考試的同學，一定要一而再，再而三地練習。

閱讀測驗拿滿分，其實很容易

　　閱讀測驗和詞彙題不一樣，不需要看懂每一個字，只要能大略抓住文章的重點，就能回答問題。在做閱讀測驗時，要特別注意每一段的第一句和最後一句，然後要邊讀文章，邊把重要的句子畫起來。此外，看到時間、地點、數字和人名時，也要特別注意，因為這些都是常考的重點。

　　看文章時，一定要有耐心。如果碰到看不懂的字，也不用緊張，先做個記號，然後繼續讀下去，後面一定有相關的解釋或同義字。最後，做題目時，如果有不確定的選項，一定要回頭查文章，不要憑印象亂猜，因為閱讀測驗的答案，其實都在文章裡。只要你能把握上述的重點，閱讀能力一定會大為提昇。

　　「高三英文閱讀測驗」集結了各校月期考試題的精華，全書共有四十篇閱讀測驗，每一篇都有詳盡的註釋及翻譯，而且針對同學最常答錯的題目，也有特別的分析，書本並附有「本書答題錯誤率分析表」。這麼重要的資料，你一定要好好利用，每一篇都確實地作答和檢討。熟讀本書，閱讀測驗必將成為你搶分的最佳利器！

　　本書編校製作過程嚴謹，但仍恐有疏失之處，尚祈各界先進不吝指正。

編者　謹識

TEST 1

Read the following passage and choose the best answer for each question.

Colonies of fire ants consist of eggs, brood, polymorphic workers, winged males, winged females and one or more reproductive queens. The queen lives up to seven years and produces an average of 1,600 eggs per day throughout her life.

Fire ants are most notorious for their stinging behavior. A single fire ant can sting repeatedly. Initially, the stings result in a localized intense burning sensation (hence the name "fire" ant). This is followed within 24-48 hours by the formation of a white pustule at the sting site. A minority of those stung by fire ants are hypersensitive to the venom and can react quite strongly, suffering chest pains, nausea, dizziness, shock or, in rare cases, lapsing into coma. Some deaths have been documented as having been caused by fire ant stings but these cases are extremely rare. 【松山高中】

1. According to the passage, which statement is untrue?
   (A) There is always only one queen in an ant colony.
   (B) The queen may live for seven years.
   (C) A single fire ant can keep on stinging.
   (D) The sting of the fire ant may cause the death of some people.

2. The reason why the ants are called fire ants is that
   _____.

   (A) they enjoy dwelling near fire
   (B) they look like fire from a distance
   (C) they are the main cause of forest fires
   (D) their sting burns like fire

3. What is a white pustule?
   (A) It is a kind of poison.
   (B) It is where the fire ant dwells.
   (C) It is the wound caused by the fire ant.
   (D) It is the venom of the fire ant.

4. Which of the following is not mentioned as a possible
   result of a fire ant bite?
   (A) A burning sensation.
   (B) Scarring.
   (C) Nausea.
   (D) Death.

5. What is a polymorphic worker?
   (A) It is a fire ant medicine.
   (B) It is a person who studies fire ants.
   (C) It is one of several types of fire ants.
   (D) It is a symptom.

TEST 1 詳解

Colonies of fire ants consist of eggs, brood, polymorphic workers, winged males, winged females and one or more reproductive queens.

整群的火蟻是由卵、一窩小螞蟻、多種形態的工蟻、有翅膀的雄蟻、有翅膀的雌蟻，還有一隻或多隻負責生殖的蟻后所組成的。

colony ('kɑlənɪ) *n.* 聚落；群體　　*fire ant* 火蟻
consist of 由～所組成　　brood (brud) *n.* (動物的) 一窩
polymorphic (ˌpɑlɪ'mɔrfɪk) *adj.* 多種形態的；多種功能的
　 (= *polymorphous*)
worker ('wɜkɚ) *n.* 工蟻　　winged (wɪŋd) *adj.* 有翅膀的
male (mel) *n.* 雄性動物　　female ('fimel) *n.* 雌性動物
reproductive (ˌriprə'dʌktɪv) *adj.* 生殖的

The queen lives up to seven years and produces an average of 1,600 eggs per day throughout her life.

蟻后可以活到七年，而且她終其一生，平均每天可以產下一千六百個卵。

up to 多達　　produce (prə'djus) *v.* 生產
average ('ævərɪdʒ) *n.* 平均　　per (pɜ) *prep.* 每…
throughout (θru'aʊt) *prep.* 在整個…期間

Fire ants are most notorious for their stinging behavior. A single fire ant can sting repeatedly.

火蟻最惡名昭彰的是，牠們會螫人的行為。單單一隻火蟻就可以重覆地螫人。

notorious (no'torɪəs) *adj.* 惡名昭彰的
stinging ('stɪŋɪŋ) *adj.* 會螫人的　　single ('sɪŋgl) *adj.* 單一的
sting (stɪŋ) *v.* 刺；螫　　*n.* 刺傷；螫傷
repeatedly (rɪ'pitɪdlɪ) *adv.* 重覆地

Initially, the stings result in a localized intense burning sensation (hence the name "fire" ant). This is followed within 24-48 hours by the formation of a white pustule at the sting site.

一開始，被火蟻螫到會導致局部強烈的灼熱感（所以才有「火」蟻這個名稱）。接下來的二十四到四十八小時，被螫到的地方會形成一個白色的膿包。

initially (ɪ'nɪʃəlɪ) adv. 起初　　result in 導致
localized ('lokḷ,aɪzd) adj. 局部化　　intense (ɪn'tɛns) adj. 強烈的
burning ('bɜnɪŋ) adj. 灼熱的　　sensation (sɛn'seʃən) n. 感覺
hence (hɛns) adv. 因此；所以
hence the name… 因此有…之名（= hence comes the name… ）
formation (fɔr'meʃən) n. 形成
pustule ('pʌstʃul) n. 膿包　　site (saɪt) n. 部位；位置

A minority of those stung by fire ants are hypersensitive to the venom and can react quite strongly, suffering chest pains, nausea, dizziness, shock or, in rare cases, lapsing into coma.

那些被火蟻螫到的人當中，有少數人會對毒液過敏，並且產生強烈的反應，他們會經歷胸部疼痛、噁心、暈眩、休克，或是有些極少數案例會陷入昏迷狀態。

minority (maɪ'nɔrətɪ) n. 少數
hypersensitive (,haɪpə'sɛnsətɪv) adj. 過於敏感的
venom ('vɛnəm) n. 毒液　　react (rɪ'ækt) v. 反應
suffer ('sʌfə) v. 遭受；經歷　　chest (tʃɛst) n. 胸腔
nausea ('nɔʒə) n. 反胃；噁心　　dizziness ('dɪzɪnɪs) n. 暈眩
shock (ʃɑk) n. 休克　　rare (rɛr) adj. 極少的；罕見的
case (kes) n. 情況；病例　　lapse (læps) v. 陷入
coma ('komə) n. 昏迷（狀態）

Some deaths have been documented as having been caused by fire ant stings but these cases are extremely rare.

有些因為被火蟻螫而死亡的情況已經被記錄下來，但是這種病例非常少。

document ('dɑkjə,mɛnt) v. 詳細記錄
extremely (ɪk'strimlɪ) adv. 非常

1. (**A**) 根據本文，哪一個敘述為非？

    (A) 一群螞蟻中，一定只有一隻蟻后。

    (B) 蟻后可以活七年。

    (C) 一隻火蟻可以一直螫人。

    (D) 被火蟻螫到可能會導致某些人死亡。

    * *keep on* + *V-ing* 一直~   cause〔kɔz〕*v.* 導致

2. (**D**) 這些螞蟻被稱為火蟻的原因是 _____。

    (A) 牠們喜歡住在火旁邊

    (B) 牠們遠看像火一樣

    (C) 牠們是導致森林火災的主因

    (D) 被牠們螫到，就像被火燒一樣

    * dwell〔dwɛl〕*v.* 居住   distance〔'dɪstəns〕*n.* 遠處

    main cause 主因   forest〔'fɔrɪst〕*adj.* 森林的

3. (**C**) 什麼是白色膿包？

    (A) 它是一種毒藥。   (B) 它是火蟻居住的地方。

    (C) 它是火蟻造成的傷口。   (D) 它是火蟻的毒液。

    * poison〔'pɔɪzn̩〕*n.* 毒藥   wound〔wund〕*n.* 傷口

4. (**B**) 本文沒有提到下列何者是被火蟻螫傷可能會有的結果？

    (A) 灼熱的感覺。   (B) 留下疤痕。

    (C) 噁心。   (D) 死亡。

    * bite〔baɪt〕*v.* 咬；螫   scar〔skɑr〕*v.* 留下疤痕

5. (**C**) 什麼是多種功能的工蟻？

    (A) 是一種治療火蟻螫傷的藥。   (B) 是一個研究火蟻的人。

    (C) 是幾種火蟻中的一種。   (D) 是一種症狀。

    * symptom〔'sɪmptəm〕*n.* 症狀

TEST 2

Read the following passage and choose the best answer for each question.

Twenty-five percent of Taipei City's franchised soft drinks are said to have failed tests on sanitation and nutritional value, according to the latest report issued by the Consumer's Foundation (CF). Of the 142 drink samples collected from the tested stands, 12 were found to contain bacteria counts that exceed legal limits. To help consumers protect themselves, CF officials suggested shoppers conduct their own visual inspections of the stands, making sure that the drinks appear to be clean, at least on the outside. In addition, consumers are advised to make sure the plastic seals of the beverages they purchase from the stands are intact. To lower the chance of food poisoning, a drink should be drunk immediately and should never be stored in the refrigerator overnight, CF officials said. 【華江高中】

1. _____ of the franchised soft drinks did not pass the tests on sanitation and nutritional value.
   (A) Half   (B) One-third
   (C) A quarter   (D) Two-thirds

2. What's the best title for this passage?

(A) What the Consumer's Foundation Does

(B) Food Poisoning

(C) Soft Drink Stands Fail Tests

(D) Thirst Quenchers

3. Of what did the Consumer's Foundation measure legal limits?

(A) Expiration date.

(B) Bacteria counts.

(C) Visual inspection.

(D) Cleanliness.

4. What did the Consumer's Foundation NOT suggest?

(A) Make sure the outside of the items is clean.

(B) Make sure plastic seals are intact.

(C) Make sure the store itself is clean.

(D) Drink immediately after purchase.

5. Which of the following is CORRECT?

(A) Drinks should be drunk immediately or stored in bags overnight.

(B) Drinks should be kept outside for a while.

(C) Drinks should be drunk immediately.

(D) Consumers should drink water only.

TEST 2 詳解

 Twenty-five percent of Taipei City's franchised soft drinks are said to have failed tests on sanitation and nutritional value, according to the latest report issued by the Consumer's Foundation (CF).

 根據消費者基金會所公布的最新報告指出，台北市連鎖加盟店的清涼飲料中，有百分之二十五未通過衛生與營養值的檢測。

  percent (pɚ'sɛnt) *n.* 百分比
  franchise ('fræntʃaɪz) *v.* 授權加盟
  soft drink ('sɔft'drɪŋk) *n.* 不含酒精飲料；清涼飲料
  be said to 據說 fail (fel) *v.* ～不及格
  test (tɛst) *n.* 檢測 sanitation (ˌsænə'teʃən) *n.* 衛生
  nutritional (nju'trɪʃənl) *adj.* 營養的 value ('vælju) *n.* 價值
  according to 根據 latest ('letɪst) *adj.* 最新的
  issue ('ɪʃju) *v.* 發行；公布 consumer (kən'sjumɚ) *n.* 消費者
  foundation (faʊn'deʃən) *n.* 基金會

 Of the 142 drink samples collected from the tested stands, 12 were found to contain bacteria counts that exceed legal limits.

 從接受檢驗的攤位所收集的一百四十二個飲料樣本中，發現有十二個含菌量超過法定限制。

  sample ('sæmpl) *n.* 樣本 collect (kə'lɛkt) *v.* 收集
  tested ('tɛstɪd) *adj.* 接受檢驗的 stand (stænd) *n.* 攤位
  contain (kən'ten) *v.* 含有
  bacteria (bæk'tɪrɪə) *n. pl.* 細菌 count (kaʊnt) *n.* 總數
  exceed (ɪk'sid) *v.* 超過 legal ('ligl) *adj.* 法定的
  limits ('lɪmɪts) *n. pl.* 限制

To help consumers protect themselves, CF officials suggested shoppers conduct their own visual inspections of the stands, making sure that the drinks appear to be clean, at least on the outside.

為了幫助消費者保護自己,消基會的人員建議,購買者要自行對攤販進行目視檢測,以確定至少飲料的外觀看起來是乾淨的。

official (ə'fɪʃəl) *n.* 職員;行政人員　　suggest (sə'dʒɛst) *v.* 建議
shopper ('ʃɑpɚ) *n.* 購買者　　conduct (kən'dʌkt) *v.* 進行
visual ('vɪʒuəl) *adj.* 視覺的;只靠肉眼觀察的
inspection (ɪn'spɛkʃən) *n.* 檢查
make sure 確定　　*at least* 至少
appear (ə'pɪr) *v.* 看來好像　　outside ('aut'saɪd) *n.* 外部

In addition, consumers are advised to make sure the plastic seals of the beverages they purchase from the stands are intact.

此外,還建議消費者,要確定從攤販買來的飲料,其塑膠封套是完好無缺的。

in addition 此外　　advise (əd'vaɪz) *v.* 建議
plastic ('plæstɪk) *adj.* 塑膠的　　seal (sil) *n.* 封套
beverage ('bɛvərɪdʒ) *n.* 飲料　　purchase ('pɜtʃəs) *v.* 購買
intact (ɪn'tækt) *adj.* 完整無缺的

To lower the chance of food poisoning, a drink should be drunk immediately and should never be stored in the refrigerator overnight, CF officials said.

消基會的人員說,要降低食物中毒的機率,就應該要馬上把飲料喝完,而且絕對不要放在冰箱裡放過夜。

lower ('loɚ) *v.* 降低　　poisoning ('pɔɪznɪŋ) *n.* 中毒
immediately (ɪ'midɪɪtlɪ) *adv.* 馬上　　store (stor) *v.* 儲藏
refrigerator (rɪ'frɪdʒəˌretɚ) *n.* 冰箱
overnight ('ovɚ'naɪt) *adv.* 過夜

1. (**C**) 有 ＿＿＿＿＿ 的連鎖清涼飲料店，沒通過衛生與營養值檢測。

    (A) 一半   (B) 三分之一

    (C) 四分之一   (D) 三分之二

    * quarter ('kwɔrtɚ) *n.* 四分之一

2. (**C**) 最適合本文的標題爲何？

    (A) 消基會做的事   (B) 食物中毒

    (C) 清涼飲料攤販未通過檢測   (D) 解渴飲料

    * title ('taɪtḷ) *n.* 標題   passage ('pæsɪdʒ) *n.* 文章

    thirst (θɝst) *n.* 口渴   quencher ('kwɛntʃɚ) *n.* 飲料

3. (**B**) 消基會測量了什麼東西的法定限制？

    (A) 到期日。   (B) 含菌量。

    (C) 目視檢測。   (D) 乾淨程度。

    * measure ('mɛʒɚ) *v.* 測量

    expiration (,ɛkspə'reʃən) *n.* 到期

    cleanliness ('klɛnlɪnɪs) *n.* 乾淨；清潔

4. (**C**) 消基會不建議做下列哪一件事？

    (A) 確定商品的外觀是乾淨的。

    (B) 確定塑膠封套完好無缺。

    (C) 確定商店本身是乾淨的。

    (D) 購買之後馬上喝掉。

    * item ('aɪtəm) *n.* 物品；項目

5. (**C**) 下列何者正確？

    (A) 飲料應該馬上喝，或是放在袋子裡放過夜。

    (B) 飲料應該放在外面一會兒。

    (C) 飲料應該馬上喝完。

    (D) 消費者應該只喝水。

TEST 3

Read the following passage and choose the best answer for each question.

Stopping by Woods on a Snowy Evening

Whose woods these are I think I know.
His house is in the village though;
He will not see me stopping here
To watch his woods fill up with snow.

My little horse must think it <u>queer</u>
To stop without a farmhouse near
Between the woods and frozen lake
The darkest evening of the year.

He gives his harness bells a shake
To ask if there is some mistake.
The only other sound's the sweep
Of easy wind and downy flake.

The woods are lovely, dark and deep,
But I have promises to keep,
And miles to go before I sleep,
And miles to go before I sleep.

【復興高中】

1. The setting of the poem is _____.

   (A) spring   (B) summer

   (C) autumn   (D) winter

2. In this poem, which of the following words was used to rhyme with "know"?

   (A) sleep   (B) though

   (C) here   (D) shake

3. The poem is about a traveler who _____.

   (A) is afraid of the universal struggle between freedom and duty

   (B) wants to take a rest but chooses to fulfill his responsibilities

   (C) decides to stop for a break and enjoy a pleasant winter scene

   (D) is unable to make a decision

4. What does the word "queer" mean in the poem?

   (A) polished   (B) serene

   (C) equal   (D) strange

5. Which of the following is most likely true about the poet?

   (A) He enjoyed the company of people.

   (B) He was a very lonely person.

   (C) He was a great farmer.

   (D) He liked to be close to Nature.

TEST 3 詳解

Stopping by Woods on a Snowy Evening

Whose woods these are I think I know.
His house is in the village though;
He will not see me stopping here
To watch his woods fill up with snow.

駐馬雪夜林邊

我想我知道這是誰的森林。
雖然他的房子是在村裡；
他不會看到我停在這裡
注視他落滿雪花的森林。

woods〔wʊdz〕*n. pl.* 森林　　snowy〔'snoɪ〕*adj.* 下雪的
village〔'vɪlɪdʒ〕*n.* 村莊　　*fill up with* 充滿了～

My little horse must think it <u>queer</u>
To stop without a farmhouse near
Between the woods and frozen lake
The darkest evening of the year.

我的小馬一定覺得奇怪
停在附近沒有農舍的地方
就在森林與冰凍的湖泊間
在一年中最漆黑的夜晚。

queer〔kwɪr〕*adj.* 奇怪的　　farmhouse〔'fɑrm,haʊs〕*n.* 農舍
frozen〔'frozn̩〕*adj.* 結冰的

He gives his harness bells a shake
To ask if there is some mistake.
The only other sound's the sweep
Of easy wind and downy flake.

牠搖了一下馬具上的鈴鐺，
問是不是弄錯了。
唯一的回響是輕風
與柔軟雪花的吹拂。

harness ('hɑrnɪs) *n.* 馬具　　bell (bɛl) *n.* 鈴鐺
shake (ʃek) *n.* 搖動　　some (sʌm) *adj.* 某個
mistake (mə'stek) *n.* 錯誤
sound (saʊnd) *n.* 回響；聲音
sweep (swip) *n.* 吹拂　　easy ('izɪ) *adj.* 輕柔的
downy ('daʊnɪ) *adj.* 柔軟的　　flake (flek) *n.* 雪花

The woods are lovely, dark and deep,
But I have promises to keep,
And miles to go before I sleep,
And miles to go before I sleep.

樹林迷人、幽暗而深沉，
但是我有承諾要履行，
就寢之前還要走許多哩路，
就寢之前還要走許多哩路。

lovely ('lʌvlɪ) *adj.* 迷人的　　deep (dip) *adj.* 深沉的
promise ('prɑmɪs) *n.* 承諾　　keep (kip) *v.* 履行

1. (**D**) 這首詩的背景是在 ＿＿＿＿＿＿ 。

(A) 春天　　　　(B) 夏天　　　　(C) 秋天　　　　(D) <u>冬天</u>

　　* setting (ˈsɛtɪŋ) *n.* 背景　　poem (ˈpo‧ɪm) *n.* 詩

2. (**B**) 在這首詩中，下列哪一個字與 "know" 押韻？

(A) 睡覺　　　　(B) <u>雖然</u>　　　　(C) 這裡　　　　(D) 搖動

　　* rhyme (raɪm) *v.* 押韻

3. (**B**) 這首詩是講一個旅人他 ＿＿＿＿＿＿ 。

(A) 害怕在自由與義務之間，普遍存在的掙扎

(B) <u>想要休息一下，但還是選擇履行義務</u>

(C) 決定停下來休息一下，好欣賞令人愉悅的冬景

(D) 無法做決定

　　* universal (ˌjunəˈvɝsḷ) *adj.* 普遍的　　struggle (ˈstrʌgḷ) *n.* 掙扎
　　freedom (ˈfridəm) *n.* 自由　　duty (ˈdjutɪ) *n.* 義務
　　take a rest 休息一下　　fulfill (fʊlˈfɪl) *v.* 履行
　　responsibility (rɪˌspɑnsəˈbɪlətɪ) *n.* 責任　　break (brek) *n.* 休息
　　pleasant (ˈplɛznt) *adj.* 愉悅的；令人愉快的
　　scene (sin) *n.* 景色　　***be unable to V.*** 無法~

4. (**D**) 在這首詩中，"queer" 的意思為何？

(A) polished (ˈpɑlɪʃt) *adj.* 有光澤的

(B) serene (səˈrin) *adj.* 寧靜的

(C) equal (ˈikwəl) *adj.* 相等的

(D) <u>奇怪的</u>

5. (**D**) 下列哪一個關於這位詩人的敘述，最有可能是事實？

(A) 他喜歡有人作伴。　　　　(B) 他是個非常寂寞的人。

(C) 他是個很了不起的農夫。　　(D) <u>他喜歡接近大自然。</u>

　　* likely (ˈlaɪklɪ) *adv.* 有可能　　poet (ˈpo‧ɪt) *n.* 詩人
　　company (ˈkʌmpənɪ) *n.* 陪伴　　lonely (ˈlonlɪ) *adj.* 寂寞的
　　be close to 接近　　nature (ˈnetʃə) *n.* 大自然

TEST 4

Read the following passage and choose the best answer for each question.

George Bernard Shaw and Winston Churchill apparently disliked each other. It is said the playwright once sent Churchill two tickets for the opening night of one of his plays, together with a card, which said, "Bring a friend (if you have one)."

Churchill, however, managed to get the better of this exchange. He returned the tickets, enclosing a note, which said, "I shall be busy that evening. Please send me two tickets for the second night (if there is one)."

There is no record of whether Shaw ever sent the tickets. 【永春高中】

1. What was Shaw trying to say to Churchill on his card?
   (A) Churchill should not bring too many people.
   (B) Churchill should not go to the play alone.
   (C) Churchill did not have any friends.
   (D) Churchill might have to waste the two tickets.

2. Why didn't Churchill want the tickets for the first night?

   (A) He couldn't find a friend to go with him the first night.

   (B) He didn't want to take Shaw's insult.

   (C) He was busy on the first night of the show.

   (D) The theater would not be as crowded the second night.

3. Why did Shaw send Churchill the tickets?

   (A) He wanted to increase the size of his audience.

   (B) It was his turn to treat Churchill.

   (C) He wanted to insult Churchill.

   (D) He wanted to encourage Churchill to make more friends.

4. What did Churchill mean by his reply?

   (A) He would rather attend the second performance.

   (B) He wanted to know how long the play would be run.

   (C) He hoped Shaw's play would be successful.

   (D) He believed the show might be a failure.

5. How would you describe the tone of Shaw's and Churchill's notes?

   (A) Sarcastic.   (B) Complimentary.

   (C) Informational.   (D) Angry.

TEST 4 詳解

George Bernard Shaw and Winston Churchill apparently disliked each other.

喬治・蕭伯納和溫斯頓・邱吉爾顯然不喜歡對方。

> ***George Bernard Shaw*** 蕭伯納（英國劇作家，1856-1950）
> ***Winston Churchill*** 邱吉爾（英國首相，1874-1965）
> apparently〔ə'pɛrəntlɪ〕*adv.* 顯然地
> dislike〔dɪs'laɪk〕*v.* 不喜歡

It is said the playwright once sent Churchill two tickets for the opening night of one of his plays, together with a card, which said, "Bring a friend (if you have one)."

聽說這位劇作家曾經寄給邱吉爾兩張票，請他來看一部戲劇作品的首映，而且還附上一張卡片，上面寫著：「帶位朋友來（如果你有的話）。」

> ***It is said that~*** 聽說~
> playwright〔'ple,raɪt〕*n.* 劇作家
> ***opening night*** （電影、戲劇等的）首映
> play〔ple〕*n.* 戲劇　　***together with*** 連同

Churchill, however, managed to get the better of this exchange. He returned the tickets, enclosing a note, which said, "I shall be busy that evening. Please send me two tickets for the second night (if there is one)."

然而，邱吉爾卻設法要在這次的交手中佔上風。他把票退了回去，還附上一張紙條，上面寫著：「我那天晚上將會很忙。請寄給我兩張第二天晚上的票（如果有第二場的話。）」

manage to V. 設法～

get the better of 佔…的上風；勝過；擊敗

exchange (ɪks'tʃendʒ) *n.* (言詞激烈、辛辣或詼諧的) 交談；交流

return (rɪ'tɜn) *v.* 退回；歸還

enclose (ɪn'kloz) *v.* (隨函) 附寄

note (not) *n.* 紙條；短箋

There is no record of whether Shaw ever sent the tickets.

至於蕭伯納是否曾經把票寄出去，則無記錄可循。

record ('rɛkəd) *n.* 記載；記錄   ever ('ɛvə) *adv.* 曾經

1. (**C**) 蕭伯納在卡片上試圖要對邱吉爾說什麼？
   (A) 邱吉爾不應該帶太多朋友來。
   (B) 邱吉爾不應該單獨前往看戲。
   (C) 邱吉爾沒有任何朋友。
   (D) 邱吉爾可能必須浪費那兩張票。

   * alone (ə'lon) *adv.* 獨自地

2. (**B**) 邱吉爾為什麼不要第一天晚上的票？
   (A) 他第一天晚上找不到朋友和他一起去。
   (B) 他不想被蕭伯納羞辱。
   (C) 他在演出的第一天晚上很忙。
   (D) 第二天晚上劇院就不會那麼擁擠。

   * take (tek) *v.* 遭受；忍受
     insult ('ɪnsʌlt) *n.* 羞辱   as (æz) *adv.* 一樣地
     crowded ('kraʊdɪd) *adj.* 擁擠的

3. (**C**) 蕭伯納為什麼要把票寄給邱吉爾？

    (A) 他想要增加觀眾人數。

    (B) 輪到他要招待邱吉爾。

    (C) <u>他想要羞辱邱吉爾。</u>

    (D) 他想要鼓勵邱吉爾多交一點朋友。

      * size (saɪz) *n.* (數量) 多少

      audience ('ɔdɪəns) *n.* 觀眾

      it is one's turn 輪到某人

      treat (trit) *v.* 招待；請 (客)   insult (ɪn'sʌlt) *v.* 羞辱

      encourage (ɪn'kɝɪdʒ) *v.* 鼓勵   *make friends* 交朋友

4. (**D**) 邱吉爾的回答是什麼意思？

    (A) 他寧願出席第二場演出。

    (B) 他想知道這齣戲會上演多久。

    (C) 他希望蕭伯納的戲能成功。

    (D) <u>他認為那場演出可能會失敗。</u>

      * reply (rɪ'plaɪ) *n.* 回答   *would rather V.* 寧願～

      attend (ə'tɛnd) *v.* 參加；出席

      performance (pɚ'fɔrməns) *n.* 表演

      run (rʌn) *v.* (戲等) 連演   failure ('feljɚ) *n.* 失敗

5. (**A**) 你會怎麼描述蕭伯納和邱吉爾他們紙條上的語氣？

    (A) *sarcastic* (sɑr'kæstɪk) *adj.* 諷刺的

    (B) complimentary (,kɑmplə'mɛntərɪ) *adj.* 恭維的

    (C) informational (,ɪnfɚ'meʃənḷ) *adj.* 資訊的

    (D) angry ('æŋgrɪ) *adj.* 生氣的

      * describe (dɪ'skraɪb) *v.* 描述

      tone (ton) *n.* 語氣

TEST 5

Read the following passage and choose the best answer for each question.

The energy content of food is measured in calories. The calorie is defined as the heat energy needed to raise the temperature of 1 kilogram of water from 14.5°C to 15.5°C. The calorie used in nutrition is sometimes spelled with a capital "C" to distinguish it from the much smaller energy calorie used in physics and chemistry, but it is more properly called the kilogram calorie, or kilocalorie, because it is precisely 1,000 times the smaller unit, or gram calorie. The energy content of food is stored in the chemical bonds that link its atoms and molecules. 【成淵高中】

1. What is the main subject of the passage?
   (A) A branch of chemistry.
   (B) A type of food.
   (C) A unit of energy.
   (D) An alphabet system.

2. What does the author define in the first two sentences?
   (A) The molecule.   (B) The kilogram.
   (C) The gram calorie.   (D) The kilocalorie.

3. In the last sentence, the word, "its" could best be replaced by _____.

   (A) the energy's
   (B) the food's
   (C) the link's
   (D) the molecule's

4. What does the passage imply about food with a high calorie content?

   (A) It can yield a lot of heat energy.
   (B) It has a high percentage of water.
   (C) It should be stored only in cool places.
   (D) It is hotter than food that has fewer calories.

5. What is the difference between a gram calorie and a kilocalorie?

   (A) One is a unit of energy and one is not.
   (B) One gram calorie equals 1000 kilocalories.
   (C) The former is used when discussing chemistry while the latter is used when talking about nutrition.
   (D) The latter is stored in links between atoms and molecules, while the former is not.

TEST 5 詳解

The energy content of food is measured in calories. The calorie is defined as the heat energy needed to raise the temperature of 1 kilogram of water from 14.5°C to 15.5°C.

食物所含的能量，是用大卡來衡量的。大卡的定義，是讓一公斤的水，溫度從 14.5°C 提高到 15.5°C 所需要的熱量。

energy ('ɛnədʒɪ) *n.* 能量　　content ('kɑntɛnt) *n.* 含量
measure ('mɛʒ&) *v.* 測量；衡量
calorie ('kælərɪ) *n.* 大卡（等於 1000 卡路里）；卡路里
define (dɪ'faɪn) *v.* 下定義
heat (hit) *n.* 熱　　raise (rez) *v.* 提高
temperature ('tɛmprətʃə) *n.* 溫度
kilogram ('kɪlə,græm) *n.* 公斤

The calorie used in nutrition is sometimes spelled with a capital "C" to distinguish it from the much smaller energy calorie used in physics and chemistry, but it is more properly called the kilogram calorie, or kilocalorie, because it is precisely 1,000 times the smaller unit, or gram calorie.

營養學裡所用的大卡，有時候會寫成大寫的 C，這是為了和在物理及化學上，所使用的較小的能量卡路里做個區別，但是稱之為仟卡或大卡會比較適當，因為它正好是比較小的那個單位，也就是小卡的一千倍。

nutrition (nju'trɪʃən) *n.* 營養學
spell (spɛl) *v.* 拼寫　　capital ('kæpətl) *n.* 大寫字母
distinguish (dɪ'stɪŋgwɪʃ) *v.* 加以區別；辨別
physics ('fɪzɪks) *n.* 物理學
chemistry ('kɛmɪstrɪ) *n.* 化學

properly〔'prɑpəlɪ〕*adv.* 適當地　　***kilogram calorie* 仟卡**
kilocalorie〔'kɪlə,kælərɪ〕*n.* 大卡
precisely〔prɪ'saɪslɪ〕*adv.* 恰好；正是
time〔taɪm〕*n.* 倍　　unit〔'junɪt〕*n.* 單位
***gram calorie* 小卡；卡路里**

The energy content of food is stored in the chemical bonds that link its atoms and molecules.

食物所含的能量，被儲存在連結其原子與分子的化學鍵裡。

store〔stor〕*v.* 儲存　　chemical〔'kɛmɪkl̩〕*adj.* 化學的
bond〔bɑnd〕*n.* 鍵　　link〔lɪŋk〕*v.* 連結
atom〔'ætəm〕*n.* 原子　　molecule〔'mɑlə,kjul〕*n.* 分子

1.(**C**) 本文的主題是什麼？

(A) 化學的一個分科。　　(B) 一種食物。
(C) 能量單位。　　(D) 一個字母系統。

　*main〔men〕*adj.* 主要的　subject〔'sʌbdʒɪkt〕*n.* 主題
　branch〔bræntʃ〕*n.* 分科
　alphabet〔'ælfə,bɛt〕*n.* 字母（系統）

2.(**D**) 作者在開頭的前兩句話中，是在定義什麼？

(A) 分子。　　(B) 公斤。
(C) 小卡。　　(D) 仟卡。

　*author〔'ɔθɚ〕*n.* 作者
　【註】　本題有 35% 的同學選 (C)，但根據文章內容，前兩句是在
　　　　定義大卡，也就是仟卡。

3. (**B**) 在最後一句話中，"its" 被替換成下列何者最適當？

    (A) 熱量的   (B) 食物的

    (C) 連結物的   (D) 分子的

    * replace〔rɪ'ples〕*v.* 替換   link〔lɪŋk〕*n.* 連結物

4. (**A**) 本文暗示，含大量卡路里的食物會怎樣？

    (A) 它可以產生很多熱量。

    (B) 它的含水比例很高。

    (C) 它應該只能被存放在涼爽的地方。

    (D) 它比含較少卡卡路里的食物還熱。

    * imply〔ɪm'plaɪ〕*v.* 暗示   yield〔jild〕*v.* 產生
     percentage〔pɚ'sɛntɪdʒ〕*n.* 百分比；比例
     cool〔kul〕*adj.* 涼爽的

5. (**C**) 小卡和大卡有什麼不同？

    (A) 一個是能量的單位，而一個不是。

    (B) 一小卡等於一千大卡。

    (C) 當談到化學時，會用前者，而談到營養學時，會用後者。

    (D) 後者是被存放在連結原子和分子的物質裡，而前者不是。

    * equal〔'ikwəl〕*v.* 等於   former〔'fɔrmɚ〕*adj.* 前者的
     latter〔'lætɚ〕*adj.* 後者的

    【註】 本題有 31% 的同學選 (B)，但根據文章內容，應該是一大
           卡等於一千小卡。

TEST 6

Read the following passage and choose the best answer for each question.

Suppose you lived in Egypt 4,500 years ago. How would your life be different? For one thing, you wouldn't go to school. You wouldn't have hair, either! Your head would be shaved, except for one lock behind your right ear. You would eat with your fingers instead of forks and knives. On hot nights, you wouldn't have air conditioning. You would sleep on the roof of your home.

But not everything would be so different. You would spend time with your family. You might have a pet dog or cat. You would also play games such as tug of war, leapfrog, and arm wrestling. 【陽明高中】

1. What is true about most Egyptians 4,500 years ago?
   (A) They ate with forks and knives.
   (B) They slept on the roofs of their homes with electric fans on.
   (C) Children spent time in school playing games.
   (D) They shaved their heads, but left one lock behind their right ear.

2. Many children in both ancient Egypt and today's society might _____.
   (A) play games like leapfrog and arm wrestling
   (B) wear many hairstyles
   (C) borrow books from the library
   (D) use air conditioning to keep cool

3. We can infer which of the following about ancient Egypt from the passage?
   (A) Egyptians worshipped cats, dogs and frogs.
   (B) Children were required to do physical exercise.
   (C) The ancient Egyptians had terrible table manners.
   (D) There was no electricity.

4. According to the passage, why did the ancient Egyptians shave their heads?
   (A) The weather was too hot.
   (B) It was fashionable.
   (C) Everyone wanted to look the same.
   (D) It is not stated in the passage.

5. What might a child in ancient Egypt and a child in modern Egypt have in common?
   (A) Their education.
   (B) Their hobbies.
   (C) Their clothing.
   (D) Their hairstyle.

TEST 6 詳解

Suppose you lived in Egypt 4,500 years ago. How would your life be different? For one thing, you wouldn't go to school. You wouldn't have hair, either!

假如你是活在四千五百年前的埃及。你的生活會有多大的差異？首先，你不會去上學。你也不會有頭髮！

> suppose〔sə'poz〕*v.* 假如　　Egypt〔'idʒɪpt〕*n.* 埃及
> different〔'dɪfərənt〕*adj.* 不同的　*for one thing* 首先
> either〔'iðə〕*adv.* 也（不）

Your head would be shaved, except for one lock behind your right ear. You would eat with your fingers instead of forks and knives. On hot nights, you wouldn't have air conditioning. You would sleep on the roof of your home.

你的頭會被剃光，除了右耳後面的一絡頭髮。你會用手指吃飯，而不是用刀叉。在炎熱的夜晚，你也沒有空調設備。你會睡在你家的屋頂上。

> shave〔ʃev〕*v.* 剃（頭）　*except for* 除了
> lock〔lɑk〕*n.* 一絡頭髮；一撮　*instead of* 而不是
> fork〔fɔrk〕*n.* 叉子　　knife〔naɪf〕*n.* 刀子
> *air conditioning* 空調設備　roof〔ruf〕*n.* 屋頂

But not everything would be so different. You would spend time with your family. You might have a pet dog or cat. You would also play games such as tug of war, leapfrog, and arm wrestling.

　　但並不是每件事都會差這麼多。你會花時間陪家人。你可能會養狗或貓當寵物。你還會玩遊戲，像是拔河比賽、跳背遊戲，和比腕力。

　　pet〔pɛt〕*adj.* (作) 寵物的；寵愛的　　***such as*** 像是

　　tug〔tʌg〕*n.* 強拉；拖扯　　***tug of war*** 拔河比賽

　　leap〔lip〕*v.* 跳　　frog〔frɑg〕*n.* 青蛙

　　leapfrog〔'lip,frɑg〕*n.* 跳背遊戲 (跳躍彎身的人的一種遊戲)

　　wrestle〔'rɛsl〕*v.* 扭打；角力　　***arm wrestling*** 比腕力

1. (**D**) 關於大多數四千五百年前的埃及人生活，何者是正確的？

　　(A) 他們會用刀叉吃東西。

　　(B) 他們會睡在自己家的屋頂上，然後吹電風扇。

　　(C) 孩子們會花時間在學校裡玩遊戲。

　　(D) <u>他們會剃頭，但是右耳後面會留一絡頭髮。</u>

　　　* Egyptian〔ɪ'dʒɪpʃən〕*n.* 埃及人

　　　electric〔ɪ'lɛktrɪk〕*adj.* 電動的

　　　fan〔fæn〕*n.* 扇子；風扇　　***electric fan*** 電風扇

　　　on〔ɑn〕*adv.* 開著

2. (**A**) 在古埃及和現今的社會，很多學生都可能會 ＿＿＿＿＿＿＿ 。

　　(A) <u>玩像是跳蛙和比腕力的遊戲</u>

　　(B) 留很多不同的髮型

　　(C) 從圖書館借書

　　(D) 用空調設備來保持涼爽

　　　* ancient〔'enʃənt〕*adj.* 古代的

　　　wear〔wɛr〕*v.* 留 (鬍子、頭髮)

　　　hairstyle〔'hɛr,staɪl〕*n.* 髮型　　borrow〔'bɑro〕*v.* 借

3. (**D**) 我們可以從本文中，推論出下列哪一個關於古埃及的敘述？

(A) 埃及人膜拜貓、狗和青蛙。

(B) 孩子們被要求要做運動。

(C) 古埃及人的餐桌禮節很糟。

(D) <u>當時沒有電。</u>

* infer (ɪn'fɜ) v. 推論　worship ('wɜʃəp) v. 膜拜
require (rɪ'kwaɪr) v. 要求
physical ('fɪzɪkl̩) adj. 身體的　exercise ('ɛksə‚saɪz) n. 運動
physical exercise 體操；運動　terrible ('tɛrəbl̩) adj. 很糟的
manners ('mænəz) n. pl. 禮節　*table manners* 餐桌上的禮節
electricity (ɪ‚lɛk'trɪsətɪ) n. 電

4. (**D**) 根據本文，爲什麼古埃及人要剃頭？

(A) 天氣太熱了。

(B) 當時很流行。

(C) 每個人都想要看來是一樣的。

(D) <u>本文沒有說明。</u>

* *according to* 根據　weather ('wɛðə) n. 天氣
fashionable ('fæʃənəbl̩) adj. 流行的
same (sem) adj. 相同的　state (stet) v. 敘述；說明

5. (**B**) 古埃及和現在埃及的小孩，可能有什麼共同點？

(A) 他們的教育。　　　　(B) <u>他們的嗜好。</u>

(C) 他們的衣服。　　　　(D) 他們的髮型。

* modern ('mɑdən) adj. 現代的　*in common* 共同的
education (‚ɛdʒə'keʃən) n. 教育　hobby ('hɑbɪ) n. 嗜好
clothing ('kloðɪŋ) n. 衣服

TEST 7

Read the following passage, and choose the best answer for each question.

When drawing human figures, children often make the head too large for the rest of the body. A recent study offers some insights into this common disproportion in children's illustrations. As part of the study, researchers asked children between 4 and 7 years old to make several drawings of men. When <u>they</u> drew front views of male figures, the size of the heads was <u>markedly</u> enlarged. However, when the children drew rear views of men, the size of the heads was not so exaggerated. The researchers suggest that children draw bigger heads when they know they must leave room for facial details. Therefore, the odd head size in children's illustrations is a form of planning ahead and not an indication of a poor sense of scale. 【南港高中】

1. The main subject of the passage is _____.
   (A) what the results of an experiment revealed
   (B) how children learn to draw
   (C) how researchers can gather data from works of art
   (D) what can be done to correct a poor sense of scale

2. It can be inferred that, during the research project, the children drew _____.

 (A) pictures of men from different angles

 (B) figures without facial expressions

 (C) sketches of both men and women

 (D) only the front view of men

3. The word "they" in line 6 refers to _____.

 (A) researchers   (B) men

 (C) illustrations   (D) children

4. The word "markedly" in line 7 is closest in meaning to _____.

 (A) modestly   (B) noticeably

 (C) merely   (D) newly

5. The findings of the experiment described in the passage would probably be of LEAST interest to which of the following groups?

 (A) teachers of art to children

 (B) commercial artists

 (C) experts in child development

 (D) parents of young children

TEST 7 詳解

When drawing human figures, children often make the head too large for the rest of the body. A recent study offers some insights into this common disproportion in children's illustrations.

在畫人物的時候，相對於身體其他部分，小孩子常常會把頭畫得太大。最近有個研究提出了一些見解，說明孩童的圖畫中常見的不成比例的情況。

* When drawing human figures,…. 是 When <u>children are</u> drawing human figures 的省略，因爲副詞子句中，句意很明顯時，可將主詞與 be 動詞同時省略。

human ('hjumən) *adj.* 人的　　figure ('fɪgjə) *n.* 人物；人像
rest (rɛst) *n.* 其餘部分　　recent ('risṇt) *adj.* 最近的
study ('stʌdɪ) *n.* 研究　　offer ('ɔfə) *v.* 提出
insight ('ɪn,saɪt) *n.* 深刻見解　　common ('kɑmən) *adj.* 常見的
disproportion (,dɪsprə'pɔrʃən) *n.* 不成比例
illustration (ɪ,ləs'treʃən) *n.* 圖案

As part of the study, researchers asked children between 4 and 7 years old to make several drawings of men. When <u>they</u> drew front views of male figures, the size of the heads was <u>markedly</u> enlarged.

在這項研究中的某一部份，研究人員要求四到七歲的小孩，畫幾張男人的圖。當他們畫男人正面的樣子時，頭部的尺寸很明顯地被放大。

researcher (rɪ'sɜtʃə) *n.* 研究人員
drawing ('drɔ·ɪŋ) *n.* 圖畫；素描
make a drawing 畫畫　　front (frʌnt) *adj.* 正面的
view (vju) *n.* 外觀；外表　　male (mel) *adj.* 男人的
size (saɪz) *n.* 尺寸；大小　　markedly ('mɑrkɪdlɪ) *adv.* 明顯地
enlarge (ɪn'lɑrdʒ) *v.* 放大

However, when the children drew rear views of men, the size of the heads was not so exaggerated. The researchers suggest that children draw bigger heads when they know they must leave room for facial details.

但是，當這些孩子們畫男人背面的樣子時，頭部的尺寸就沒有這麼誇張。研究人員說，孩子們把頭畫得比較大，是因為他們知道，必須要留空間來畫臉部的細節。

rear (rɪr) *adj.* 背部的　　exaggerated (ɪg'zædʒə,retɪd) *adj.* 誇張的
suggest (sə'dʒɛst) *v.* 委婉地說；暗示　　leave (liv) *v.* 留下
room (rum) *n.* 空間　　facial ('feʃəl) *adj.* 臉部的
detail ('ditel) *n.* 細節

Therefore, the odd head size in children's illustrations is a form of planning ahead and not an indication of a poor sense of scale.

因此，在孩子們的畫中，奇怪的頭部尺寸是一種預先計劃的方式，而不是表示判斷比例的能力不好。

therefore ('ðɛr,for) *adv.* 因此　　odd (ɑd) *adj.* 奇怪的
form (fɔrm) *n.* 方式　　ahead (ə'hɛd) *adv.* 事先
indication (,ɪndə'keʃən) *n.* 指示；表示　　poor (pʊr) *adj.* 不好的
sense (sɛns) *n.* 辨識力；判斷力　　scale (skel) *n.* 比例

1. (**A**) 本文的主題是 ＿＿＿＿＿＿＿＿ 。

(A) 一場實驗顯示的結果　　　(B) 孩子們如何學會畫圖
(C) 研究人員如何從藝術作品中收集資料
(D) 要怎麼做才能矯正不良的判斷比例能力

* main (men) *adj.* 主要的　　subject ('sʌbdʒɪkt) *n.* 主題
result (rɪ'zʌlt) *n.* 結果　　experiment (ɪk'spɛrəmənt) *n.* 實驗
reveal (rɪ'vil) *v.* 顯示　　gather ('gæðə) *v.* 收集
data ('detə) *n. pl.* 資料　　work (wɜk) *n.* 作品
correct (kə'rɛkt) *v.* 改正；矯正

2. (**A**) 我們可以推論，在這個研究計劃中，孩子們畫了 _____。

    (A) 不同角度的人像   (B) 沒有臉部表情的人像

    (C) 男人和女人的素描   (D) 只有男人正面的樣子

   * infer (ɪn'fɜ) *v.* 推論   research (rɪ'sɜtʃ) *n.* 研究

    project ('prɑdʒɛkt) *n.* 計劃   angle ('æŋgl̩) *n.* 角度

    expression (ɪk'sprɛʃən) *n.* 表情   sketch (skɛtʃ) *n.* 素描

   【註】 本題有 28% 的同學選 (B)，但文章內容有提到，孩子們把頭畫

           得比較大，是因為要留空間來畫臉部的細節，所以可以推論

           孩子們有畫臉部表情。另外，有 31% 的同學選 (D)，而文章中

           也有提到，孩子們有畫男人的背面，所以這個選項也是錯的。

3. (**D**) 第六行的 "they" 指的是 _____。

    (A) 研究人員   (B) 男人   (C) 圖畫   (D) 孩子們

   * ***refer to*** 是指

4. (**B**) 第七行的 "markedly" 意思和 _____ 最接近。

    (A) 謙虛地   (B) 顯著地   (C) 僅僅   (D) 最近

   * modestly ('mɑdɪstlɪ) *adv.* 謙虛地

    noticeably ('notɪsəblɪ) *adv.* 顯著地

    merely ('mɪrlɪ) *adv.* 僅僅   newly ('njulɪ) *adv.* 最近

5. (**B**) 對本文所描述的實驗研究結果最沒興趣的，可能是下列哪一個團體？

    (A) 孩子的美術老師   (B) 商業美術家

    (C) 兒童發展專家   (D) 幼兒的父母

   * findings ('faɪndɪŋz) *n.* 研究的結果

    describe (dɪ'skraɪb) *v.* 描述

    probably ('prɑbəblɪ) *adv.* 可能   least (list) *adj.* 最少的

    interest ('ɪntrɪst) *n.* 興趣   commercial (kə'mɜʃəl) *adj.* 商業的

    artist ('ɑrtɪst) *n.* 藝術家；美術家；畫家

    expert ('ɛkspɜt) *n.* 專家

    development (dɪ'vɛləpmənt) *n.* 發展；發育

TEST 8

Read the following passage and choose the best answer for each question.

My father, an occasional golfer, one day hit a straight drive quite a way down the fairway. When he got to the ball, he found that a woman was about to hit it. "Pardon me," he said, "you're addressing my ball."

"This is my ball!" she replied.

"Ma'am," Dad said, "if you pick it up, you'll find my name on it."

The woman scooped the ball up and examined it. "What's your name doing on my ball?" she said.

【西松高中】

1. Where did this event probably happen?
   (A) On a tennis court.
   (B) In a park.
   (C) On a golf course.
   (D) On a playground.

2. Whose name was on the ball?
   (A) The author's.
   (B) The man's.
   (C) The woman's.
   (D) We can't be sure whose name was on it.

3. The author's father was a(n) _____.
   (A) professional billiards player
   (B) basketball player
   (C) occasional golfer
   (D) golf cart driver

4. What did the woman do after arguing with the author's father?
   (A) hit the ball anyway
   (B) scooped up the ball
   (C) kicked the ball away
   (D) buried the ball even deeper

5. The author's father hit the golf ball down the _____.
   (A) woodland
   (B) bunker
   (C) the green
   (D) fairway

TEST 8 詳解

My father, an occasional golfer, one day hit a straight drive quite a way down the fairway. When he got to the ball, he found that a woman was about to hit it. "Pardon me," he said, "you're addressing my ball."

我父親偶爾會打打高爾夫球，有一天，他擊出又直又遠的一球，距離相當遠，就落在平坦的球道上。當他走到球那邊時，發現有一名女士正要將球擊出。「很抱歉，」他說，「妳要擊出的是我的球。」

* an occasional golfer 是同位語，用來補充說明主詞 **My father**。

occasional〔ə'keʒənḷ〕*adj.* 偶爾的
golfer〔'gɑlfɚ〕*n.* 打高爾夫球的人
straight〔stret〕*adj.* 直的　　drive〔draɪv〕*n.* (高爾夫球) 長打
quite〔kwaɪt〕*adj.* 相當大或多的　　way〔we〕*n.* 路程；距離
fairway〔'fɛr,we〕*n.* (高爾夫球) 美好區；平坦的球道 (在開球區和
　果嶺之間)　　***get to*** 前往
be about to V. 正要～　　pardon〔'pɑrdṇ〕*v.* 原諒
address〔ə'drɛs〕*v.* 準備擊 (球)

"This is my ball!" she replied.
"Ma'am," Dad said, "if you pick it up, you'll find my name on it."

「這是我的球！」她回答道。
「女士，」我爸爸說，「如果妳把球拿起來，妳會看到我的名字就在上面。」

reply〔rɪ'plaɪ〕*v.* 回答　　ma'am〔mæm〕*n.* 女士；小姐
pick up 拿起來；撿起來

The woman scooped the ball up and examined it. "What's your name doing on my ball?" she said.

那位女士就把球拿起來檢查，結果她說：「你的名字在我的球上幹嘛？」

scoop〔skup〕*v.* 挖起；撈起　　examine〔ɪg'zæmɪn〕*v.* 檢查

1.(**C**) 這件事可能發生在哪裡？
    (A) 網球場上。   (B) 公園裡。
    (C) <u>高爾夫球場上。</u>   (D) 遊樂場上。
    * ***tennis court*** 網球場   ***golf course*** 高爾夫球場
    playground ('ple,graʊnd) *n.* 運動場；遊樂場

2.(**B**) 誰的名字在高爾夫球上？
    (A) 作者的。
    (B) <u>那位男士的。</u>
    (C) 那位女士的。
    (D) 我們無法確定誰的名字在那上面。

3.(**C**) 作者的父親是個 ＿＿＿＿＿＿＿＿＿。
    (A) 職業撞球選手   (B) 籃球選手
    (C) <u>偶爾打高爾夫球的人</u>   (D) 高爾夫球車的駕駛人
    * professional (prə'fɛʃənḷ) *adj.* 職業的
    billiards ('bɪljədz) *n.* 撞球
    golf cart 高爾夫球車

4.(**B**) 那位女士和作者的父親吵完架之後做了什麼？
    (A) 還是把球打出去了   (B) <u>把球拿起來</u>
    (C) 把球踢開   (D) 把球埋得更深
    * argue ('ɑrgju) *v.* 爭論；爭吵   anyway ('ɛnɪ,we) *adv.* 仍然；還是
    kick (kɪk) *v.* 踢   bury ('bɛrɪ) *v.* 埋葬；掩埋

5.(**D**) 作者的父親把高爾夫球打到 ＿＿＿＿＿＿＿＿。
    (A) 林地裡   (B) 沙坑裡
    (C) 果嶺上   (D) <u>平坦的球道上</u>
    * woodland ('wʊd,lænd) *n.* 林地
    bunker ('bʌŋkə) *n.* 【高爾夫球】沙坑（球道上人工造成的障礙區域）
    the green 【高爾夫球】球洞區；果嶺

TEST 9

Read the following passage and choose the best answer for each question.

Dear Annie,

I am a 33-year-old woman, married, with two children. My friend "Barb" asked me to baby-sit for her two-year-old son full-time (about 45 hours a week). However, I was shocked when she offered me only $25 a week. I was thinking more along the lines of $75-$100. Barb said she couldn't afford that.

Barb and her husband both have full-time, decent-paying jobs. They just spent quite a bit of money to "super size" their truck, but somehow don't have enough to pay me to care for their son.

I love Barb and her little boy, but I think 45 hours is a lot of time for so little money. Am I being selfish to ask for more?

—— Crying Baby Blues

Dear Crying,

Of course you aren't being selfish. She expects you to be a full-time baby sitter for part-time wages. If Barb truly has financial problems and you can afford to help her out for $25 a week, go ahead and do it, but otherwise, she is taking advantage of you. 【中正高中】

1. Why was the 33-year-old woman shocked?
   (A) "Barb" asked her to baby-sit for her two-year-old son full-time.
   (B) She got a decent-paying job.
   (C) "Barb" offered her only $25 a week for baby-sitting her son.
   (D) "Barb" spent quite a bit of money on a big truck.

2. According to the passage, which of the following statements is incorrect?
   (A) Crying Baby Blues is not being selfish to want more money.
   (B) Barb expects the woman to be a full-time babysitter for part-time wages.
   (C) If Barb has financial problems, the woman should help her.
   (D) Annie asks the woman to take advantage of her friend Barb.

3. Annie is probably _____.

   (A) the 33-year-old woman's mother

   (B) an advice-giver

   (C) Barb's sister

   (D) the woman's close friend

4. Why does Barb want a full-time babysitter for her son?

   (A) She cannot afford to care for her son herself.

   (B) A full-time sitter is cheaper than a part-time one.

   (C) She wants her son to have other children to
       play with.

   (D) Both she and her husband work all day.

5. What can we infer from the letter?

   (A) Barb and her husband have no money left.

   (B) Barb and her husband could probably afford to
       pay babysitter more.

   (C) Barb and her husband prefer their truck to
       their son.

   (D) Barb and her husband think babysitters should
       not be paid at all.

TEST 9 詳解

Dear Annie,

I am a 33-year-old woman, married, with two children. My friend "Barb" asked me to baby-sit for her two-year-old son full-time (about 45 hours a week).

親愛的安妮：

我今年 33 歲，已婚，有兩個小孩。我的朋友「芭」要求我專職（大約一週四十五個小時）照顧她兩歲的兒子。

> **married** ('mærɪd) *adj.* 已婚的　　**baby-sit** ('bebɪ,sɪt) *v.* 充當臨時褓母
> **full-time** ('fʊl'taɪm) *adv.* 專職地；專任地

However, I was shocked when she offered me only $25 a week. I was thinking more along the lines of $75-$100. Barb said she couldn't afford that.

但是，當她說一週只給我 25 元時，我非常震驚。我以為會更多，大概是 75 到 100 元之間。芭說她負擔不起。

> **shocked** (ʃɑkt) *adj.* 震驚的　　**offer** ('ɔfɚ) *v.* 提供
> ***along the lines of*** ~ 介於~之間
> **afford** (ə'fɔrd) *v.* 付得起；負擔得起

Barb and her husband both have full-time, decent-paying jobs. They just spent quite a bit of money to "super size" their truck, but somehow don't have enough to pay me to care for their son.

芭和她先生都有全職而且薪水相當不錯的工作。他們剛花了不少錢來「換更大的」卡車，但是不知道為什麼，卻沒有足夠的錢，請我照顧他們的兒子。

> **decent** ('disn̩t) *adj.* 相當不錯的　　***quite a bit of*** 相當多的
> ***super size*** 換更大的　　**somehow** ('sʌm,haʊ) *adv.* 不知道為什麼
> ***care for*** 照顧

I love Barb and her little boy, but I think 45 hours is a lot of time for so little money.　Am I being selfish to ask for more?

　　　　　　　　　　　　　　　　　—— Crying Baby Blues

　我很喜歡芭和她的小兒子，但是我認為對這麼少的薪資而言，四十五個小時的工作時間很多。我如果要求更多的錢，會不會太自私？

　　　　　　　　　　　　　　　　　—— 哭泣的眼睛

　　　selfish〔'sɛlfɪʃ〕adj. 自私的　　***ask for*** 要求
　　　baby blues 【俚】眼睛（可指任何顏色的）

Dear Crying,

　　Of course you aren't being selfish.　She expects you to be a full-time baby sitter for part-time wages.　If Barb truly has financial problems and you can afford to help her out for $25 a week, go ahead and do it, but otherwise, she is taking advantage of you.

親愛的哭泣者：

　　妳當然不會太自私。她希望妳拿兼差的薪水，做全職的褓母。如果芭真的有財務上的困難，而妳又負擔得起以週薪 25 元的方式來幫她，那就放手去做吧，但是若非如此，那麼她就只是在佔妳便宜而已。

　　　full-time〔'fʊl'taɪm〕adj. 專職的
　　　part-time〔'pɑrt'taɪm〕adj. 兼差的　　wage〔wedʒ〕n. 薪水
　　　financial〔faɪ'nænʃəl〕adj. 財務上的　　***help sb. out*** 幫助某人
　　　go ahead 進行；做吧
　　　otherwise〔'ʌðɚ,waɪz〕adv. 若非如此；否則
　　　take advantage of 佔～便宜

1. (**C**) 爲何這位 33 歲的女士十分震驚？

(A) 「芭」要求她全職照顧她兩歲的兒子。

(B) 她得到一份薪水相當不錯的工作。

(C) 「芭」只付週薪 25 元，請她照顧她的兒子。

(D) 「芭」花了很多錢買一輛大卡車。

2. (**D**) 根據本文，下列哪一項敘述是錯的？

(A) 哭泣的眼睛想要更多的錢並不自私。

(B) 芭期待這位女士拿兼差的薪水，做全職的褓母。

(C) 如果芭有財務困難，這位女士應該幫她。

(D) 安妮叫這位女士佔她朋友芭的便宜。

* babysitter ('bebɪ͵sɪtɚ) n. 褓母 (= baby-sitter)

3. (**B**) 安妮可能是 ＿＿＿＿＿＿＿ 。

(A) 這位 33 歲的女士的媽媽　　(B) 一位顧問

(C) 芭的姊妹　　(D) 這位女士的密友

* advice-giver 給建議者；顧問　　close (klos) adj. 親密的

4. (**D**) 芭爲何要替兒子找一位全職的褓母？

(A) 她無法自己照顧兒子。　　(B) 全職褓母比兼職的便宜。

(C) 她希望他兒子可以跟其他小孩一起玩。

(D) 她跟她先生都要整天上班。

* cannot afford to V. 無法～

sitter ('sɪtɚ) n. 褓母 (= babysitter)　　all day 整天

5. (**B**) 我們可由信中推論出什麼？

(A) 芭跟她先生沒錢了。

(B) 芭跟她先生可能有能力多付褓母一點錢。

(C) 芭跟她先生喜歡卡車勝過自己的兒子。

(D) 芭跟她先生認爲不應該付任何錢給褓母。

* infer (ɪnˈfɝ) v. 推論　　left (lɛft) adj. 剩下的

prefer A to B 喜歡 A 勝過 B　　not…at all 一點也不…

TEST 10

Read the following passage and choose the best answer for each question.

Mr. Gordon is an employee in a bank. He knows the banking business very well, but the bank president is not satisfied with him because he always becomes very tired in the afternoon and works too slowly. For this reason the president has decided to fire Mr. Gordon. The other employees in the bank feel sorry for him, but they agree that Mr. Gordon's tiredness is his "Achilles' heel." What do they mean by this?

Achilles is the hero of an ancient Greek epic, *the Iliad*. When Achilles was born, his mother, a goddess, decided to make him invincible. She took him to the underworld to dip his body into the river Styx because its water protects people. But because she was holding onto his heel, the magical water did not touch that part. Later, during the Trojan War, Achilles was shot in the heel by an arrow and died. His heel was the weakness that brought about his downfall.

Thus when people refer to any kind of serious weakness or flaw in a person, they often call it an "Achilles' heel." 【麗山高中】

1. What caused Mr. Gordon to get fired from his job at the bank?

   (A) He made too many different mistakes.
   (B) He didn't sleep enough at the office.
   (C) His sleepiness prevented him from working well.
   (D) His sore heel made him work slower.

2. Why did Achilles' mother dip her son in the river Styx?

   (A) She wanted her son to have a bath.
   (B) She wanted her son to learn how to swim.
   (C) Its magical water would help him sleep.
   (D) Its magical water would make him undefeatable.

3. What caused Achilles' downfall?

   (A) He was not able to swim across the river Styx.
   (B) An arrow hit him while he was sleeping.
   (C) He never learned to shoot arrows.
   (D) An arrow struck the weakest part of his body.

4. An "Achilles' heel" _____.

   (A) is a flaw in the heel that causes one to be fired
   (B) is a flaw that causes one to be shot by an arrow
   (C) is a flaw in any part of the foot that causes one's downfall
   (D) is any kind of flaw that causes one's downfall

5. The purpose of this passage is to _____.

   (A) tell Mr. Gordon's story
   (B) tell the story of Achilles
   (C) warn people about the danger of an "Achilles' heel"
   (D) explain the origin of the idiom "Achilles' heel"

TEST 10 詳解

Mr. Gordon is an employee in a bank. He knows the banking business very well, but the bank president is not satisfied with him because he always becomes very tired in the afternoon and works too slowly.

高登先生是銀行的雇員。他對銀行的業務非常熟悉,但是銀行的總裁卻對他不滿意,因為他到了下午總是變得非常疲倦,做起事來慢吞吞的。

employee (ˌɛmplɔɪˈi) *n.* 雇員;員工
banking (ˈbæŋkɪŋ) *n.* 銀行業務
president (ˈprɛzədənt) *n.* 總裁　　***be satisfied with*** 對～感到滿意

For this reason the president has decided to fire Mr. Gordon. The other employees in the bank feel sorry for him, but they agree that Mr. Gordon's tiredness is his "Achilles' heel." What do they mean by this?

因為這個原因,總裁決定開除高登先生。銀行裡其他的雇員都為他感到難過,但是他們都一致認為,疲倦是高登先生的「致命傷」。他們這麼說的意思是什麼?

fire (faɪr) *v.* 開除　　sorry (ˈsɔrɪ) *adj.* 難過的;遺憾的
agree (əˈgri) *v.* 一致認為;同意
tiredness (ˈtaɪrdnɪs) *n.* 疲倦;倦怠　　heel (hil) *n.* 腳後跟
Achilles' heel 唯一的弱點;阿基里斯腱;致命傷 (= *Achilles heel*)

Achilles is the hero of an ancient Greek epic, *the Iliad.* When Achilles was born, his mother, a goddess, decided to make him invincible.

阿基里斯是古希臘敘事詩「伊里亞德」中的英雄。當阿基里斯出生時，他的媽媽，她是位女神，決定要讓他所向無敵。

Achilles〔ə'kıliz〕n. 阿基里斯　　epic〔'εpık〕n. 敘事詩；史詩
the Iliad 伊里亞德（歌詠特洛伊戰爭的敘事詩）
goddess〔'gɑdıs〕n. 女神　　invincible〔ın'vınsəbļ〕adj. 無敵的

She took him to the underworld to dip his body into the river Styx
because its water protects people. But because she was holding
onto his heel, the magical water did not touch that part.

她帶他去冥界，把他的身體浸到冥河裡，因爲冥河的水可以保護人們。但是因爲她抓著他的腳後跟，所以具有魔力的水沒有碰到那個部分。

underworld〔'ʌndɚˌwɝld〕n. 地獄；冥界　　dip〔dıp〕v. 浸；泡
Styx〔stıks〕n. 冥河　　protect〔prə'tεkt〕v. 保護
hold onto 抓住　　magical〔'mædʒıkļ〕adj. 神奇的；有魔力的

Later, during the Trojan War, Achilles was shot in the heel by an
arrow and died. His heel was the weakness that brought about his
downfall.

之後在特洛伊戰爭期間，阿基里斯被弓箭射中了腳後跟，然後死亡。他的腳後跟就是造成他滅亡的弱點。

Trojan War 特洛伊戰爭（古希臘人與特洛伊人之間的戰爭）
shoot〔ʃut〕v. 射（箭）
arrow〔'æro〕n. 箭　　weakness〔'wiknıs〕n. 弱點
bring about 造成；導致　　downfall〔'daʊnˌfɔl〕n. 滅亡

Thus when people refer to any kind of serious weakness or
flaw in a person, they often call it an "Achilles' heel."

因此，當人們提到一個人嚴重的弱點或缺陷時，他們經常稱之爲「阿基里斯的腳後跟」（致命傷）。

refer to 提到　　flaw〔flɔ〕n. 缺點

1. (**C**) 導致高登先生被銀行開除的原因為何？

(A) 他犯了太多不同的錯誤。　　(B) 他在辦公室沒有睡飽。

(C) <u>他的睡意使他不能好好工作。</u>

(D) 他疼痛的腳跟使得他工作得更慢。

* sleepiness ('slipɪnɪs) *n.* 睡意
prevent (prɪ'vɛnt) *v.* 阻礙　　sore (sor) *adj.* 疼痛的

2. (**D**) 阿基里斯的媽媽為什麼要把她的兒子浸在冥河裡？

(A) 她想要她兒子洗個澡。　　(B) 她想要她兒子學習如何游泳。

(C) 它具有魔力的水有助於使他睡著。

(D) <u>它具有魔力的水會讓他所向無敵。</u>

* undefeatable (ˌʌndɪ'fitəbļ) *adj.* 無法打敗的

3. (**D**) 是什麼導致阿基里斯滅亡？

(A) 他不能夠游過冥河。　　(B) 在他睡覺時，有支箭射中他。

(C) 他從來沒有學過射箭。

(D) <u>有支箭射中他身體最脆弱的部分。</u>

* strike (straɪk) *v.* 擊中；襲擊 (三態變化為：strike-struck-struck)

4. (**D**) 「阿基里斯的腳後跟」 (致命傷) 是 ＿＿＿＿＿＿＿。

(A) 腳跟上一個會使人被解僱的瑕疵

(B) 會使人被箭射中的缺點

(C) 位於腳上任何部分，會使人滅亡的缺點

(D) <u>會使人滅亡的任何一種缺點</u>

5. (**D**) 這篇文章的目的是要 ＿＿＿＿＿＿＿。

(A) 講高登先生的故事　　(B) 講阿基里斯的故事

(C) 警告人們「阿基里斯的腳後跟」的危險性

(D) <u>解釋「阿基里斯的腳後跟」這個成語的由來</u>

* warn (wɔrn) *v.* 警告　　danger ('dendʒɚ) *n.* 危險
explain (ɪk'splen) *v.* 解釋　　origin ('ɔrədʒɪn) *n.* 起源；由來
idiom ('ɪdɪəm) *n.* 成語

TEST 11

Read the following passage and choose the best answer for each question.

American poet Sara Teasdale won a Pulitzer Prize
in 1918. As you read the poem below, think about what
Teasdale has to say about life. Use information from the
poem to answer the questions that follow.

Barter

Life has loveliness to sell,
　All beautiful and splendid things,
　Blue waves whitened on a cliff,
　Soaring fire that sways and sings,
　And children's faces looking up
　Holding wonder like a cup.

Life has loveliness to sell,
　Music like a curve of gold,
　Scent of pine trees in the rain,
　Eyes that love you, arms that hold,
　And for your spirit's still delight,
　Holy thoughts that star the night.

Spend all you have for loveliness,

Buy it and never count the cost;

For one white singing hour of peace

Count many a year of strife well lost,

And for a breath of ecstasy

Give all you have been, or could be.

—— Sara Teasdale 【成功高中】

1. What is emphasized in lines 1 and 2?

   (A) the beauty of life

   (B) reasons for the reader to take action

   (C) the importance of reevaluating one's life

   (D) the poet's affection for children

2. Which of the following figures of speech is used in line 8?

   (A) simile   (B) metaphor

   (C) overstatement   (D) understatement

3. What does line 10 suggest to the reader?

   (A) the surprises one can find in nature

   (B) the need for aggressive action

   (C) the warmth of human affection

   (D) the unpredictability of kindness

4. Which of the following lines from the poem states that beauty is worth any sacrifice?

   (A) "Life has loveliness to sell"

   (B) "Holy thoughts that star the night"

   (C) "Spend all you have for loveliness"

   (D) "Holding wonder like a cup"

5. In which collection might this poem be found?

   (A) Humorous Poems

   (B) Inspirational Poems for Quiet Moments

   (C) Travel Poems from Many Lands

   (D) Children's Poetry Collection

【劉毅老師的話】

    多背單字是增強閱讀能力的不二法門，熟背「電腦統計常考字彙」和「考前必背字彙」，你將成為閱測高手。

TEST 11 詳解

American poet Sara Teasdale won a Pulitzer Prize in 1918.
As you read the poem below, think about what Teasdale has to say
about life. Use information from the poem to answer the questions
that follow.

美國詩人莎拉・帝絲戴爾在一九一八年贏得普立茲獎。當你閱讀以下這
首詩時,想一想關於生命這個主題,帝絲戴爾想要說些什麼。利用這首詩的
資訊,來回答之後的問題。

poet (ˈpo·ɪt) *n.* 詩人　　Pulitzer (ˈpjulɪtsə) *n.* 普立茲
Pulitzer Prize 普立茲獎 (美國新聞、文學、音樂方面的獎項)
poem (ˈpo·ɪm) *n.* 詩　　below (bəˈlo) *adv.* 以下
follow (ˈfɑlo) *v.* 跟隨在後

Barter

Life has loveliness to sell,
All beautiful and splendid things,
Blue waves whitened on a cliff,
Soaring fire that sways and sings,
And children's faces looking up
Holding wonder like a cup.

以物易物

生命有許多美好的事物可販賣,
所有美麗的、華麗的東西,
藍色的波浪打在懸崖上變成白色,
高漲的火焰搖曳歌唱,
孩子們的臉抬頭看,
像杯子一樣裝著驚嘆。

* 這一段只有第一行是主要子句，其餘都是同位語的結構，作者舉出 blue waves, soaring fire, children's faces，來說明生命的 loveliness。最後一行 Holding wonder like a cup，是形容第五行 children's faces，用來描述孩子們的天眞無邪。

barter ('bɑrtɚ) n. 以物易物

loveliness ('lʌvlɪnɪs) n. 可愛；美好

splendid ('splɛndɪd) adj. 華麗的；極好的

wave (wev) n. 波浪　　hold (hold) v. 盛裝

whiten ('hwaɪtn̩) v. 變白　　cliff (klɪf) n. 懸崖；峭壁

soaring ('sorɪŋ) adj. 翱翔的；高漲的

sway (swe) v. 搖晃；搖動　　***look up*** 抬頭看

wonder ('wʌndɚ) n. 驚嘆；驚奇

Life has loveliness to sell,

Music like a curve of gold,

Scent of pine trees in the rain,

Eyes that love you, arms that hold,

And for your spirit's still delight,

Holy thoughts that star the night.

生命有許多美好的事物可販賣，

音樂就像金色的曲線，

雨中的松樹氣味，

愛你的眼神，擁抱你的雙臂，

爲了你精神上的寧靜喜悅，

聖潔的思想像星星般滿布夜空。

* 這一段與上一段相同，只有第一行是主要子句，music, scent of pine trees, eyes, arms, holy thoughts，仍然是生命中 loveliness 的實例。最後一行 Holy thoughts that star the night，是為了第五 行 your spirit's still delight 而存在。

curve〔kɜv〕*n.* 曲線 scent〔sɛnt〕*n.* 氣味
pine〔paɪn〕*n.* 松樹（= *pine tree*）
spirit〔'spɪrɪt〕*n.* 精神
still〔stɪl〕*adj.* 寂靜的；靜止的
delight〔dɪ'laɪt〕*n.* 高興；喜悅
holy〔'holɪ〕*adj.* 神聖的；聖潔的
star〔stɑr〕*v.* 如星星般布滿

<blockquote>

Spend all you have for loveliness,

Buy it and never count the cost;

For one white singing hour of peace

Count many a year of strife well lost,

And for a breath of ecstasy

Give all you have been, or could be.

</blockquote>

把你的一切都花費在美好的事物上面，

買下它，而且永遠不要計算代價；

為了一小時純真而平靜的歌唱時光，

把用在爭吵上的許多年都視為是值得的，

為了一絲絲欣喜若狂，

要傾盡你的一切，或你可能擁有的一切。

* 最後一行的 give 是「用盡；犧牲」，all you have been 指的是你 的一切，包括你所擁有的、你的成就，你未做、已做，將做之事 等等。

count〔kaʊnt〕v. 計算；將…視爲；認爲
cost〔kɔst〕n. 成本；代價
white〔hwaɪt〕adj. 純眞無邪的　　peace〔pis〕n. 平靜
「*many a* + 單數名詞」表「許多的～」。
strife〔straɪf〕n. 爭吵
well〔wɛl〕adv. 良好地；適當地
breath〔brɛθ〕n. 呼吸；氣息　　*a breath of* 一絲；些許
ecstasy〔'ɛkstəsɪ〕n. 狂喜；欣喜若狂

1.(**A**) 第一行和第二行強調的是什麼？

(A) 生命之美

(B) 讀者要採取行動的原因

(C) 重新評估生活的重要性

(D) 詩人對小孩子的愛

　* emphasize〔'ɛmfə,saɪz〕v. 強調
　take action 採取行動
　reevaluate〔,riɪ'væljʊ,et〕v. 重新評估
　affection〔ə'fɛkʃən〕n. 愛；感情

2.(**A**) 第八行用的是下列何種修辭方法？

(A) simile〔'sɪmə,li〕n. 明喻 (有用 as 或 like 的比喻法)

(B) metaphor〔'mɛtəfə〕n. 暗喻 (沒有用 as 或 like 的比喻法)

(C) overstatement〔,ovə'stetmənt〕n. 誇張

(D) understatement〔,ʌndə'stetmənt〕n. 含蓄的說法；
輕描淡寫

　* *figure of speech* 修辭

3. (**C**) 第十行暗示讀者什麼？

(A) 一個人在大自然中可以發現的驚奇

(B) 攻擊性行為的必要性

(C) 人類感情的溫暖

(D) 仁慈的不可預測性

* suggest (sə'dʒɛst) *v.* 暗示
aggressive (ə'grɛsɪv) *adj.* 具攻擊性的
warmth (wɔrmθ) *n.* 溫暖
unpredictability (ˌʌnprɪˌdɪktə'bɪlətɪ) *n.* 不可預測性
kindness ('kaɪndnɪs) *n.* 親切；仁慈

4. (**C**) 在本詩中，下列哪一行提到美是值得任何犧牲的？

(A) 「生命有許多美好的事物可販賣」

(B) 「聖潔的思想像星星般滿布夜空」

(C) 「把你的一切都花費在美好的事物上」

(D) 「像杯子一樣裝著驚嘆」

* state (stet) *v.* 陳述；說明　　worth (wɜθ) *adj.* 值得的
sacrifice ('sækrəˌfaɪs) *n.* 犧牲

5. (**B**) 這首詩可能會在哪一種詩集裡被發現？

(A) 幽默詩

(B) 在寧靜時刻鼓舞人心的詩

(C) 來自許多國家的旅遊詩

(D) 兒童詩集

* collection (kə'lɛkʃən) *n.* 集合；收集（在此指「詩集」）
humorous ('hjumərəs) *adj.* 幽默的
inspirational (ˌɪnspə'reʃənḷ) *adj.* 鼓舞人心的
moment ('momənt) *n.* 時刻　　travel ('trævḷ) *n.* 旅行
land (lænd) *n.* 國家　　poetry ('po‧ɪtrɪ) *n.* 詩

TEST 12

Read the following passage and choose the best answer for each question.

In 1990, an 11-year-old girl with the immune disease ADA underwent the first successful gene therapy treatment. Since then, the therapy has been used in trials to treat a host of other diseases, such as cancer and hemophilia. So far, it has been most successful in growing new blood vessels in heart patients.

But there are still considerable obstacles to overcome before your local doctor starts injecting you with fresh genes. One major problem is delivering the genetic material into the cells. Early trials used viruses to slip the new DNA past the body's immune system. Problems arose because in many cases the virus would transfer material in random, even harmful ways. Alternate methods aim at harnessing the body's own genetic repair processes to spot defects in the DNA, remove them and stitch in replacements.

Then there are children. Parents can already select a baby's sex and screen for genetic illness. From there it's a short step to selecting for things like intelligence, beauty and athleticism, which begins to raise disturbing moral questions. 【景美女中】

1. How has the gene therapy treatment proved successful and effective?

   (A) Heart patients can grow new blood vessels.

   (B) The new genes easily slip into the sick cells.

   (C) The injected genes strengthen the human immune system.

   (D) Viruses are transformed in a random and harmful way.

2. The writer is worried that _____.

   (A) parents might break moral codes to select a perfect baby

   (B) good qualities will fail to be passed down to the coming generations

   (C) moral questions will be a public concern

   (D) the sex of human beings might become indecisive

3. As mentioned in the report, what is a major technical difficulty for gene therapy?

   (A) Patients' willingness to try an alternative treatment.

   (B) Finding a way to deliver the genetic material into the cells.

   (C) The asymmetry of the sexes in human society.

   (D) The harmful viruses which kill fresh genes.

4. In what way might scientists overcome the problem of random transfer of genetic material?

   (A) Select only "good" genes for transfer despite moral objections.

   (B) First grow new blood vessels through which to pass the genes.

   (C) First eliminate all viruses from the body.

   (D) Use the body's own repair process to replace defective genes.

5. What kinds of genes might future parents be able to select for their children?

   (A) Moral genes.

   (B) Genes for height.

   (C) Genes for wealth.

   (D) Genes for replacement.

【劉毅老師的話】

   多做閱讀測驗，熟能生巧，閱測滿分就不再是夢想。

TEST 12 詳解

In 1990, an 11-year-old girl with the immune disease ADA underwent the first successful gene therapy treatment.　Since then, the therapy has been used in trials to treat a host of other diseases, such as cancer and hemophilia.　So far, it has been most successful in growing new blood vessels in heart patients.

在一九九〇年時，一位得了 ADA 免疫疾病的十一歲女孩，接受了首次成功的基因治療法。此後，這種治療法就被試著用來治療許多其他疾病，像是癌症和血友病。到目前為止，此療法最成功之處，就在於替心臟病患者培植新的血管。

immune〔ɪ'mjun〕*adj.* 免疫的　　disease〔dɪ'ziz〕*n.* 疾病
ADA immune disease ADA 酵素缺乏免疫疾病，俗稱「泡泡兒」
undergo〔ˌʌndə'go〕*v.* 接受　　gene〔dʒin〕*n.* 基因
therapy〔'θɛrəpɪ〕*n.* 治療法　　treatment〔'tritmənt〕*n.* 治療
since then 此後　　trial〔'traɪəl〕*n.* 試驗　　treat〔trit〕*v.* 治療
a host of 許多的　　cancer〔'kænsə〕*n.* 癌症
hemophilia〔ˌhimə'fɪlɪə〕*n.* 血友病　　***so far*** 到目前為止
grow〔gro〕*v.* 栽培；使生長　　vessel〔'vɛsl̩〕*n.* 血管
patient〔'peʃənt〕*n.* 病人

But there are still considerable obstacles to overcome before your local doctor starts injecting you with fresh genes.　One major problem is delivering the genetic material into the cells.

但是，在你當地的醫生開始替你注射新生的基因前，仍有相當多的阻礙要克服。主要的問題，是在於將基因物質放入細胞裡面。

considerable〔kən'sɪdərəbl̩〕*adj.* 相當多的
obstacle〔'ɑbstəkl̩〕*n.* 阻礙　　overcome〔ˌovə'kʌm〕*v.* 克服
local〔'lokl̩〕*adj.* 當地的　　inject〔ɪn'dʒɛkt〕*v.* 注射
fresh〔frɛʃ〕*adj.* 新生的　　major〔'medʒə〕*adj.* 主要的
deliver〔dɪ'lɪvə〕*v.* 遞送
genetic〔dʒə'nɛtɪk〕*adj.* 基因的；遺傳上的　　cell〔sɛl〕*n.* 細胞

Early trials used viruses to slip the new DNA past the body's
immune system. Problems arose because in many cases the virus
would transfer material in random, even harmful ways.
早期的試驗是利用病毒，來使新的 DNA 避開身體的免疫系統。問題出現了，
因為在許多病例中，病毒會隨意地，甚至是以有害的方式轉移物質。

> virus ('vaɪrəs) *n.* 病毒　　slip (slɪp) *v.* 擺脫；躲避
> *DNA* 去氧核醣核酸　　arise (ə'raɪz) *v.* 產生
> transfer (træns'fɝ) *v.* 轉移
> random ('rændəm) *adj.* 隨意的；漫無目的的
> harmful ('hɑrmfəl) *adj.* 有害的

Alternate methods aim at harnessing the body's own genetic repair
processes to spot defects in the DNA, remove them and stitch in
replacements.
其他方法的目的是在於，要運用身體本身的基因修補過程，來找出 DNA 中
的缺陷，去除這些缺陷之後，再用替代物來修補。

> alternate ('ɔltɚnɪt) *adj.* 另外的　　*aim at* 目的在於
> harness ('hɑrnɪs) *v.* 運用　　process ('prɑsɛs) *n.* 過程
> spot (spɑt) *v.* 找到　　defect ('difɛkt) *n.* 缺陷
> remove (rɪ'muv) *v.* 除去　　stitch (stɪtʃ) *v.* 修補
> replacement (rɪ'plesmənt) *n.* 代替物

Then there are children. Parents can already select a baby's
sex and screen for genetic illness. From there it's a short step to
selecting for things like intelligence, beauty and athleticism, which
begins to raise disturbing moral questions.
　　然後還有小孩的問題。父母已經可以選擇孩子的性別，並且過濾遺傳疾
病。距離選擇像是智力、美貌和對運動的愛好這些特質，就只剩一小步了，
而這些都會開始產生令人不安的道德問題。

select (sə'lɛkt) *v.* 選擇   sex (sɛks) *n.* 性別
screen (skrin) *v.* 過濾   intelligence (ɪn'tɛlədʒəns) *n.* 智力
athleticism (æθ'lɛtə,sɪzəm) *n.* 愛好運動
raise (rez) *v.* 產生   disturbing (dɪ'stɝbɪŋ) *adj.* 令人不安的
moral ('mɔrəl) *adj.* 道德的

1. (**A**) 基因治療法已經如何被證實是成功又有效的？
   (A) 心臟病患者能長出新的血管。
   (B) 新的基因很容易就潛入生病的細胞。
   (C) 注入的基因能強化人的免疫系統。
   (D) 病毒被以隨意且有害的方式加以改變。

   * prove (pruv) *v.* 證實；顯示   *slip into* 潛入
     strengthen ('strɛŋθən) *v.* 強化   *immune system* 免疫系統
     transform (træns'fɔrm) *v.* 轉變；改變

2. (**A**) 作者擔心 ＿＿＿＿＿＿＿＿。
   (A) 父母會打破道德規範，去挑選一個完美的小孩
   (B) 好的特質會無法被傳遞給下一代
   (C) 道德問題將成為大家關切的事
   (D) 人類的性別可能是非決定性的

   * *moral code* 道德規範   quality ('kwɑlətɪ) *n.* 特質
     fail to 未能   *pass down* 傳遞
     coming ('kʌmɪŋ) *adj.* 下一個的
     generation (,dʒɛnə'reʃən) *n.* 一代
     concern (kən'sɝn) *n.* 關切之事
     indecisive (,ɪndɪ'saɪsɪv) *adj.* 非決定性的

   【註】 本題有 42% 的同學選 (C)，但根據文章最後一段，作者是先表達
        出他擔心父母將會選擇某些特質，然後才說這樣的做法，會引
        起令人不安的道德問題，所以本題應該選 (A)。而且你想想，如
        果這個議題真的成為大家關切的道德問題，那麼就可以加以防
        範，作者就不需要擔心了。

3. (**B**) 本篇報告提到，基因療法在技術上的主要困難是什麼？

   (A) 病人嘗試另一種療法的意願。

   (B) <u>找到將基因物質放進細胞的方法。</u>

   (C) 人類社會男女人數的不平衡。

   (D) 會殺死新生基因的有害病毒。

     * major ('medʒɚ) *adj.* 主要的

       technical ('tɛknɪkḷ) *adj.* 技術上的

       willingness ('wɪlɪŋnɪs) *n.* 意願

       asymmetry (ə'sɪmɪtrɪ) *n.* 不對稱

4. (**D**) 科學家可能要用什麼方法來克服基因物質隨意轉移的問題？

   (A) 不管道德上的禁忌，只選擇「好的」基因轉移。

   (B) 先培植新血管，並透過它們來傳送基因。

   (C) 先除去身體裡的所有病毒。

   (D) <u>藉著身體本身的修補過程來取代有缺陷的基因。</u>

     * despite (dɪ'spaɪt) *prep.* 不管；不顧

       objection (əb'dʒɛkʃən) *n.* 禁止   through (θru) *prep.* 透過

       eliminate (ɪ'lɪmə,net) *v.* 除去

       defective (dɪ'fɛktɪv) *adj.* 有缺陷的

5. (**B**) 未來父母能為子女選擇什麼基因？

   (A) 道德基因。   (B) <u>身高基因。</u>

   (C) 財富基因。   (D) 替代基因。

     * height (haɪt) *n.* 身高   wealth (wɛlθ) *n.* 財富

    【註】本題有 24% 的同學選 (D)，其實這個答案，可能包含了文章最後
        一段所提到的智力、美貌和運動特質，但是跟 (B) 選項相較之
        下，後者是更直接的答案。

TEST 13

Read the following passage and choose the best answer for each question.

Greek mythology begins with Homer, an epic poet generally believed to have lived no earlier than a thousand years before Christ. The first written record of Greece by Homer, *The Iliad*, is a heroic poem in which heroes like Achilles and Hector fight <u>valiantly</u> for their honor. Written in rich and beautiful language, *The Iliad* has been hailed as indisputable proof of the greatness of ancient Greek civilization. However, the tales of Greek mythology do not throw much light on what other early cultures were like. Rather, they throw an abundance of light upon what early Greeks were like. Perhaps that's the reason why the ancient Greeks seem so familiar to us; we are their descendants intellectually, artistically, and politically.

Early Greeks were preoccupied with the visible. Sculptors watched athletes competing in games and felt that nothing imaginable could be as beautiful as those young bodies. So the statue of Apollo was made to embody the perfect combination of the physical and artistic beauty of youth. Through this brilliant image of a god, Greek artists and poets expressed how splendid man could be. He was the fulfillment of their search for beauty. Actually, despite all the admiration of and reference to gods, all the art and thought of ancient Greece centered on human beings. 【中正高中】

1. Which statement about *The Iliad* is correct?

   (A) It was written in coarse language.

   (B) It reflected a civilized society.

   (C) The name of the author is unknown.

   (D) It was written about 1,000 years ago.

2. Which statement about the tales of Greek mythology is correct?

   (A) They depict the world before the Greek civilization.

   (B) They provide little information about ancient Greece.

   (C) They reflect the beliefs of several early cultures.

   (D) They had a great and lasting influence on many generations to follow.

3. Who was the ideal image of youth for the ancient Greeks?

   (A) Homer (B) Achilles

   (C) Zeus (D) Apollo

4. What was considered the center of the world from the viewpoint of the ancient Greeks?

   (A) Gods and goddesses. (B) The invisible.

   (C) Human beings. (D) Artists and poets.

5. The underlined word "valiantly" can best be replaced by _____.

   (A) cowardly (B) encouragingly

   (C) stubbornly (D) bravely

TEST 13 詳解

Greek mythology begins with Homer, an epic poet generally believed to have lived no earlier than a thousand years before Christ.

希臘神話始於史詩詩人荷馬，一般認爲他的年代不早於西元前一千年。

* no earlier than a thousand years before Christ 字面的意思是「不早於西元前一千年」，也就是「還不到西元前一千年」。

　　Greek〔grik〕adj. 希臘的　　n. 希臘人
　　mythology〔mɪˈθɑlədʒɪ〕n. 神話（集合名詞）
　　Homer〔ˈhomɚ〕n. 荷馬（古希臘詩人）
　　epic〔ˈɛpɪk〕n. 史詩；敘事詩　　poet〔ˈpo·ɪt〕n. 詩人
　　generally〔ˈdʒɛnərəlɪ〕adv. 一般地　　Christ〔kraɪst〕n. 基督
　　before Christ 西元前（= B.C.）

The first written record of Greece by Homer, *The Iliad*, is a heroic poem in which heroes like Achilles and Hector fight <u>valiantly</u> for their honor.

荷馬所寫的第一部希臘的文字紀錄，即「伊里亞德」，是一部歌頌英雄的史詩，其中許多英雄，像阿基里斯和赫克特等，都爲了自己的榮譽而英勇奮戰。

* in which 引導形容詞子句 heroes…honor，修飾先行詞 a heroic poem。

　　written〔ˈrɪtn̩〕adj. 書面的　　Greece〔gris〕n. 希臘
　　Iliad〔ˈɪlɪəd〕n. 伊里亞德（荷馬的史詩作品，描述特洛伊戰爭）
　　heroic〔hɪˈroɪk〕adj. 英勇的；歌頌英雄的
　　Achilles〔əˈkɪliz〕n. 阿基里斯（特洛伊戰爭中的英雄之一）
　　Hector〔ˈhɛktɚ〕n. 赫克特（特洛伊戰爭中的英雄之一，被阿基里斯所殺）
　　fight〔faɪt〕v. 打仗；戰鬥　　valiantly〔ˈvæljəntlɪ〕adv. 英勇地
　　honor〔ˈɑnɚ〕n. 榮譽

Written in rich and beautiful language, *The Iliad* has been hailed as indisputable proof of the greatness of ancient Greek civilization.

「伊里亞德」的措辭豐富而優美，被認定是非常確實的證據，能證明古希臘文明的偉大。

> rich (rɪtʃ) *adj.* 豐富的   hail (hel) *v.* 歡呼；致敬
> *be hailed as* 被譽為；被認定為
> indisputable (ˌɪndɪ'spjutəb!) *adj.* 不容爭辯的；確實的
> proof (pruf) *n.* 證據   greatness ('gretnɪs) *n.* 偉大
> ancient ('enʃənt) *adj.* 古代的   civilization (ˌsɪvl̩ə'zeʃən) *n.* 文明

However, the tales of Greek mythology do not throw much light on what other early cultures were like. Rather, they throw an abundance of light upon what early Greeks were like.

不過，希臘神話的故事並沒有很清楚地說明其他早期文化的情況。反之，它們充分說明了早期的希臘人是什麼樣子。

> tale (tel) *n.* 故事   *throw light (up)on* 說明；解釋
> culture ('kʌltʃə) *n.* 文化   rather ('ræðə) *adv.* 反而；反之
> abundance (ə'bʌndəns) *n.* 豐富   *an abundance of* 很多
> early ('ɜlɪ) *adj.* 早期的

Perhaps that's the reason why the ancient Greeks seem so familiar to us; we are their descendants intellectually, artistically, and politically.

或許這就是古希臘人對我們而言，是如此熟悉的原因；我們在智慧上、藝術上，和政治上，都是他們的繼承者。

> seem (sim) *v.* 似乎   familiar (fə'mɪljə) *adj.* 熟悉的
> descendant (dɪ'sɛndənt) *n.* 子孫；繼承者
> intellectually (ˌɪntl̩'ɛktʃʊəlɪ) *adv.* 智慧上
> artistically (ɑr'tɪstɪkəlɪ) *adv.* 藝術上
> politically (pə'lɪtɪkəlɪ) *adv.* 政治上

Early Greeks were preoccupied with the visible. Sculptors watched athletes competing in games and felt that nothing imaginable could be as beautiful as those young bodies.

早期的希臘人都專注於看得見的事物。雕刻家看著參加比賽的運動員，覺得沒有一樣可想到的東西，能像那些年輕的身軀一樣優美。

preoccupy (pri'ɑkjəˌpaɪ) v. 使專注
be preoccupied with 專注於
visible ('vɪzəbḷ) adj. 看得見的   sculptor ('skʌlptɚ) n. 雕刻家
athlete ('æθlit) n. 運動員   compete (kəm'pit) v. 競爭；比賽
imaginable (ɪ'mædʒɪnəbḷ) adj. 可想像的

So the statue of Apollo was made to embody the perfect combination of the physical and artistic beauty of youth. Through this brilliant image of a god, Greek artists and poets expressed how splendid man could be. He was the fulfillment of their search for beauty.

所以，他們製作出阿波羅神像，以具體呈現，年輕人這種體格和藝術之美的完美結合。透過這樣一個出色的形象，希臘藝術家和詩人所表現的是，人類有多麼美好。他實現了他們不斷在追求的美的境界。

statue ('stætʃu) n. 雕像   Apollo (ə'pɑlo) n. (太陽神) 阿波羅
embody (ɪm'bɑdɪ) v. 具體表現   perfect ('pɝfɪkt) adj. 完美的
combination (ˌkɑmbə'neʃən) n. 結合
physical ('fɪzɪkḷ) adj. 身體的   artistic (ɑr'tɪstɪk) adj. 藝術的
youth (juθ) n. 年輕；年輕人   through (θru) prep. 透過
brilliant ('brɪljənt) adj. 卓越的；出色的
image ('ɪmɪdʒ) n. 形象   god (gɑd) n. 神
express (ɪk'sprɛs) v. 表達
splendid ('splɛndɪd) adj. 壯觀的；極好的   man (mæn) n. 人
fulfillment (fʊl'fɪlmənt) n. 實現   search (sɝtʃ) n. 尋找；追求

Actually, despite all the admiration of and reference to gods, all the art and thought of ancient Greece centered on human beings.

事實上，儘管希臘人對眾神非常崇拜，也常常提及，但是古希臘所有的藝術和思想，都是以人為中心。

> actually ('ækt∫uəlɪ) adv. 事實上
> despite (dɪ'spaɪt) prep. 儘管 (= in spite of)
> admiration (ˌædmə'reʃən) n. 欽佩；讚賞
> reference ('rɛfərəns) n. 提及 < to >　　center ('sɛntɚ) v. 集中
> **center on** 集中於；以…為中心；以…為主題
> **human beings** 人類

1. (**B**) 關於「伊里亞德」的敘述哪一個是正確的？
   (A) 它是以粗俗的語言寫成的。　　(B) 它反映文明的社會。
   (C) 作者的姓名不詳。　　　　　　(D) 它是在大約一千年前寫成的。

   > * coarse (kɔrs) adj. 粗俗的　　reflect (rɪ'flɛkt) v. 反映
   >   civilized ('sɪvḷˌaɪzd) adj. 文明的
   >   unknown (ʌn'non) adj. 未知的；不詳的

2. (**D**) 關於希臘神話的敘述哪一個是正確的？
   (A) 它們描繪希臘文明之前的世界。
   (B) 它們提供極少有關古希臘的資訊。
   (C) 它們反映出數種早期文化的信仰。
   (D) 它們對後代有深遠的影響。

   > * depict (dɪ'pɪkt) v. 描繪　　belief (bɪ'lif) n. 信仰
   >   lasting ('læstɪŋ) adj. 持久的；永遠的
   >   **have an influence on** 對～有影響
   >   generation (ˌdʒɛnə'reʃən) n. 世代
   >   **generations to follow** 後代

   > 【註】 本題有 21% 的同學選 (B)，但根據文章第一段最後，可知這個
   >   選項是錯誤的。另外，還有 24% 的同學選 (C)，同樣根據文章第
   >   一段第八行，也可以證明這個選項是錯的。

3. (**D**) 對古希臘人來說，誰是最理想的年輕人形象？

    (A) 荷馬   (B) 阿基里斯

    (C) 宙斯   (D) <u>阿波羅</u>

    * ideal〔aɪ'diəl〕*adj.* 理想的

      Zeus〔zus〕*n.* 宙斯（希臘神話中的眾神之王）

4. (**C**) 從古希臘人的觀點來看，什麼被認爲是世界的中心？

    (A) 眾神。

    (B) 看不見的事物；靈界。

    (C) <u>人。</u>

    (D) 藝術家和詩人。

    * consider〔kən'sɪdɚ〕*v.* 認爲

      viewpoint〔'vju,pɔɪnt〕*n.* 觀點

      goddess〔'gɑdɪs〕*n.* 女神

      invisible〔ɪn'vɪzəbḷ〕*n.* 看不見的人或物

      the invisible 靈界

    【註】 本題有 24% 的同學選 (A)，24% 的同學選 (D)，但根據文章的最後
         一段可知，古希臘所有的藝術和思想，都是以人爲中心的。

5. (**D**) 畫底線的字 "valiantly" 用哪一個字代換最適合？

    (A) cowardly〔'kaʊɚdlɪ〕*adv.* 膽怯地

    (B) encouragingly〔ɪn'kɝɪdʒɪŋlɪ〕*adv.* 鼓勵地

    (C) stubbornly〔'stʌbɚnlɪ〕*adv.* 固執地

    (D) *bravely*〔'brevlɪ〕*adv.* 勇敢地

    * underline〔ʌndɚ'laɪn〕*v.* 畫底線

      replace〔rɪ'ples〕*v.* 代換

TEST 14

Read the following passage and choose the best answer for each question.

The most prestigious award in American writing and music is the Pulitzer Prize, set up in 1917. The prize gets its name from Joseph Pulitzer. As the publisher of the *New York World* and *St. Louis Post-Dispatch* newspapers in the late 1800s, Pulitzer was the first to suggest university-level training for journalists. He was a widely respected figure in the newspaper industry. A year after his death, in 1912, the Columbia School of Journalism was founded in New York. Five years later, the first Pulitzer Prizes were awarded. The prizes were set up according to instructions in Pulitzer's will; he hoped they would be an incentive to achieve excellence.

Poetry was not included as a prize category at first. It was not until 1922 that a Pulitzer Prize was awarded to a poet, and the first winner was Edwin Arlington Robinson. He was one of a handful of American poets who won the prize more than once. Robert Frost was honored four times with a Pulitzer—in 1924, 1931, 1937, and 1943. Archibald MacLeish (1933 and 1953) and Robert Lowell (1947 and 1974) also won more than one. 【內湖高中】

1. Joseph Pulitzer was _____.
   (A) the first dean of the Columbia School of Journalism
   (B) a famous novelist who was born in Hungary
   (C) the publisher of the St. Louis Post-Dispatch
   (D) a newspaper publisher in the eighteenth century

2. When was the Pulitzer Prize established?
   (A) 1912   (B) 1917
   (C) 1922   (D) 1946

3. The Pulitzer Prizes were organized according to _____.
   (A) the Columbia School of Journalism
   (B) the wishes of Joseph Pulitzer
   (C) the standards of American writers and musicians
   (D) the newspaper industry in New York

4. Which of the following statements is FALSE?
   (A) Edwin Arlington Robinson was the first poet to win a Pulitzer Prize.
   (B) Robert Lowell's two Pulitzers came twenty-seven years apart.
   (C) Archibald MacLeish was a two-time winner of the Pulitzer Prize.
   (D) Robert Frost won two Pulitzer Prizes.

5. How many Pulitzer Prizes were awarded in the first year?
   (A) Five.
   (B) Only four because poetry was not included.
   (C) Twelve.
   (D) The passage does not say.

TEST 14 詳解

The most prestigious award in American writing and music is the Pulitzer Prize, set up in 1917. The prize gets its name from Joseph Pulitzer.

美國最有名的寫作和音樂獎，就是一九一七年創立的普立茲獎。這個獎的名字來自約瑟夫・普立茲。

* set up in 1917 源自於 *which was* set up in 1917，爲補述用法的形容詞子句，用來補充說明 the Pulitzer Prize。

> prestigious (prɛs'tɪdʒɪəs) *adj.* 有聲望的；有名的
> award (ə'wɔrd) *n.* 獎 (= *prize*)
> Pulitzer ('pjulɪtsɚ) *n.* 普立茲 (1847-1911；美國新聞記者及慈善家，
> 出生於匈牙利)　　*Pulitzer Prize* 普立茲獎
> *set up* 設立；創立

As the publisher of the *New York World* and *St. Louis Post-Dispatch* newspapers in the late 1800s, Pulitzer was the first to suggest university-level training for journalists.

在十九世紀末，普立茲身爲「紐約世界報」和「聖路易斯郵報」兩份報紙的發行人，他第一個提議記者應該接受大學程度的教育。

> publisher ('pʌblɪʃɚ) *n.* 發行人　　post (post) *n.* 郵政；郵報
> dispatch (dɪ'spætʃ) *n.* 特派；特遣
> suggest (sə'dʒɛst) *v.* 提議　　*in the late 1800s* 在十九世紀末
> level ('lɛvl) *n.* 程度；水準
> training ('trenɪŋ) *n.* 訓練；教育
> journalist ('dʒɝnl̩ɪst) *n.* 記者

He was a widely respected figure in the newspaper industry. A
year after his death, in 1912, the Columbia School of Journalism
was founded in New York.

他在報業界是個廣受尊敬的人物。在他過世後一年，也就是一九一二年，哥
倫比亞新聞學院在紐約創立了。

figure ('fɪgɚ) n. 人物　　industry ('ɪndəstrɪ) n. 企業
death (dɛθ) n. 死亡　　journalism ('dʒɝnḷ,ɪzəm) n. 新聞學
found (faʊnd) v. 創立 (= set up)

Five years later, the first Pulitzer Prizes were awarded. The prizes
were set up according to instructions in Pulitzer's will; he hoped
they would be an incentive to achieve excellence.

五年後，頒發了第一屆普立茲獎。這些獎項是根據普立茲遺囑中的指示所創
立的；他希望這些獎項能做為追求卓越的動機。

award (ə'wɔrd) v. 頒發　　*according to* 根據
instructions (ɪn'strʌkʃənz) n. pl. 指示　　will (wɪl) n. 遺囑
incentive (ɪn'sɛntɪv) n. 動機；刺激
achieve (ə'tʃiv) v. 達成；獲得
excellence ('ɛksḷəns) n. 優秀；卓越

Poetry was not included as a prize category at first. It was not
until 1922 that a Pulitzer Prize was awarded to a poet, and the first
winner was Edwin Arlington Robinson. He was one of a handful
of American poets who won the prize more than once.

起初，詩並沒有被包括在獎項的種類裡。直到一九二二年，才頒發普立
茲獎給詩人，而第一位得獎者是愛德溫・阿靈頓・羅賓森。他是少數美國詩
人當中，得獎不只一次的人。

* "It was not until…that~" 表「直到…才~」，"It was…that~"
  為強調句型，強調 not until…「直到…（時間）」。

> poetry ('po·ɪtrɪ) n. 詩（集合名詞，不可數）
> category ('kætə,gorɪ) n. 分類；種類　　*at first* 起初
> handful ('hænd,fʊl) n. 一把；少量　　*a handful of* 少數的

Robert Frost was honored four times with a Pulitzer—in 1924, 1931,
1937, and 1943. Archibald MacLeish (1933 and 1953) and Robert
Lowell (1947 and 1974) also won more than once.

羅伯・佛斯特榮獲普立茲獎四次 —— 在一九二四、一九三一、一九三七和一
九四三年。阿爾奇伯德・麥克力許（一九三三和一九五三年）得獎，還有羅
伯・洛威（一九四七和一九七四年），他們的得獎次數都不只一次。

> honor ('ɑnɚ) v. 給予榮譽；授與

1.(**C**) 約瑟夫・普立茲是 ＿＿＿＿＿＿＿。

　　(A) 哥倫比亞新聞學院的首任院長

　　(B) 出生於匈牙利的著名小說家

　　(C) 聖路易郵報的發行人

　　(D) 十八世紀的一位報紙發行人

> * dean (din) n. 院長　　novelist ('nɑvḷɪst) n. 小說家
>   Hungary ('hʌŋgərɪ) n. 匈牙利
>   century ('sɛntʃərɪ) n. 世紀

2.(**B**) 普立茲獎何時創立？

　　(A) 一九一二年　　　　　(B) 一九一七年

　　(C) 一九二二年　　　　　(D) 一九四六年

> * establish (ə'stæblɪʃ) v. 建立；創立

3. (**B**) 普立茲獎的創立是根據 ＿＿＿＿＿＿＿。

(A) 哥倫比亞新聞學院

(B) 約瑟夫・普立茲的願望

(C) 美國作家和音樂家的標準

(D) 紐約的報業界

* organize (ˈɔrgənˌaɪz) v. 組織；創立
 wish (wɪʃ) n. 意願；願望

4. (**D**) 下列敘述何者爲非？

(A) 愛德溫・阿靈頓・羅賓森是第一位贏得普立茲獎的詩人。

(B) 羅伯・洛威的兩座普立茲獎相隔了二十七年。

(C) 阿爾奇伯德・麥克力許是兩次普立茲獎的得主。

(D) 羅伯・佛斯特贏得兩次普立茲獎。

* apart (əˈpart) adv. 分開地
 two-time (ˈtuˌtaɪm) adj. 發生過兩次的
 winner (ˈwɪnə) n. 得獎者

5. (**D**) 普立茲獎第一年頒發了幾座獎項？

(A) 五座。

(B) 只有四座，因爲不包括詩。

(C) 十二座。

(D) 本文沒有提到。

* passage (ˈpæsɪdʒ) n. 文章

TEST 15

Read the following passage and choose the best answer for each question.

Even though they were written 150 years ago, Alexander Dumas' action novels still excite millions of readers around the world in close to a hundred languages. Dumas's two most famous stories, *The Three Musketeers* and *The Count of Monte Cristo*, have inspired more than 100 films. His 1848 novel, *The Man in the Iron Mask*, was recently made into a movie.

Few people know, however, that the author was the grandson of a Haitian slave. Even fewer people know that Dumas' father rose rapidly from a soldier to a general in the French Army before he was 31. The general died young, leaving Alexander penniless. But Dumas overcame poverty, the lack of formal education, and the hardship of racism to become one of the world's most popular writers.

Dumas's life was sometimes just like his action novels. He participated in three revolutions and fought with people when he was insulted. After making a fortune by writing novels, he built a mansion outside Paris and kept it open to starving artists, friends, and even strangers. 【復興高中】

1. Which of the following books was not written by
   Alexander Dumas?

   (A) The Man in the Iron Mask
   (B) The Three Musketeers
   (C) Alexander the General
   (D) The Count of Monte Cristo

2. Alexander Dumas's novels _____.

   (A) have fascinated readers around the world
   (B) have lasted for less than 100 years
   (C) were all made into movies
   (D) have been translated into more than 100 languages

3. In this passage, the word penniless means _____.

   (A) powerful   (B) poor
   (C) healthy   (D) alone

4. This passage was written mainly to describe _____.

   (A) a great novelist and his life
   (B) a well-known actor and his action movies
   (C) a Haitian slave and his father
   (D) a soldier who rose rapidly to the rank of a general

5. We may infer from the article that Dumas _____.

   (A) was a man who kept his money for himself
   (B) was a peace-loving writer
   (C) did not lead a colorful life
   (D) was a generous and kind-hearted man

TEST 15 詳解

Even though they were written 150 years ago, **Alexander**
Dumas' action novels still excite millions of readers **around the**
world in close to a hundred languages.

即使大仲馬的動作小說是在一百五十年前完稿的，其將近上百種文字的
翻譯本，仍然使全世界數百萬的讀者感到興奮。

> *even though* 即使
> *Alexander Dumas* 亞歷山大・仲馬（1802-70，法國小說家及劇作家，
> 　中文習慣翻譯為「大仲馬」）　*action novel* 動作小說
> excite〔ɪkˊsaɪt〕*v.* 使興奮
> *around the world* 全世界　　*close to* 接近於

Dumas's two most famous stories, *The Three Musketeers* and *The*
Count of Monte Cristo, have inspired more than 100 films. His 1848
novel, *The Man in the Iron Mask*, was recently made into a movie.

大仲馬最有名的兩部小說，即「三劍客」與「基督山恩仇記」，已經給了一
百多部電影靈感。他在一八四八年完成的小說「鐵面人」，最近被拍成電影。

> musketeer〔͵mʌskəˊtɪr〕*n.* 步兵（小說名）
> *The Three Musketeers* 三劍客
> count〔kaʊnt〕*n.*（除英國外，西歐地區的）伯爵
> *The Count of Monte Cristo* 基督山恩仇記（小說名）
> inspire〔ɪnˊspaɪr〕*v.* 啟發；給予靈感
> iron〔ˊaɪən〕*adj.* 鐵的　　mask〔mæsk〕*n.* 面具
> *The Man in the Iron Mask* 鐵面人（小說名）
> recently〔ˊrisn̩tlɪ〕*adv.* 最近　　*be made into* 被製作成

Few people know, however, that the author was the grandson of a Haitian slave. Even fewer people know that Dumas' father rose rapidly from a soldier to a general in the French Army before he was 31.

不過，卻很少有人知道，作者的祖父是個海地奴隸。而更少人知道，大仲馬的父親在三十一歲之前，就在法國軍隊中，快速地從士兵晉升到將軍。

author (ˈɔθɚ) *n.* 作者　　Haitian (ˈhetɪən) *adj.* 海地的
slave (slev) *n.* 奴隸　　rise (raɪz) *v.* 晉升
rapidly (ˈræpɪdlɪ) *adv.* 快速地　　soldier (ˈsoldʒɚ) *n.* 士兵
general (ˈdʒɛnərəl) *n.* 將軍　　army (ˈɑrmɪ) *n.* 軍隊

The general died young, leaving Alexander penniless. But Dumas overcame poverty, the lack of formal education, and the hardship of racism to become one of the world's most popular writers.

這位將軍英年早逝，留下身無分文的大仲馬。不過大仲馬克服了貧窮、缺乏正規教育及種族歧視的困境，而成為全世界最受歡迎的作家之一。

die young 早死　　leave (liv) *v.* 使處於（某種狀態）
penniless (ˈpɛnɪlɪs) *adj.* 身無分文的
lack (læk) *n.* 缺乏　　overcome (ˌovɚˈkʌm) *v.* 克服
poverty (ˈpɑvɚtɪ) *n.* 貧窮　　formal (ˈfɔrml̩) *adj.* 正規的
hardship (ˈhɑrdʃɪp) *n.* 困境
racism (ˈresɪzəm) *n.* 種族主義；種族歧視

Dumas's life was sometimes just like his action novels. He participated in three revolutions and fought with people when he was insulted.

大仲馬的人生有時就像他的動作小說一樣。他參與了三次革命，而且當他被侮辱的時候，也會跟人決鬥。

participate (pɑrˈtɪsəˌpet) *v.* 參加 < *in* >
revolution (ˌrɛvəˈluʃən) *n.* 革命　　fight (faɪt) *v.* 決鬥
insult (ɪnˈsʌlt) *v.* 侮辱

After making a fortune by writing novels, he built a mansion outside Paris and kept it open to starving artists, friends, and even strangers.

在以寫小說致富之後，他在巴黎的市區外蓋了一座豪宅，並且將它開放給挨餓的藝術家、朋友，甚至陌生人。

> fortune ('fɔrtʃən) n. 財富　　***make a fortune*** 致富；發財
> mansion ('mænʃən) n. 豪宅　　starving ('stɑrvɪŋ) adj. 挨餓的
> artist ('ɑrtɪst) n. 藝術家　　stranger ('strendʒɚ) n. 陌生人

1. (**C**) 下列哪一本書不是大仲馬寫的？
    (A) 鐵面人　　　　　　(B) 三劍客
    (C) <u>亞歷山大將軍</u>　(D) 基督山恩仇記

2. (**A**) 大仲馬的小說 _____。
    (A) <u>使全球的讀者著迷</u>　(B) 延續了不到一百年
    (C) 全都拍成電影　　　　　(D) 已經被翻譯成一百多種語言

    * fascinate ('fæsn̩,et) v. 使著迷　　last (læst) v. 延續
    translate (træns'let) v. 翻譯 < *into* >

3. (**B**) 在本文中，penniless 的意思是 _____。
    (A) powerful ('pauɚfəl) adj. 有力的
    (B) <u>貧窮的</u>
    (C) 健康的
    (D) alone (ə'lon) adj. 單獨的；獨自的

    * passage ('pæsɪdʒ) n. 文章

    【註】本題有 40% 的同學選 (D)，雖然文章中沒有提示 penniless 這個字的意思，但是仔細看這個字，其實是由 penny 和 less 組合而成的，而 penny 是「一便士銅幣」，所以可推知 penniless 就是沒錢的意思，故選 (B)。

4. (**A**) 本文最主要是要描寫 ＿＿＿＿＿＿。

    (A) 一位偉大的小說家及其生平

    (B) 一位著名的演員及其動作片

    (C) 一個海地奴隸及其父親

    (D) 一個迅速晉升到將軍階級的士兵

    * mainly ('menlɪ) *adv.* 主要地

      describe (dɪ'skraɪb) *v.* 描寫

      novelist ('nɑvḷɪst) *n.* 小說家

      well-known ('wɛl'non) *adj.* 著名的

      actor ('æktɚ) *n.* 演員   *action movie* 動作片

      rank (ræŋk) *n.* 階級

5. (**D**) 我們可以從這篇文章中，推論出大仲馬 ＿＿＿＿＿＿。

    (A) 是個只會把錢留給自己的人

    (B) 是個愛好和平的作家

    (C) 沒有過著多采多姿的生活

    (D) 是個慷慨而且仁慈的人

    * infer (ɪn'fɝ) *v.* 推論

      peace-loving ('pis'lʌvɪŋ) *adj.* 愛好和平的

      lead a ~ life 過～的生活

      colorful ('kʌlɚfəl) *adj.* 多采多姿的

      generous ('dʒɛnərəs) *adj.* 慷慨的

      kind-hearted ('kaɪnd'hɑrtɪd) *adj.* 好心腸的；仁慈的

TEST 16

Read the following passage and choose the best answer for each question.

(Santiago, Reuters)

A 10-year-old Chilean boy who had been abandoned by his parents survived for two years in a cave with a pack of stray dogs who scavenged for food with him and may even have <u>suckled</u> him, child care workers said on Monday.

The boy, thrown out of his home by abusive parents at the age of five, ran with 15 strays in the southern port town of Talcahuano after he escaped from a care center two years ago.

He lived in a cave with dogs and roamed the streets for food with them. "He would eat out of garbage cans and find leftovers," Delia Delgatto, head of Chile's National Child-Care Service, told Reuters.

The boy, who has not been named, threw himself into the wintry cold waters of the southern Pacific Ocean on Saturday to escape from police who had been alerted to his case by the municipality.

" A police officer dived into the water and saved him," a spokesman for the police said.

The child, dubbed "Dog Boy" by the Chilean media, spent a day in hospital in the city of Conception and was then taken to a childcare center. "He is showing signs of depression, is aggressive and is not speaking much though he does know how to speak," Delgatto said. "He was dressed almost in rags, was dirty and had filthy hair."

【華江高中】

1. "Dog Boy" _____.
   (A) was brought up by stray dogs
   (B) has no parents
   (C) ran to the mountains to escape from the police
   (D) was abandoned by his parents about five years ago

2. In line four, the word "suckle" probably means to _____.
   (A) hurt
   (B) attack
   (C) feed with milk
   (D) be scared of

3. This story reported by Reuters _____.

(A) happened in Brazil

(B) is mainly about 15 stray dogs

(C) is about a Chilean boy

(D) is made up

4. How did "Dog Boy" feed himself?

(A) He begged on the street.

(B) He found leftovers in garbage cans.

(C) A kind-hearted woman offered him some food.

(D) A child care center provided food for him.

5. When the police officer saved the boy, he _____.

(A) was wearing torn clothes

(B) was gentle and well-mannered

(C) didn't know how to speak

(D) was cheerful

【劉毅老師的話】

　　閱讀測驗的答案，都在文章裡，仔細對照，才能拿高分！

TEST 16 詳解

(Santiago, Reuters)

A 10-year-old Chilean boy who had been abandoned by his parents survived for two years in a cave with a pack of stray dogs who scavenged for food with him and may even have <u>suckled</u> him, child care workers said on Monday.

（聖地牙哥，路透社）

　　兒童保護人士在星期一指出，一個被父母遺棄的十歲智利男孩，和一群流浪狗，在洞穴中生活了兩年，這些狗和小男孩一起覓食，甚至可能還餵奶給小男孩吃。

> Santiago〔͵sæntɪ'ɑgo〕*n.* 聖地牙哥（智利首都）
> Reuters〔'rɔɪtəz〕*n.* 路透社（位於英國的通訊社）
> Chilean〔'tʃɪlɪən〕*adj.* 智利的　　abandon〔ə'bændən〕*v.* 遺棄
> survive〔sə'vaɪv〕*v.* 存活　　cave〔kev〕*n.* 洞穴
> pack〔pæk〕*n.* 一群　　stray〔stre〕*adj.* 迷失的；流浪的
> scavenge〔'skævɪndʒ〕*v.* 搜尋　　suckle〔'sʌkl̩〕*v.* 餵…奶
> ***child care*** 兒童保護的；幼兒保育的（ = *child-care* = *childcare*）

The boy, thrown out of his home by abusive parents at the age of five, ran with 15 strays in the southern port town of Talcahuano after he escaped from a care center two years ago.

　　這名小男孩五歲時，被虐待他的父母攆出家門，他兩年前從保護中心逃走之後，就跟十五隻流浪狗在一個叫做塔卡瓦諾的南部港市到處跑。

> * …in the southern port town of Talcahuano….介系詞 of 表示同格關係，作「叫做…的」解，如 the city of Rome「羅馬市」。
>
> ***throw out*** 扔掉；攆走　　abusive〔ə'bjusɪv〕*adj.* 虐待的
> run〔rʌn〕*v.* 到處跑　　stray〔stre〕*n.* 流浪狗　　port〔port〕*n.* 港口
> ***port town*** 港市　　escape〔ə'skep〕*v.* 逃走；逃避

He lived in a cave with dogs and roamed the streets for food with them. "He would eat out of garbage cans and find leftovers," Delia Delgatto, head of Chile's National Child-Care Service, told Reuters.

他和狗住在洞穴中，而且還和牠們在街上遊蕩覓食。智利國立兒童保護局局長 Delia Delgatto 告訴路透社說：「他會從垃圾桶中找剩菜吃。」

roam (rom) *v.* 在…遊蕩　　***garbage can*** 垃圾桶
leftovers ('lɛft,ovɚz) *n.pl.* 剩飯；剩菜
head (hɛd) *n.* 首長　　Chile ('tʃɪlɪ) *n.* 智利
service ('sɝvɪs) *n.* (政府的) 部門；局

The boy, who has not been named, threw himself into the wintry cold waters of the southern Pacific Ocean on Saturday to escape from police who had been alerted to his case by the municipality.

星期六時，因爲市政機關提醒警方注意他這個案例，結果那個沒有名字的男孩，爲了逃避警方的追捕，縱身跳入南太平洋的冰冷海水中。

name (nem) *v.* 命名　　***throw oneself into*** 投身於
wintry ('wɪntrɪ) *adj.* 寒冷的；冷冰冰的
the Pacific Ocean 太平洋
alert (ə'lɝt) *v.* 提醒　　case (kes) *n.* 案例；情況
municipality (,mjunɪsə'pælətɪ) *n.* 市政機關

"A police officer dived into the water and saved him," a spokesman for the police said.

「有位警察跳入水中救他，」警方的發言人說。

dive (daɪv) *v.* 跳水　　spokesman ('spoksmən) *n.* 發言人

The child, dubbed "Dog Boy" by the Chilean media, spent a day in hospital in the city of Conception and was then taken to a childcare center.

這位被智利媒體稱爲「狗仔」的孩子，在康塞普森市的醫院待了一天，然後就被帶往兒童保護中心。

dub〔dʌb〕v. 稱爲　　media〔'midɪə〕n. pl. 媒體

"He is showing signs of depression, is aggressive and is not speaking much though he does know how to speak," Delgatto said. "He was dressed almost in rags, was dirty and had filthy hair."

「他表現出很沮喪的樣子，具有攻擊性，而且話不多，雖然他確實知道如何說話，」Delgatto 說：「他幾乎是穿得破破爛爛，髒兮兮，而且頭髮也很髒。」

sign〔saɪn〕n. 徵兆；跡象
depression〔dɪ'prɛʃən〕n. 沮喪
aggressive〔ə'grɛsɪv〕adj. 具有攻擊性的
「do + 原形 V.」作「真的～」解，do 加強語氣用。
rags〔rægz〕n. pl. 破衣服　　*in rags* 衣衫襤褸的；穿著舊衣服的
dirty〔'dɝtɪ〕adj. 髒的　　filthy〔'fɪlθɪ〕adj. 污穢的

1. (**D**)　「狗仔」＿＿＿＿＿＿。
   (A) 是由流浪狗撫養長大的
   (B) 沒有父母
   (C) 爲了逃避警方而跑到山裡去
   (D) 大約五年前被他的父母遺棄

   * *bring up* 撫養長大

   【註】本題有 45%的同學選 (A)，但根據文章內容，狗仔這個小男孩，是和狗一起覓食，而且還會自己從垃圾桶找剩菜吃，所以 (A) 這個選項並沒有完全正確。

2. (**C**) 第四行中的 "suckle" 這個字，意思可能是 _____。

(A) 傷害   (B) 攻擊

(C) 餵奶   (D) 害怕

    * attack (ə'tæk) v. 攻擊   feed (fid) v. 餵食

      scared (skɛrd) adj. 害怕的

3. (**C**) 這個由路透社所報導的故事 _____。

(A) 發生在巴西

(B) 主要是關於十五隻流浪狗

(C) 是關於一個智利男孩

(D) 是編造出來的

    * Brazil (brə'zɪl) n. 巴西

      mainly ('menlɪ) adv. 主要地   ***make up*** 編造

4. (**B**) 「狗仔」如何養活他自己？

(A) 他在街上乞討。

(B) 他在垃圾桶找剩飯。

(C) 一位好心的女士提供他一些食物。

(D) 兒童保護中心提供食物給他。

    * beg (bɛg) v. 乞討   kind-hearted ('kaɪnd'hɑrtɪd) adj. 好心的

      offer ('ɔfə) v. 提供   provide (prə'vaɪd) v. 提供

5. (**A**) 當警察救起男孩時，他 _____。

(A) 穿著破爛的衣服   (B) 既溫和又有禮貌

(C) 不知道如何說話   (D) 很高興

    * torn (tɔrn) adj. 破掉的   gentle ('dʒɛntl) adj. 溫和的

      well-mannered ('wɛl'mænəd) adj. 有禮貌的

      cheerful ('tʃɪrfəl) adj. 高興的

    【註】 本題有 56% 的同學選 (C)，根據文章最後一段倒數第二行有提

         到，狗仔話很少，但是的確會說話，所以這個選項是錯的。

TEST 17

Read the following passage, and choose the best answer for each question.

Here are some things you can do to improve your chances of finding meaningful employment:

First, identify your skills and abilities in great detail. Don't give yourself a professional label, such as accountant or typist, because this may limit the jobs open to you. Be able to define what makes you a better applicant than another. Communicate this clearly and politely to the interviewer. Be well-groomed at all times. You never know when you will be interviewed.

Secondly, take the initiative and meet face to face with employers. Learn about a company before you visit it. Apply at different organizations and businesses to increase your chances. Use many avenues to find a job: answer job ads, make phone calls, etc. Let your friends and relatives know that you are looking for a job. They may know of companies offering positions that fit your qualifications.

Thirdly, be persistent without being obnoxious. Send short thank-you notes to those who have interviewed you. And give enough time to job-hunting, at least 30 hours a week.

Above all, have the right attitude. Nobody owes you a job. You have to convince an employer you are the best man for the job. 【南港高中】

1. A good title for the passage would be _____.
   (A) Job-hunting Is a Snap
   (B) Be a Success on the Job
   (C) The Job Market
   (D) Steps to Successful Job-hunting

2. The author suggests that _____.
   (A) anyone can find a job
   (B) you can improve your chances of getting a job
   (C) job-hunting is lots of fun
   (D) some job-hunting formulas never fail

3. The most important point the author makes is that you should _____.
   (A) communicate your abilities
   (B) get the help of friends and relatives
   (C) be persistent
   (D) have the right attitude

4. The author apparently feels that persistence is _____.
   (A) a negative characteristic
   (B) a positive characteristic
   (C) not important
   (D) useless

5. The words "take the initiative" in this article mean to _____.
   (A) be the last one
   (B) wait to be called
   (C) take the first step
   (D) provide references

TEST 17 詳解

Here are some things you can do to improve your chances of finding meaningful employment:

你可以做以下這些事情，來提高自己找到有意義的工作的機會：

improve (ɪm'pruv) v. 改善；增加；提高
chance (tʃæns) n. 機會　　**meaningful** ('minɪŋfl̩) adj. 有意義的
employment (ɪm'plɔɪmənt) n. 職業；工作

First, identify your skills and abilities in great detail. Don't give yourself a professional label, such as accountant or typist, because this may limit the jobs open to you.

首先，要非常仔細地確認自己所擁有的技能與能力。不要給自己貼上專業的標籤，像是會計師或打字員，因為這樣可能會使你可以應徵的工作受限。

identify (aɪ'dɛntə,faɪ) v. 確認；確定
skill (skɪl) n. 技能；技術
ability (ə'bɪlətɪ) n. 能力　　**detail** ('ditel) n. 細節
in detail 詳細地　　**professional** (prə'fɛʃənl̩) adj. 專業的
label ('lebl̩) n. 標籤　　*such as* 像是
accountant (ə'kauntənt) n. 會計師
typist ('taɪpɪst) n. 打字員　　**limit** ('lɪmɪt) v. 限制
open ('opən) adj. 開放的　　*be open to* ~ 提供給~

Be able to define what makes you a better applicant than another. Communicate this clearly and politely to the interviewer. Be well-groomed at all times. You never know when you will be interviewed.

要能夠表明，你有哪些特點，讓你比其他應徵者更好。要能夠清楚而且有禮貌地把這個訊息傳達給面試者。隨時都要穿戴整齊。你永遠不知道，自己何時將會去面試。

> **be able to V.** 能夠　　define (dɪˋfaɪn) v. 表明
> applicant (ˋæpləkənt) n. 應徵者
> communicate (kəˋmjunəˏket) v. 傳達
> clearly (ˋklɪrlɪ) adv. 清楚地
> politely (pəˋlaɪtlɪ) adv. 有禮貌地
> interviewer (ˋɪntɚˏvjuɚ) n. 面試者
> well-groomed (ˋwɛlˋgrumd) adj. 穿戴整齊的
> **at all times** 隨時；總是　　interview (ˋɪntɚˏvju) v. 面試

　　Secondly, take the initiative and meet face to face with employers. Learn about a company before you visit it. Apply at different organizations and businesses to increase your chances.

　　第二，要主動和你的雇主見面。在你拜訪一家公司之前，要了解這家公司的情況。要到不同的機構和企業應徵，以增加自己的機會。

> secondly (ˋsɛkəndlɪ) adv. 第二
> initiative (ɪˋnɪʃɪˏetɪv) n. 主動權
> **take the initiative** 採取主動　　*face to face* 面對面地
> employer (ɪmˋplɔɪɚ) n. 雇主　　*learn about* 知道關於…的事
> visit (ˋvɪzɪt) v. 拜訪　　apply (əˋplaɪ) v. 應徵
> organization (ˏɔrgənəˋzeʃən) n. 機構
> business (ˋbɪznɪs) n. 企業；公司

　　Use many avenues to find a job: answer job ads, make phone calls, etc. Let your friends and relatives know that you are looking for a job. They may know of companies offering positions that fit your qualifications.

要用很多方法來找工作：回覆徵才廣告、打電話等。讓你的親朋好友知道你
正在找工作。他們可能會知道，哪些公司有提供符合你的資格的職位。

avenue ('ævə,nju) n. 方法；途徑　　answer ('ænsə) v. 回覆
ad (æd) n. 廣告 (= advertisement)
etc. (ɛt'sɛtərə) 等等 (= et cetera)
relative ('rɛlətɪv) n. 親戚
know of 知道有；聽說過　　offer ('ɔfə) v. 提供
position (pə'zɪʃən) n. 工作；職位
fit (fɪt) v. 適合；符合
qualifications (,kwɑləfə'keʃənz) n. pl. 資格；條件

Thirdly, be persistent without being obnoxious. Send short
thank-you notes to those who have interviewed you. And give
enough time to job-hunting, at least 30 hours a week.

第三，要以不討人厭的方式，不屈不撓地找工作。要寄簡短的感謝函給
那些面試過你的人。而且要花足夠的時間來找工作，一星期至少要花三十個
小時。

thirdly ('θɝdlɪ) adv. 第三
persistent (pə'zɪstənt) adj. 不屈不撓的；持續的
obnoxious (əb'nɑkʃəs) adj. 討厭的；令人不愉快的
send (sɛnd) v. 寄　　thank-you ('θæŋk,ju) adj. 感謝的
note (not) n. 短箋　　**a thank-you note** 感謝函
job-hunting ('dʒɑb,hʌntɪŋ) n. 找工作　　**at least** 至少

Above all, have the right attitude. Nobody owes you a job.
You have to convince an employer you are the best man for the job.

最重要的是，要有正確的態度。沒有人欠你一份工作。你必須要使雇主
相信，你是最適合這份工作的人。

above all 最重要的是　　attitude ('ætə,tjud) n. 態度
owe (o) v. 欠　　convince (kən'vɪns) v. 使確信；說服

1. (**D**) 適合本文的標題是 ＿＿＿＿＿＿＿＿ 。

    (A) 找工作是件輕鬆的事　　　　(B) 做個事業成功的人

    (C) 就業市場　　　　　　　　　(D) <u>成功找到工作的步驟</u>

    * title ('taɪtl) *n.* 標題　　snap (snæp) *n.* 輕鬆的工作

    success (sək'sɛs) *n.* 成功的人　　market ('morkɪt) *n.* 市場

    step (stɛp) *n.* 步驟　　successful (sək'sɛsfəl) *adj.* 成功的

2. (**B**) 作者指出 ＿＿＿＿＿＿＿＿ 。

    (A) 任何人都可以找到工作

    (B) <u>你可以增加自己找到工作的機會</u>

    (C) 找工作很有趣

    (D) 有些找工作的方法永遠不會失敗

    * author ('ɔθɚ) *n.* 作者　　suggest (sə'dʒɛst) *v.* 提出

    formula ('fɔrmjələ) *n.* 公式；方式　　fail (fel) *v.* 失敗

3. (**D**) 作者指出，最重要的一點，就是你應該要 ＿＿＿＿＿＿＿＿＿ 。

    (A) 表達你的能力　　　　　　　(B) 得到親朋好友的幫助

    (C) 不屈不撓　　　　　　　　　(D) <u>有正確的態度</u>

    * point (pɔɪnt) *n.* 要點

4. (**B**) 作者顯然覺得不屈不撓是 ＿＿＿＿＿＿＿ 。

    (A) 不好的特質　　(B) <u>好的特質</u>　　(C) 不重要的　　(D) 無用的

    * apparently (ə'pɛrəntlɪ) *adv.* 顯然

    persistence (pɚ'zɪstəns) *n.* 不屈不撓

    negative ('nɛgətɪv) *adj.* 不好的；負面的

    characteristic (ˌkærɪktə'rɪstɪk) *n.* 特質

    positive ('pazətɪv) *adj.* 正面的　　useless ('juslɪs) *adj.* 無用的

5. (**C**) 本文中的「採取主動」意思是 ＿＿＿＿＿＿＿ 。

    (A) 當最後一個　　　　　　　　(B) 等著被叫到

    (C) <u>走出第一步</u>　　　　　　　(D) 提供參考

    * provide (prə'vaɪd) *v.* 提供　　reference ('rɛfərəns) *n.* 參考

TEST 18

Read the following passage, and choose the best answer for each question.

There was a man called "Uncle Sam" Wilson. He was born in Anington, Mass., Sept.13, 1766. His father and older bothers fought in the American Revolution. Sam himself enlisted at the age of 14 and served until the end of the war. Then he moved to Troy, NY, and began a meat-packing business.

On Oct.2, 1822, a group of visitors came to his plant. One of them, Governor Daniel D. Tomplins of New York, asked what the initials "EA-US" on the barrels of meat stood for. A workman replied the "EA" stood for the contractor for whom Wilson worked "Elbert Anderson." And he added jokingly that the "US" (actually an abbreviation for United States) stood for "Uncle Sam" Wilson.

An account of this incident appeared in the May 12, 1830 issue of the New York Gazette and General Advertiser. Since Wilson was a popular man, and was an example of a hard-working and patriotic American, the idea of "Uncle Sam" as a name for this kind of man caught on quickly.

By the end of the war of 1812, "Uncle Sam" had come to symbolize the character of the nation and the government. In 1961, Congress adopted a resolution saluting "Uncle Sam" Wilson of Troy, NY, as the "progenitor of America's national symbol." 【西松高中】

1. What does "Uncle Sam" mean?
   (A) It was the nickname for the man named "Uncle Sam" Wilson.
   (B) It is a name for a hard-working and patriotic American.
   (C) It symbolizes the character of the United States of America.
   (D) All of the three statements above are true.

2. Which statement is NOT true?
   (A) Americans are proud of the image that "Uncle Sam" has.
   (B) Americans enjoy having "Uncle Sam" as their national symbol.
   (C) Uncle Sam Wilson was later a Congressman.
   (D) Elbert Anderson was a businessman.

3. The name "Uncle Sam" gains public recognition
when _____.

  (A) the New York Gazette and General Advertiser
published the story

  (B) a group of visitors came to Wilson's plant

  (C) the War of 1812 ended

  (D) Wilson was born

4. This passage can most likely be found in a
_____.

  (A) newspaper

  (B) textbook

  (C) brochure

  (D) travel guide

5. The phrase "caught on" in paragraph three means
_____.

  (A) to be understood

  (B) to become symbolic

  (C) to become popular

  (D) to become amusing

TEST 18 詳解

There was a man called "Uncle Sam" Wilson. He was born in
Anington, Mass., Sept.13, 1766. His father and older brothers
fought in the American Revolution.

　　有一個人叫「山姆叔叔」威爾遜。他於一七六六年九月十三日出生在麻
薩諸塞州的阿寧頓。他的父親和哥哥曾參與過獨立戰爭。

> ***Mass.*** 麻薩諸塞州（Massachusetts 的縮寫，位於美國東北部）
> revolution (ˌrɛvə'luʃən) *n.* 革命
> ***the American Revolution*** （美國）獨立戰爭

Sam himself enlisted at the age of 14 and served until the end of
the war. Then he moved to Troy, NY, and began a meat-packing
business.

　　山姆本身在十四歲時入伍，並服役到戰爭結束爲止。之後他搬到紐約州的特
洛伊，並開始從事肉類加工業。

> enlist (ɪn'lɪst) *v.* 從軍；入伍
> serve (sɝv) *v.* 服役　　move (muv) *v.* 搬家
> meat-packing ('mit,pækɪŋ) *n.* 肉類加工（業）

On Oct.2, 1822, a group of visitors came to his plant. One of
them, Governor Daniel D. Tomplins of New York, asked what the
initials "EA-US" on the barrels of meat stood for.

　　在一八二二年的十月二日，有一群訪客來到他的工廠。紐約州州長丹尼
爾・湯普林斯是其中之一，他問說裝肉的桶子上的開頭字母「EA-US」代表
什麼。

> plant (plænt) *n.* 工廠
> governor ('gʌvənɚ) *n.* 州長　　initial (ɪ'nɪʃəl) *n.* 開頭字母
> barrel ('bærəl) *n.* 大桶　　***stand for*** 代表

A workman replied the "EA" stood for the contractor for whom
Wilson worked "Elbert Anderson."

有個工人回答，"EA" 是代表威爾遜的老闆，也就是承包商「艾伯特・安德森」。

> workman (ˈwɜkmən) *n.* 工人　　reply (rɪˈplaɪ) *v.* 回答
> contractor (ˈkɑntræktə) *n.* 立契約者；承包商

And he added jokingly that the "US" (actually an abbreviation for
United States) stood for "Uncle Sam" Wilson.

然後他開玩笑地補充說，US（事實上是美國的縮寫）代表「山姆叔叔」威
爾遜。

> add (æd) *v.* 補充說明　　jokingly (ˈdʒokɪŋlɪ) *adv.* 開玩笑地
> actually (ˈæktʃuəlɪ) *adv.* 事實上
> abbreviation (ə,brivɪˈeʃən) *n.* 縮寫字

An account of this incident appeared in May 12, 1830 issue
of the New York Gazette and General Advertiser.

這件事的報導，後來出現在一八三〇年五月十二日發行的紐約報和大
眾報。

> account (əˈkaʊnt) *n.* 描述；報導
> incident (ˈɪnsədənt) *n.* 事件
> appear (əˈpɪr) *v.* 出現
> issue (ˈɪʃju) *n.* (雜誌、報紙等的)⋯期；⋯版
> gazette (gəˈzɛt) *n.* ⋯報(通常用於報紙名稱)
> general (ˈdʒɛnərəl) *adj.* 大眾的；一般的
> advertiser (,ædvəˈtaɪzə) *n.* ⋯報 (用於以廣告為主的報紙名稱)

Since Wilson was a popular man, and was an example of a hard-
working and patriotic American, the idea of "Uncle Sam" as a
name for this kind of man caught on quickly.

因為威爾遜是個受歡迎的人，還有他是個努力工作且愛國的典型美國人，所以「山姆叔叔」的意思，就變成這種人的別稱，並很快地流行起來。

example (ɪgˈzæmpḷ) *n.* 例子；典範
hard-working (ˈhɑrdˌwɜkɪŋ) *adj.* 努力工作的；勤勉的
patriotic (ˌpetrɪˈɑtɪk) *adj.* 愛國的　　name (nem) *n.* 別稱；綽號
catch on 流行起來

By the end of the war of 1812, "Uncle Sam" had come to symbolize the character of the nation and the government.

到一八一二年戰爭結束時，「山姆叔叔」已經變成用來象徵美國這個國家和政府的特性。

symbolize (ˈsɪmbḷˌaɪz) *v.* 象徵　　***come to*** 成為（某種狀態）
character (ˈkærɪktə) *n.* 特性；身份

In 1961, Congress adopted a resolution saluting "Uncle Sam" Wilson of Troy, NY, as the "progenitor of America's national symbol."

在一九六一年，美國國會通過一個決議案，要向紐約州特洛伊市的「山姆叔叔」威爾遜致敬，因為他是「美國國家象徵的創始人」。

Congress (ˈkɑŋgrəs) *n.* 美國國會
adopt (əˈdɑpt) *v.* 採用（意見）；批准（提案）
resolution (ˌrɛzəˈluʃən) *n.* 決議案　　salute (səˈlut) *v.* 向…致敬
progenitor (proˈdʒɛnətə) *n.* 祖先；創始人
symbol (ˈsɪmbḷ) *n.* 象徵

1. (**D**)　「山姆叔叔」代表什麼意思？
　　(A) 是一個叫「山姆叔叔」威爾遜的人的綽號。
　　(B) 是努力工作又愛國的美國人的別稱。
　　(C) 象徵美國的特質。
　　(D) 以上三個敘述都是正確的。
　　　* nickname (ˈnɪkˌnem) *n.* 暱稱；綽號
　　　　statement (ˈstetmənt) *n.* 敘述

2. (**C**) 哪一項敘述是錯的？

    (A) 美國人以「山姆叔叔」的形象為榮。

    (B) 美國人很樂意有「山姆叔叔」這個國家象徵。

    (C) 山姆叔叔威爾遜後來當了美國國會議員。

    (D) 艾伯特‧安德森是個商人。

    * *be proud of* 以～為榮   image ('ɪmɪdʒ) *n.* 形象

      Congressman ('kɑŋgrəsmən) *n.* 國會議員

3. (**A**) 「山姆叔叔」這個名字被大家所認可是在 ＿＿＿＿＿＿＿。

    (A) 紐約報和大眾報刊登這則報導時

    (B) 一群訪客到威爾遜的工廠時

    (C) 一八一二年的戰爭結束時

    (D) 威爾遜出生時

    * public ('pʌblɪk) *adj.* 大眾的

      recognition (ˌrɛkəg'nɪʃən) *n.* 承認

      publish ('pʌblɪʃ) *v.* 刊登   story ('storɪ) *n.* 新聞報導

4. (**B**) 這篇文章最有可能可以在 ＿＿＿＿＿＿ 找到。

    (A) 報紙   (B) 教科書

    (C) 小冊子   (D) 旅遊指南

    * textbook ('tɛkstˌbʊk) *n.* 教科書

      brochure (bro'ʃʊr) *n.* 小冊子

      guide (gaɪd) *n.* 指南

5. (**C**) 第三段中的片語 "caught on" 意思是 ＿＿＿＿＿＿＿。

    (A) 被理解   (B) 變成象徵性的

    (C) 變得受歡迎   (D) 變得有趣

    * phrase (frez) *n.* 片語

      symbolic (sɪm'bɑlɪk) *adj.* 象徵性的

      amusing (ə'mjuzɪŋ) *adj.* 有趣的；好玩的

TEST 19

Read the following passage and choose the best answer for each question.

Louis Braille is today regarded and respected as the greatest benefactor of blind people. Louis Braille was born on January 4th, 1809 in a French village not far from Paris called Coupvray. At the age of three, while playing in his father's workshop he injured his eye. Infection set in and this quickly spread to the other eye. He became totally blind. While in school he proved to be a gifted student. While pursuing his normal studies he became interested in developing an alphabet for blind people. In 1824, at the age of fifteen, he invented a system of touch writing and reading for the blind. This system was eventually to bear his name.

The foundation for his invention was laid by an artillery captain in the army of Louis XV, Charles Barbier de la Sere. He designed a system of raised dots and dashes for night writing to be used by soldiers on night maneuvers. A group in favor of making Braille the official international system for reading and writing for blind people met in Paris in 1878. In 1918, the United States of America realized that Braille was superior to other methods. In 1922 an agreement was reached which is known today as Standard English Braille.

Louis Braille's health started deteriorating at the age of 26 when he contracted tuberculosis, a contagious lung disease, for which there was no cure at the time. In December 1851 he became very ill and he never recovered. He died on the 6th of January, 1852. He was buried in the village of his birth, Coupvray. One century later, in 1952, he was reburied in the Pantheon. This is the highest honor that France **bestows on** its citizens. 【明倫高中】

1. What is the topic of the passage?
   (A) The life of Louis Braille.
   (B) The production of Braille books.
   (C) The building of the Pantheon in France.
   (D) The rise of the French army.

2. Which of the following is not included in this passage?
   (A) When and where Braille invented the system.
   (B) The cause of Braille's death.
   (C) What inspired Braille to invent the system.
   (D) Where Braille was hospitalized.

3. The system invented by Charles Barbier de la Sere was originally for _____.

    (A) educational purposes

    (B) military use

    (C) medical operations

    (D) entertaining

4. The phrase "bestow on" is most likely to mean _____.

    (A) give to

    (B) take away

    (C) suffer from

    (D) cope with

5. Where was Louis Braille first buried?

    (A) Where he died.

    (B) At the Pantheon.

    (C) Where he was born.

    (D) In Paris.

TEST 19 詳解

Louis Braille is today regarded and respected as the greatest benefactor of blind people. Louis Braille was born on January 4th, 1809 in a French village not far from Paris called Coupvray.

路易士・布雷爾現今被視爲，和尊爲盲人最大的恩人。路易士・布雷爾生於一八〇九年一月四日，他出生在一個離巴黎不遠的法國村莊，叫做普伯雷。

> regard (rɪ'gɑrd) v. 認爲 < *as* >
> respect (rɪ'spɛkt) v. 尊敬
> benefactor (,bɛnə'fæktɚ) n. 恩人
> blind (blaɪnd) adj. 盲的　　village ('vɪlɪdʒ) n. 村莊

At the age of three, while playing in his father's workshop he injured his eye. Infection set in and this quickly spread to the other eye.

三歲的時候，他在父親的工廠玩耍時，弄傷了一隻眼睛。後來發生感染，而且很快就蔓延到另一隻眼睛了。

> *at the age of* 在～歲的時候
> workshop ('wɝk,ʃɑp) n. 工作場所；小工廠
> injure ('ɪndʒɚ) v. 使受傷
> infection (ɪn'fɛkʃən) n. 感染
> *set in* 開始　　spread (sprɛd) v. 蔓延

He became totally blind. While in school he proved to be a gifted student. While pursuing his normal studies he became interested in developing an alphabet for blind people.

他變成全盲了。在學校，他是個有天賦的學生。當他在接受正規的學校教育時，對於發展出一套盲人專用的字母表很有興趣。

totally（'totlɪ）*adv.* 完全地　　prove（pruv）*v.* 顯示；結果（成為）
gifted（'gɪftɪd）*adj.* 有天賦的　pursue（pə'su）*v.* 追求；從事
normal（'nɔrml）*adj.* 正規的　　studies（'stʌdɪz）*n. pl.* 求學；學業
develop（dɪ'vɛləp）*v.* 發展　　alphabet（'ælfə,bɛt）*n.* 字母表

In 1824, at the age of fifteen, he invented a system of touch writing and reading for the blind. This system was eventually to bear his name.

在一八二四年，十五歲的他發明了一套系統，讓盲人能以觸摸的方式來書寫與閱讀。最後這套系統就冠上了他的名字。

invent（ɪn'vɛnt）*v.* 發明　　***the blind*** 盲人（= *blind people*）
eventually（ɪ'vɛntʃuəlɪ）*adv.* 最後；終於
bear（bɛr）*v.* 擁有

The foundation for his invention was laid by an artillery captain in the army of Louis XV, Charles Barbier de la Sere. He designed a system of raised dots and dashes for night writing to be used by soldiers on night maneuvers.

替他的發明奠定基礎的是查理・巴比爾・德・拉・塞爾，他是路易十五軍隊裡的砲兵上尉。他設計了一套系統，這套系統能在晚上書寫凸起的點和長劃，好讓夜間演習的士兵使用。

foundation（faun'deʃən）*n.* 基礎
invention（ɪn'vɛnʃən）*n.* 發明　　lay（le）*v.* 奠定
artillery（ɑr'tɪlərɪ）*n.* 砲兵　　captain（'kæptɪn）*n.* 上尉
army（'ɑrmɪ）*n.* 軍隊　　design（dɪ'zaɪn）*v.* 設計
raised（rezd）*adj.* 凸起的　　dot（dɑt）*n.* 小點
dash（dæʃ）*n.* 長劃　　maneuver（mə'nuvə）*n.* 演習

A group in favor of making Braille the official international system for reading and writing for blind people met in Paris in 1878.

在一八七八年，一個支持讓布雷爾點字法成為正式的國際盲人讀寫系統的團體在巴黎聚會。

in favor of 支持　　Braille〔brel〕*n.* 布雷爾點字（法）；盲人點字法
official〔ə'fɪʃəl〕*adj.* 官方的；正式的
international〔ˌɪntɚ'næʃənḷ〕*adj.* 國際的　　meet〔mit〕*v.* 聚會

In 1918, the United States of America realized that Braille was superior to other methods. In 1922 an agreement was reached which is known today as Standard English Braille.

在一九一八年，美國了解到布雷爾點字法優於其他的方法。在一九二二年，達成了現今稱為「標準英文布雷爾點字法」的協議。

superior〔sə'pɪrɪɚ〕*adj.* 較優良的 < *to* >
agreement〔ə'grimənt〕*n.* 協議　　reach〔ritʃ〕*v.* 達成
be known as 以…為人所知；被稱為
standard〔'stændɚd〕*adj.* 標準的

Louis Braille's health started deteriorating at the age of 26 when he contracted tuberculosis, a contagious lung disease, for which there was no cure at the time.

路易士‧布雷爾的健康，在他二十六歲時開始惡化，當時他感染了肺結核，那是一種會傳染的肺部疾病，而且在當時是無法治療的。

deteriorate〔dɪ'tɪrɪəˌret〕*v.* 惡化
contract〔kən'trækt〕*v.* 感染（疾病）
tuberculosis〔tjuˌbɝkjə'losɪs〕*n.* 肺結核（= *TB* ）
contagious〔kən'tedʒəs〕*adj.* 接觸傳染的；易感染的
lung〔lʌŋ〕*n.* 肺部　　disease〔dɪ'ziz〕*n.* 疾病
cure〔kjʊr〕*n.* 治療法　　*at the time* 當時

In December 1851 he became very ill and he never recovered. He died on the 6th of January, 1852. He was buried in the village of his birth, Coupvray.

在一八五一年十二月，他的病情變得很嚴重，而且永遠無法康復。他死於一八五二年一月六日。他被埋在他出生的那個村莊 — 普伯雷。

> recover (rɪ'kʌvɚ) v. 康復　　bury ('bɛrɪ) v. 埋葬
> birth (bɝθ) n. 出生

One century later, in 1952, he was reburied in the Pantheon. This is the highest honor that France **bestows on** its citizens.

一世紀之後，在一九五二年時，他被改葬在法國先賢祠。這是法國授與其國民的最高榮譽。

> century ('sɛntʃərɪ) n. 世紀；一百年
> rebury (ri'bɛrɪ) v. 改葬　　Pantheon (pæn'θiən) n. 法國先賢祠
> honor ('ɑnɚ) n. 榮譽　　bestow (bɪ'sto) v. 授與 <*on*>
> citizen ('sɪtəzṇ) n. 公民；國民

1. (**A**) 本文的主題爲何？
  (A) 路易士・布雷爾的生平。　(B) 布雷爾點字書的製作。
  (C) 法國先賢祠的建造。　　　(D) 法國軍隊的崛起。
  　 * passage ('pæsɪdʒ) n. 文章　　production (prə'dʌkʃən) n. 製作
  　 rise (raɪz) n. 崛起

2. (**D**) 下列何者未包含在本文中？
  (A) 布雷爾發明這套系統的時間與地點。
  (B) 布雷爾的死因。
  (C) 激發布雷爾發明這系統的原因。
  (D) 布雷爾住院的地方。
  　 * cause (kɔz) n. 原因　　inspire (ɪn'spaɪr) v. 激勵；給予靈感
  　 hospitalize ('hɑspɪtḷ͵aɪz) v. 使住院

3. (**B**) 查理‧巴比爾‧德‧拉‧塞爾所發明的系統，本來是爲了
_____。

(A) 教育目的　　　　　　(B) <u>軍事用途</u>

(C) 醫療手術　　　　　　(D) 娛樂用途

* originally (ə'rɪdʒənḷɪ) *adv.* 本來

educational (,ɛdʒə'keʃənḷ) *adj.* 教育的

purpose ('pɝpəs) *n.* 目的；用途

military ('mɪlə,tɛrɪ) *adj.* 軍事的

medical ('mɛdɪkḷ) *adj.* 醫療的

operation (,ɑpə'reʃən) *n.* 手術

entertaining (,ɛntə'tenɪŋ) *adj.* 有娛樂效果的

4. (**A**) "bestow on" 這個片語最有可能的意思是 _____。

(A) <u>給予</u>

(B) take away　拿走；剝奪

(C) suffer from　遭受；罹患

(D) cope with　應付

5. (**C**) 路易士‧布雷爾一開始埋在哪裡？

(A) 他過世的地方。　　　　(B) 在法國先賢祠。

(C) <u>他出生的地方。</u>　　　　(D) 在巴黎。

TEST 20

Read the following passage and choose the best answer for each question.

Recently, a fingerprint identification program was set up in three Pennsylvania school districts. With this program, students do not need to bring cash for buying pizza, a burger, fries, etc. anymore. They can pay for lunch by placing their index finger on a machine. This is much faster and more convenient.

To activate this program, students just need to put their index finger on a small machine—a scanner that can record their fingerprints electronically. Then the image of each fingerprint, which is made up of 27 points, will be recorded in the computer. At the same time, each of the 27 points will be given a number. Only the numbers will be kept while the image will be deleted immediately, in order to prevent others from seeing students' actual fingerprints.

Milton Miller, director of food services at one of the school districts, says there are at least three benefits. First of all, there is no need for students to worry about lost cards. Second, it is impossible for anyone to use another student's PIN (personal identification number) to get into the student's account. Last but not least, parents can be sure that the money in the account is spent only on school lunches.

With this high level of technology, one may ask, "What's next?" No one knows. But we may guess what may be in the near future—we may be able to open our gym lockers with a simple finger scan! 【麗山高中】

1. What is the best title for this article?
   (A) Index Finger   (B) Finger Food
   (C) Fingernail   (D) Ring Finger

2. In this article, what does the word "identification" mean?
   (A) report   (B) recognition
   (C) reflection   (D) reputation

3. Which is not an advantage of using the new system mentioned in this article?

(A) Students don't have to worry about losing their cards.

(B) It will be difficult for students to get access to others' accounts.

(C) This system is faster and more convenient.

(D) Students can use their lunch money to buy whatever they want.

4. Why is it essential for students' fingerprint images to be deleted at once?

(A) So that other students can't copy the actual fingerprints.

(B) So that other students can get the money fast.

(C) So that students can operate other functions.

(D) So that students can change their PIN numbers.

5. What does the author imply in the last paragraph?

(A) Many other uses will be found for fingerprint scanning in the future.

(B) Students will no longer need money to open their lockers.

(C) If students do not have enough money in their accounts, they will be denied access to their lockers.

(D) We do not have enough high technology to predict the future.

TEST 20 詳解

Recently, a fingerprint identification program was set up in three Pennsylvania school districts. With this program, students do not need to bring cash for buying pizza, a burger, fries, etc. anymore.

最近，有三個位於賓夕凡尼亞州的學區，創立了指紋辨識系統。有了這個系統，學生們不再需要為了買披薩、漢堡、或薯條等，而攜帶現金。

recently (ˈrisn̩tlɪ) *adv.* 最近　　fingerprint (ˈfɪŋgɚ͵prɪnt) *n.* 指紋
identification (aɪ͵dɛntəfəˈkeʃən) *n.* 身分確認
fingerprint identification 指紋辨識
program (ˈprogræm) *n.* 計劃；系統
set up 創立　　district (ˈdɪstrɪkt) *n.* 地區
school district 學區　　cash (kæʃ) *n.* 現金
pizza (ˈpitsə) *n.* 披薩　　burger (ˈbɝgɚ) *n.* 漢堡 (= *hamburger*)
fries (fraɪz) *n. pl.* 薯條 (= *French fries*)　　etc. (ɛtˈsɛtərə) …等等

They can pay for lunch by placing their index finger on a machine. This is much faster and more convenient.

他們只要把食指放在一部機器上，就可以支付午餐費了，而且這樣做會更快、更方便。

place (ples) *v.* 放置　　*index finger* 食指 (= *forefinger*)

To activate this program, students just need to put their index finger on a small machine—a scanner that can record their fingerprints electronically.

要啟動這個系統，學生們只要把食指放在一台小型機器上 —— 這台掃描器能以電子化的方式記錄他們的指紋。

activate (ˈæktə͵vet) *v.* 使活動起來　　record (rɪˈkɔrd) *v.* 記錄
electronically (ɪ͵lɛkˈtrɑnɪklɪ) *adv.* 電子化地

Then the image of each fingerprint, which is made up of 27 points, will be recorded in the computer. At the same time, each of the 27 points will be given a number.

接著，每個由二十七個點所組成的指紋影像，就會被記錄在電腦裡。同時，這二十七個點各自都會有一個號碼。

> image ('ɪmɪdʒ) *n.* 影像　　*be make up of* 由～組成
> point (pɔɪnt) *n.* 點　　*at the same time* 同時

Only the numbers will be kept while the image will be deleted immediately, in order to prevent others from seeing students' actual fingerprints.

為了要防止別人看到學生們眞正的指紋，指紋的影像會立刻被刪除，只留下號碼。

> while (hwaɪl) *conj.* 然而　　delete (dɪ'lit) *v.* 刪除
> immediately (ɪ'midɪɪtlɪ) *adv.* 立刻
> prevent (prɪ'vɛnt) *v.* 預防
> actual ('æktʃuəl) *adj.* 眞正的

Milton Miller, director of food services at one of the school districts, says there are at least three benefits. First of all, there is no need for students to worry about lost cards.

米爾頓·米勒，是其中一個學區的供餐負責人，他表示這項計劃至少有三個好處。第一，學生們不再需要擔心遺失卡片。

> director (də'rɛktə) *n.* 管理者　　service ('sɝvɪs) *n.* 服務
> *at least* 至少　　benefit ('bɛnəfɪt) *n.* 好處
> *first of all* 首先；第一　　need (nid) *n.* 需要
> lost (lɔst) *adj.* 遺失的

Second, it is impossible for anyone to use another student's PIN (personal identification number) to get into the student's account.

第二，任何人都不可能利用別的學生的密碼（個人身分確認號碼），去侵入該名學生的帳戶。

> PIN〔pɪn〕*n.* 密碼（= *personal identification number*）
> personal〔'pɝsn̩l〕*adj.* 個人的　　account〔ə'kaʊnt〕*n.* 帳戶

Last but not least, parents can be sure that the money in the account is spent only on school lunches.

最後一項要點是，家長們可以確定該帳戶裡的錢，只是花在學校的午餐上。

> ***last but not least*** 最後一項要點是

　With this high level of technology, one may ask, "What's next?" No one knows. But we may guess what can be in the near future — we may be able to open our gym lockers with a simple finger scan!

　有了這項高科技，或許有人會問：「那接下來呢？」沒有人知道。但是我們可能會猜到，在不久的將來會怎麼樣 —— 我們或許可以用簡單的指紋掃描，打開體育館的寄物櫃！

> level〔'lɛvl̩〕*n.* 水平；程度　　***in the near future*** 在不久的將來
> technology〔tɛk'nɑlədʒɪ〕*n.* 科技　　gym〔dʒɪm〕*n.* 體育館
> locker〔'lɑkɚ〕*n.* 寄物櫃　　scan〔skæn〕*n.* 掃描

1.（**B**）本篇文章最適合的標題是什麼？
　(A) 食指　　(B) 點心　　(C) 指甲　　(D) 無名指

> ＊ title〔'taɪtl̩〕*n.* 標題　　***finger food*** 點心
> fingernail〔'fɪŋgɚ,nel〕*n.* 指甲　　***ring finger*** 無名指

> 【註】本題有超過一半的同學選(A)，但在本文中，一再提到手指（finger）
> 　　　和食物（food），所以選(B)會更完整。此外 finger food 這個片語，
> 　　　還可以作「點心」解，所以以此為題的話，更有一語雙關的趣味。

2. (**B**) 在本文中，identification（身分確認）這個字是什麼意思？

    (A) 報導

    (B) ***recognition*** 〔ˌrɛkəgˈnɪʃən〕*n.* 識別

    (C) reflection〔rɪˈflɛkʃən〕*n.* 反射

    (D) reputation〔ˌrɛpjəˈteʃən〕*n.* 名聲

3. (**D**) 下列何者不是本文中所提到，使用這個新系統的好處？

    (A) 學生們不用擔心遺失卡片。

    (B) 學生們很難侵入別人的帳戶。

    (C) 這個系統是更快速、更方便的。

    (D) <u>學生們可以用吃午餐的錢，來買任何他們想要的東西。</u>

      * advantage〔ədˈvæntɪdʒ〕*n.* 好處；優點
        mention〔ˈmɛnʃən〕*v.* 提到
        access〔ˈæksɛs〕*n.* 進入；接近或使用權　　***get access to*** 進入

4. (**A**) 為什麼立刻刪除學生們的指紋影像是非常重要的？

    (A) <u>這樣一來其他的學生就不能複製真正的指紋。</u>

    (B) 這樣一來其他的學生就可以很快拿到錢。

    (C) 這樣一來學生們就可以操作其他的功能。

    (D) 這樣一來學生們就可以更改他們的個人身份確認號碼。

      * essential〔əˈsɛnʃəl〕*adj.* 必要的；非常重要的
        at once 立刻　　　***so that*** 以便於；因此
        operate〔ˈɑpəˌret〕*v.* 操作　　function〔ˈfʌŋkʃən〕*n.* 功能

5. (**A**) 作者在最後一段暗示什麼？

    (A) <u>在未來還會發現指紋掃描的許多用途。</u>

    (B) 學生們將不再需要用錢來開寄物櫃。

    (C) 如果學生的戶頭裡沒有足夠的錢，他們將打不開寄物櫃。

    (D) 我們沒有足夠的高科技去預測未來。

      * author〔ˈɔθɚ〕*n.* 作者　　imply〔ɪmˈplaɪ〕*v.* 暗示
        paragraph〔ˈpærəˌgɪæf〕*n.* 段落　　use〔jus〕*n.* 用途
        deny〔dɪˈnaɪ〕*v.* 拒絕給予　　predict〔prɪˈdɪkt〕*v.* 預測

TEST 21

Read the following passage and choose the best answer for each question.

Five genetically identical fruit flies were produced
at the lab of Dr. Vett Lloyd at Dalhousie University in
Halifax, Nova Scotia, Canada. They join an expanding
collection of animal clones that now includes sheep,
mice, rats, cows, and even cats. Fruit flies have long
been a "model" to study reproductive biology. "That's
the only reason why you would want to do this," Dr.
Lloyd told BBC News. "There are more than enough
fruit flies in the world."

The Dalhousie fly clones were produced in a slightly
different way from the method made famous with Dolly
the sheep. In **that process**, the genetic material of the
adult animal to be copied was taken from one of its cells
and injected into an emptied egg, which later developed
into a developing embryo. For the Dalhousie flies, the
genetic material came not from an adult cell but from an
embryo cell. It is generally thought to be easier to clone
this way. Even so, it still took about eight hundred
transfers to produce the five fly clones.

Currently, many of the large animal clones experience ill health and die prematurely. This acts as an obstacle to the application of cloning technology in areas that might improve the quality of agricultural livestock or produce useful drug products in animals. It is thought that many of the problems associated with cloning result from the mis-regulation of genes that would not be found in correctly developing embryos. The Lloyd team intends to investigate this issue with their fly clones so that they can understand why cloning is often **flawed**. "If we can see in flies where the process goes wrong and these genes are present in mammals, maybe we could correct it in mammal cloning— but that is a long, long way down the road," Dr. Lloyd said.

【成功高中】

1. What is the purpose of this article?
   (A) To introduce a new development in genetics.
   (B) To comment on the latest biology book.
   (C) To tell people how fruit flies clone themselves.
   (D) To criticize the discovery made by Dr. Lloyd.

2. According to this passage, which of the following animals has NOT been cloned?
   (A) The cow.   (B) The mouse.
   (C) The mosquito.   (D) The cat.

3. What does "**that process**" refer to in the second paragraph?

   (A) Taking cells out of an egg.

   (B) The process used in cloning Dolly the sheep.

   (C) The Dalhousie fly production.

   (D) Doing 800 transfers in fruit fly cloning.

4. The word "**flawed**" in the last paragraph can be best replaced by "_____."

   (A) destructive   (B) successful

   (C) questionable   (D) imperfect

5. Which of the following is INCORRECT?

   (A) Lloyd adopted the same process to reproduce fruit flies as that used with Dolly the sheep.

   (B) Large cloned animals often suffer from bad health and die at an early age.

   (C) Genetic mis-regulation may account for the problems with clones.

   (D) Fruit flies were experimented because they are a model of reproductive biology.

TEST 21 詳解

Five genetically identical fruit flies were produced at the lab of Dr. Vett Lloyd at Dalhousie University in Halifax, Nova Scotia, Canada. They join an expanding collection of animal clones that now includes sheep, mice, rats, cows, and even cats.

在加拿大新斯科夏省，哈利法克斯市的達爾豪西大學，維特・羅伊德博士的實驗室裡，製造出了五隻基因完全相同的果蠅。牠們加入了逐漸擴大的複製動物群，這個群體目前包括綿羊、老鼠、母牛，甚至還有貓。

* 第二句中的主詞 They，即指第一句中的五隻果蠅。

> genetically (dʒə'nɛtɪkəlɪ) adv. 遺傳上；基因方面
> identical (aɪ'dɛntɪkl̩) adj. 完全相同的　　*fruit fly* 果蠅
> lab (læb) n. 實驗室 (= *laboratory*)
> expanding (ɪk'spændɪŋ) adj. 逐漸擴大的
> collection (kə'lɛkʃən) n. (一批) 收藏品；(一批) 收集的東西
> clone (klon) n. 被複製者　v. 複製　　sheep (ʃip) n. 綿羊
> mice (maɪs) n. pl. 老鼠 (單數為 mouse (maʊs))
> rat (ræt) n. 老鼠 (在住家內所見到的較小型老鼠為 mouse，較大型的則
> 稱為 rat)　　cow (kaʊ) n. 母牛

Fruit flies have long been a "model" to study reproductive biology. "That's the only reason why you would want to do this," Dr. Lloyd told BBC News. "There are more than enough fruit flies in the world."

長久以來，果蠅一直是生殖生物學的研究「模型」。「這麼做的唯一原因，」羅伊德博士告訴 BBC 新聞說。「世界上有太多果蠅了。」

> model ('mɑdl̩) n. 模型；模範
> reproductive (ˌriprə'dʌktɪv) adj. 繁殖的
> biology (baɪ'ɑlədʒɪ) n. 生物學　　news (njuz) n. 新聞節目
> *more than enough* 超過所需的；太多的

The Dalhousie fly clones were produced in a slightly different way from the method made famous with Dolly the sheep.

達爾豪西複製果蠅的方法，與有名的桃莉羊稍微不同。

> slightly (ˈslaɪtlɪ) *adv.* 稍微　　method (ˈmɛθəd) *n.* 方法

In **that process**, the genetic material of the adult animal to be copied was taken from one of its cells and injected into an emptied egg, which later developed into a developing embryo.

在複製桃莉羊那個過程中，他們將欲複製的成年動物的基因物質，從其中一個細胞抽出，注射到一個空的卵子裡，之後這個卵子就會發育成一個成長中的胚胎。

> * 不定詞片語 to be copied，用來修飾 the adult animal。which later…embryo 為形容詞子句，修飾先行詞 an emptied egg。
>
> genetic (dʒəˈnɛtɪk) *adj.* 遺傳的；基因的
> material (məˈtɪrɪəl) *n.* 物質　　adult (əˈdʌlt) *adj.* 成年的
> copy (ˈkɑpɪ) *v.* 複製　　cell (sɛl) *n.* 細胞
> inject (ɪnˈdʒɛkt) *v.* 注射　　emptied (ˈɛmptɪd) *adj.* 空的
> egg (ɛg) *n.* 卵子　　develop (dɪˈvɛləp) *v.* 發展；發育
> developing (dɪˈvɛləpɪŋ) *adj.* 成長中的　　embryo (ˈɛmbrɪˌo) *n.* 胚胎

For the Dalhousie flies, the genetic material came not from an adult cell but from an embryo cell. It is generally thought to be easier to clone this way. Even so, it still took about eight hundred transfers to produce the five fly clones.

至於達爾豪西的果蠅，基因物質並非來自成年動物的細胞，而是來自胚胎細胞。一般認為，這樣會比較容易複製。即使如此，還是做了大約八百次轉殖，才製造出這五隻複製果蠅。

> ***not~but***… 不是～而是…　　generally (ˈdʒɛnərəlɪ) *adv.* 一般地
> ***even so*** 即使如此　　transfer (ˈtrænsfɝ) *n.* 移植；轉殖

Currently, many of the large animal clones experience ill health and die prematurely. This acts as an obstacle to the application of cloning technology in areas that might improve the quality of agricultural livestock or produce useful drug products in animals.

目前，許多複製出來的大型動物，都經歷了健康不佳和夭折的情形。這會成爲複製科技運用在改善農耕家畜的品質，或是利用動物製造出有效藥品等方面的阻礙。

* that might improve…in animals 爲形容詞子句，修飾先行詞 areas。

> currently (ˈkɜəntlɪ) *adv.* 目前　　experience (ɪkˈspɪrɪəns) *v.* 經歷
> prematurely (ˌpriməˈtjʊrlɪ) *adv.* 過早地；未成熟地
> ***act as*** 作爲；充當　　obstacle (ˈɑbstəkḷ) *n.* 阻礙
> application (ˌæpləˈkeʃən) *n.* 運用
> cloning (ˈklonɪŋ) *n.* 生物的複製
> area (ˈɛrɪə) *n.* 領域　　quality (ˈkwɑlətɪ) *n.* 品質
> agricultural (ˌægrɪˈkʌltʃərəl) *adj.* 農業的
> livestock (ˈlaɪvˌstɑk) *n.* 家畜　　drug (drʌg) *n.* 藥

It is thought that many of the problems associated with cloning result from the mis-regulation of genes that would not be found in correctly developing embryos.

與複製有關的許多問題，被認爲是起因於基因的錯誤調節，因爲這種情況在正常發育的胚胎裡是不會被發現的。

* associated with cloning 是分詞片語，修飾 the problems，後面的 result from 是動詞片語。that would not…embryos 是形容詞子句，修飾先行詞 the mis-regulation of genes。

> associate (əˈsoʃɪˌet) *v.* 使有關連 < *with* >
> ***result from*** 起因於　　mis- 爲表示「不好、錯誤」的字首。
> regulation (ˌrɛgjəˈleʃən) *n.* 調整 (指胚胎發育中，物質的重新分配)
> gene (dʒin) *n.* 基因　　correctly (kəˈrɛktlɪ) *adv.* 正確地

The Lloyd team intends to investigate this issue with their fly clones so that they can understand why cloning is often **flawed**.

羅伊德博士的小組打算要利用他們的複製果蠅，來調查這個問題，這麼一來，他們就可以了解複製為何常常出現缺失。

intend (ɪn'tɛnd) v. 打算　　investigate (ɪn'vɛstə,get) v. 調查
issue ('ɪʃju) n. 議題；問題　　*so that* 如此一來；以便於
flawed (flɔd) adj. 有缺點的

"If we can see in flies where the process goes wrong and these genes are present in mammals, maybe we could correct it in mammal cloning — but that is a long, long way down the road," Dr. Lloyd said.

「如果我們能夠在果蠅身上，看出複製的過程是哪裡出錯，以及這些基因是在哺乳動物身上的哪些地方，那麼或許我們在複製哺乳類動物時，就可以加以修正 —— 但未來還有很漫長的路要走，」羅伊德博士說。

　* where the…and these…in mammals 是名詞子句，做 see 的受詞。

process ('prɑsɛs) n. 過程
go wrong 出錯　　present ('prɛznt) adj. 存在的
mammal ('mæml) n. 哺乳類動物　　correct (kə'rɛkt) v. 改正
down the road 在未來 (= *in the future*)

1. (**A**) 這篇文章的目的為何？
(A) 介紹一項遺傳學上的新發展。
(B) 評論最新的生物學書籍。
(C) 告訴人們果蠅如何自行複製。
(D) 批評羅伊德博士的發現。

　* purpose ('pɝpəs) n. 目的　　article ('ɑrtɪkl) n. 文章
comment ('kɑmɛnt) v. 評論 < on >　　latest ('letɪst) adj. 最新的
criticize ('krɪtə,saɪz) v. 批評　　discovery (dɪ'skʌvərɪ) n. 發現

2. (**C**) 根據本文，以下哪一種動物還沒有被複製過？

    (A) 母牛。   (B) 老鼠。

    (C) <u>蚊子。</u>   (D) 貓。

     * mosquito〔məˈskito〕*n.* 蚊子

3. (**B**) 第二段中的 "that process" 指的是什麼？

    (A) 從卵子中將細胞取出。   (B) <u>桃莉羊的複製過程。</u>

    (C) 達爾豪西果蠅的複製。

    (D) 在果蠅複製時做了八百次轉殖。

     * *refer to* 是指

4. (**D**) 最後一段的 "flawed"，用哪一個字代換最適合？

    (A) destructive〔dɪˈstrʌktɪv〕*adj.* 破壞性的

    (B) successful〔səkˈsɛsfəl〕*adj.* 成功的

    (C) questionable〔ˈkwɛstʃənəbl̩〕*adj.* 可疑的

    (D) *imperfect*〔ɪmˈpɝfɪkt〕*adj.* 不完美的；有缺點的

     * replace〔rɪˈples〕*v.* 代換

    【註】 本題有不少同學選 (A) 和 (C)，但根據文章最後一段，討論的是複製的問題，羅伊德複製果蠅，目的就是要找出複製過程是哪邊有問題，所以可推知 flawed 應是作「有缺點的」解，故選 (D)。

5. (**A**) 下列何者爲非？

    (A) <u>羅伊德採取和複製桃莉羊相同的方法，來複製果蠅。</u>

    (B) 大型的複製動物常常因爲健康不佳而受苦，然後很早就死掉。

    (C) 基因的錯誤調整，可能可以說明複製所發生的問題。

    (D) 果蠅被用來做實驗，因爲牠們是生殖生物學的模型。

     * adopt〔əˈdɑpt〕*v.* 採取；採用   *suffer from* 受～之苦

     account for 說明；是～的原因

     experiment〔ɪkˈspɛrəˌmɛnt〕*v.* 實驗

    【註】 本題有 23% 的同學選 (C)，要注意，本題是要你選錯誤的選項，所以應該選 (A)。

TEST 22

Read the following passage and choose the best answer for each question.

What exactly is ecotourism? In its original context, ecotourism means traveling in a way that helps to preserve the earth rather than damage the environment to please tourists. It aims to support local economies rather than international corporations. Essentially, ecotours are very different from traditional vacations.

Here is some advice for would-be ecotourists: Avoid hugely popular destinations because if too many tourists flock to an area, it will impact the environment. Look for locally owned businesses (according to the International Ecotourism Society, 80% of the price of packaged tours typically goes to airfare and corporate-owned hotels, leaving little to support local businesses). When shopping, avoid the mass-imported trinkets and buy locally-made souvenirs. Seek out accommodations that don't change the sheets every day and leave little bars of soap that are supposed to be used once and then thrown away. Look for restaurants that serve local food, which helps the economy, rather than imported food that is exactly the same as what we eat at home.

There are many other tips we can give to ecotourists. Don't harass, try to feed or touch wildlife. Don't be condescending to the local residents. Do learn a few words in the local language. Do be sensitive to local customs and attitudes, especially those that relate to acceptable public dress and conversation. 【中正高中】

1. According to the passage, which of the following does ecotourism benefit the most?
   (A) ecotourists
   (B) environmentalists
   (C) local economies
   (D) international corporations

2. According to the passage, which kind of hotel is highly recommended?
   (A) One that changes its sheets every day.
   (B) One that throws away little bars of soap.
   (C) One that helps the local economy by serving local food.
   (D) One that belongs to an international corporation.

3. According to the passage, tourists can show respect for people by _____.

    (A) showing pity for them

    (B) dressing in a locally acceptable way

    (C) helping them feed local wildlife

    (D) having lots of conversations with them

4. The word "harass" in the last paragraph most likely means _____.

    (A) love   (B) look at

    (C) feed   (D) bother

5. Why should ecotourists avoid popular destinations?

    (A) Those areas are all owned by international corporations.

    (B) The environment cannot support too many people.

    (C) There are not enough souvenirs available for all the tourists.

    (D) They will only be able to eat imported food there.

TEST 22 詳解

What exactly is ecotourism? In its original context, ecotourism means traveling in a way that helps to preserve the earth rather than damage the environment to please tourists.

生態旅遊到底是什麼？從它原本的意思看來，生態旅遊就是以有助於保護地球的方式旅遊，而不是爲了取悅遊客而破壞環境。

> exactly〔ɪg'zæktlɪ〕*adv.* 究竟；到底
> ecotourism〔,ikə'turɪzəm〕*n.* 生態旅遊
> original〔ə'rɪdʒənḷ〕*adj.* 原本的；最初的
> context〔'kɑntɛkst〕*n.* 語境；意思
> preserve〔prɪ'zɜv〕*v.* 保護　　earth〔ɜθ〕*n.* 地球
> ***rather than*** 而不是　　damage〔'dæmɪdʒ〕*v.* 破壞
> environment〔ɪn'vaɪrənmənt〕*n.* 環境
> please〔pliz〕*v.* 取悅　　tourist〔'turɪst〕*n.* 觀光客；遊客

It aims to support local economies rather than international corporations. Essentially, ecotours are very different from traditional vacations.

其目的在於支援當地的經濟，而不是國際企業。在本質上，生態旅遊與傳統的度假方式有非常大的不同。

> aim〔em〕*v.* 目的在於
> support〔sə'port〕*v.* 支持；支援
> local〔'lokḷ〕*adj.* 當地的　　economy〔ɪ'kɑnəmɪ〕*n.* 經濟
> international〔,ɪntə'næʃənḷ〕*adj.* 國際的
> corporation〔,kɔrpə'reʃən〕*n.* 公司
> essentially〔ə'sɛnʃəlɪ〕*adv.* 本質上
> ecotour〔,ikə'tur〕*n.* 生態旅遊
> traditional〔trə'dɪʃənḷ〕*adj.* 傳統的

Here is some advice for would-be ecotourists: avoid hugely popular destinations because if too many tourists flock to an area, it will impact the environment.

這裡有一些建議要給未來想從事生態旅遊的人：避免到非常受歡迎的地方，因爲如果有太多遊客湧入一個區域，則會對環境造成衝擊。

advice〔əd'vaɪs〕*n.* 建議
would-be〔'wʊd,bɪ〕*adj.* 想成爲…的；未來的
ecotourist〔,ikə'tʊrɪst〕*n.* 生態旅遊的遊客　　avoid〔ə'vɔɪd〕*v.* 避免
hugely〔'hjudʒlɪ〕*adv.* 非常　　destination〔,dɛstə'neʃən〕*n.* 目的地
flock〔flɑk〕*v.* 聚集；成群而去　　impact〔ɪm'pækt〕*v.* 衝擊

Look for locally owned businesses (according to the International Ecotourism Society, 80% of the price of packaged tours typically goes to airfare and corporate-owned hotels, leaving little to support local businesses).

要找當地人經營的企業（根據國際生態旅遊協會的說法，套裝旅遊的價格中，有百分之八十大概都花在機票與企業經營的飯店，只剩下一點點是用來支援當地的企業）。

locally-owned〔'lokəlɪ,ond〕*adj.* 當地人擁有的
business〔'bɪznɪs〕*n.* 企業　　society〔sə'saɪətɪ〕*n.* 協會
packaged〔'pækɪdʒd〕*adj.* 整套的；旅行社包辦的
tour〔tʊr〕*n.* 旅遊　　typically〔'tɪpɪklɪ〕*adv.* 一般地；通常
airfare〔'ɛr,fɛr〕*n.* 機票錢
corporate-owned〔'kɔrpərɪt,ond〕*adj.* 公司經營的

When shopping, avoid the mass-imported trinkets and buy locally-made souvenirs. Seek out accommodations that don't change the sheets every day and leave little bars of soap that are supposed to be used once and then thrown away.

在購物的時候，要避免購買大量進口的小飾品，要買當地製造的紀念品。住宿就要找不會每天換床單，而且會將原本被認為只用一次就丟掉的小塊肥皂給留下來的地方。

> mass-imported ('mæs,ɪm'portɪd) *adj.* 大量進口的
> trinket ('trɪŋkɪt) *n.* 小飾品
> locally-made ('lokəlɪ,med) *adj.* 當地製造的
> souvenir (,suvə'nɪr) *n.* 紀念品　　*seek out* 尋找
> accommodations (ə,kɑmə'deʃənz) *n. pl.* 住宿設備
> sheets (ʃits) *n. pl.* 床單
> bar (bɑr) *n.* (長方形或橢圓形的) 塊
> soap (sop) *n.* 肥皂
> supposed (sə'pozd) *adj.* 被認為應當…的
> ***throw away*** 丟掉

Look for restaurants that serve local food, which helps the economy, rather than imported food that is exactly the same as what we eat at home.

要找提供當地食物的餐廳，這樣會對其經濟有幫助，而不是吃那些跟我們自己國家吃的一模一樣的進口食物。

> serve (sɜv) *v.* 供應
> imported (ɪm'portɪd) *adj.* 進口的
> exactly (ɪg'zæktlɪ) *adv.* 完全　　home (hom) *n.* 本國；家鄉

There are many other tips we can give to ecotourists. Don't harass, try to feed or touch wildlife. Don't be condescending to the local residents.

我們還可以提供給生態遊客很多其他的建議。不要騷擾、試著餵食或觸摸野生動物。不要對當地居民抱著傲慢的態度。

tip（ tɪp ）*n.* 建議　　harass（ hə'ræs ）*v.* 騷擾
feed（ fid ）*v.* 餵食
wildlife（'waɪld,laɪf ）*n.* 野生動物
condescending（,kɑndɪ'sɛndɪŋ ）*adj.* 有優越感的；傲慢的
resident（'rɛzədənt ）*n.* 居民

Do learn a few words in the local language. Do be sensitive to
local customs and attitudes, especially those that relate to
acceptable public dress and conversation.

一定要學會當地語言的一些詞彙。對當地的習俗與看法一定要**敏感**，**特別是**
可以被接受的公共場所穿著與對話。

sensitive（'sɛnsətɪv ）*adj.* 敏感的 < *to* >
custom（'kʌstəm ）*n.* 習俗
attitude（'ætə,tjud ）*n.* 態度
especially（ ə'spɛʃəlɪ ）*adv.* 尤其；特別是
relate（ rɪ'let ）*v.* 與…有關 < *to* >
acceptable（ ək'sɛptəbḷ ）*adj.* 可接受的

1.(**C**) 根據本文，生態旅遊對下列何者最有利？
   (A) 生態遊客　　　　　　　(B) 環境保護者
   (C) 當地經濟　　　　　　　(D) 國際企業

    * passage（'pæsɪdʒ ）*n.* 文章
     benefit（'bɛnəfɪt ）*v.* 對～有益
     environmentalist（ ɪn,vaɪrən'mɛntḷɪst ）*n.* 環境保護者

2. (**C**) 根據本文，哪一種飯店被大力推薦？

　　(A) 每天換床單的飯店。

　　(B) 會將小塊肥皂丟掉的飯店。

　　(C) <u>因提供當地食物而有助於當地經濟的飯店。</u>

　　(D) 屬於國際企業的飯店。

　　　* highly〔'haɪlɪ〕*adv.* 高度地；大大地
　　　　recommend〔,rɛkə'mɛnd〕*v.* 推薦　　***belong to*** 屬於

3. (**B**) 根據本文，遊客可以用 ＿＿＿＿＿＿＿ 來表達對人們的尊重。

　　(A) 對他們表示同情

　　(B) <u>穿當地能接受的服裝</u>

　　(C) 幫他們餵食當地的野生動物

　　(D) 跟他們談很多話

　　　* respect〔rɪ'spɛkt〕*n.* 尊重；尊敬　　pity〔'pɪtɪ〕*n.* 同情

4. (**D**) 最後一段的 "harass" 最有可能的意思是 ＿＿＿＿＿＿。

　　(A) 愛　　　　　　　　　　(B) 看著

　　(C) 餵食　　　　　　　　　(D) <u>打擾</u>

　　　* bother〔'baðɚ〕*v.* 打擾

5. (**B**) 為何生態旅客應該避免去受歡迎的地方？

　　(A) 那些地區都是國際企業所擁有的。

　　(B) <u>環境無法支撐這麼多人。</u>

　　(C) 沒有足夠的紀念品給所有遊客買。

　　(D) 他們只能在那裡吃到進口的食物。

　　　* available〔ə'veləbḷ〕*adj.* 可獲得的；可買到的

TEST 23

Read the following passage and choose the best answer for each question.

POISONING

The home is loaded with poisons: Cosmetics, Detergents, Bleaches, Cleaning Solutions, Glue, Lye, Paint, Turpentine, Kerosene, Gasoline and other petroleum products, Alcohol, Aspirin and other medications, and on and on.

1. **Small children are most often the victims of accidental poisoning. If a child has swallowed or is suspected to have swallowed any substance that might be poisonous, assume the worst — TAKE ACTION.**

2. **Call your Poison Control Center. If none is in your area, call your emergency medical rescue squad. Bring the suspected item and container with you.**

3. **What you can do if the victim is unconscious:**
A. Make sure the patient is breathing. If not, tilt the head back and perform mouth-to-mouth resuscitation. Do not give anything by mouth. Do not attempt to stimulate the person. Call emergency rescue squad immediately.

4. **If the victim is vomiting:**
A. Roll him or her over onto the left side so that the person will not choke on what is brought up.

5. **Be prepared. Determine and verify your Poison Control Center and Fire Department Rescue Squad numbers and keep them near your telephone.**

【大同高中】

1. Who are most often the victims of poisoning?
   (A) children　　　　　(B) teenagers
   (C) adults　　　　　　(D) old people

2. Where is the information likely to be found?
   (A) In advertisements containing information about personal hygiene.
   (B) In magazines containing information about dizziness.
   (C) In books containing information about quality sleep.
   (D) In the front of telephone books containing information about emergencies.

3. Which of the following statements is true?
   (A) If the victim is a small child, hold him or her upside down to help him throw up.
   (B) Give unconscious victims water to help them come to their senses.
   (C) If the victim is vomiting, tilt the head back and perform mouth to mouth resuscitation.
   (D) You can call the Fire Department Rescue Squad for help in case of poisoning.

4. According to the passage, which of the following is not a poison found in the home?
   (A) Oil paint.   (B) Firewood.
   (C) Painkillers.   (D) Javex bleach.

5. If you think someone has been poisoned the passage advises you to _____.
   (A) act cautiously and be prepared
   (B) verify your Poison Control Center's number
   (C) not do anything until the emergency rescue squad arrives
   (D) contact the Poison Control Center immediately

TEST 23 詳解

POISONING

The home is loaded with poisons: Cosmetics, Detergents, Bleaches, Cleaning Solutions, Glue, Lye, Paint, Turpentine, Kerosene, Gasoline and other petroleum products, Alcohol, Aspirin and other medications, and on and on.

中 毒

家中充滿了各種毒物:化妝品、清潔劑、漂白劑、去污劑、膠水、鹼液、油漆、松節油、煤油、汽油,及其他石化製品、酒精、阿斯匹靈與其他藥物等等。

poisoning ('pɔɪznɪŋ) *n.* 中毒　　load (lod) *v.* 使充滿 < *with* >
poison ('pɔɪzn̩) *n.* 毒物　　cosmetics (kɑz'mɛtɪks) *n.pl.* 化妝品
detergent (dɪ'tɝdʒənt) *n.* 清潔劑　　bleach (blitʃ) *n.* 漂白劑
cleaning ('klinɪŋ) *n.* 去污;打掃
solution (sə'luʃən) *n.* 溶液;溶劑
cleaning solution 去污劑　　glue (glu) *n.* 膠水
lye (laɪ) *n.* 鹼液　　paint (pent) *n.* 油漆
turpentine ('tɝpən,taɪn) *n.* 松節油
kerosene ('kɛrə,sin) *n.* 煤油
gasoline ('gæsḷ,in) *n.* 汽油　　petroleum (pə'troliəm) *n.* 石油
alcohol ('ælkə,hɔl) *n.* 酒精　　aspirin ('æspərɪn) *n.* 阿斯匹靈
medication (,mɛdɪ'keʃən) *n.* 藥物　　***on and on*** 等等

1. Small children are most often the victims of accidental poisoning. If a child has swallowed or is suspected to have swallowed any substance that might be poisonous, assume the worst — TAKE ACTION.

一、 小孩子最常成為意外中毒的受害者。如果小孩已經吞下，或是懷疑有吞下任何可能有毒的物質，就要假設最壞的情形 —— 採取行動。

> victim (ˈvɪktɪm) *n.* 受害者
> accidental (ˌæksəˈdɛntḷ) *adj.* 意外的
> swallow (ˈswɑlo) *v.* 吞下
> suspect (səˈspɛkt) *v.* 懷疑
> substance (ˈsʌbstəns) *n.* 物質
> poisonous (ˈpɔɪznəs) *adj.* 有毒的
> assume (əˈsjum) *v.* 假設
> worst (wɜst) *n.* 最壞的情形　　*take action* 採取行動

2. Call your Poison Control Center. If none is in your area, call your emergency medical rescue squad. Bring the suspected item and container with you.

二、 打給中毒控制中心。如果你那一區都沒有中毒控制中心，就打電話給緊急醫療救護隊。要帶著可疑的物品與容器。

> control (kənˈtrol) *n.* 控制
> none (nʌn) *pron.* 沒有一個
> area (ˈɛrɪə) *n.* 區域
> emergency (ɪˈmɜdʒənsɪ) *n.* 緊急情況
> medical (ˈmɛdɪkḷ) *adj.* 醫療的
> rescue (ˈrɛskju) *n.* 救援　　squad (skwɑd) *n.* 小組
> *rescue squad* 救護隊；搜救隊
> suspected (səˈspɛktɪd) *adj.* 可疑的
> item (ˈaɪtəm) *n.* 物品
> container (kənˈtenɚ) *n.* 容器

3. What you can do if the victim is unconscious:

A. Make sure patient is breathing. If not, tilt head back and perform mouth-to-mouth resuscitation. Do not give anything by mouth. Do not attempt to stimulate the person. Call emergency rescue squad immediately.

三、如果中毒者失去意識該怎麼辦？

解答：　要確定病人還有呼吸。如果沒有，將頭往後仰並施行口對口人工呼吸。
不要讓病人用嘴巴吃任何東西。不要企圖刺激那個人。立刻打電話給
緊急救護隊。

unconscious (ʌn'kɑnʃəs) *adj.* 失去意識的
make sure 確定　　　patient ('peʃənt) *n.* 病人
breathe (brið) *v.* 呼吸　　　tilt (tɪlt) *v.* 使傾斜
perform (pɚ'fɔrm) *v.* 施行
resuscitation (rɪ,sʌsə'teʃən) *n.* 復甦
mouth-to-mouth resuscitation 口對口人工呼吸法
attempt (ə'tɛmpt) *v.* 企圖
stimulate ('stɪmjə,let) *v.* 刺激
immediately (ɪ'midɪɪtlɪ) *adv.* 立刻

4. If the victim is vomiting:

A. Roll him or her over onto the left side so that the person will not choke on what is brought up.

四、如果病人正在嘔吐：

解答：　將他或她的身體往左側翻，如此一來，那個人才不會被吐出來的東
西嗆到。

vomit ('vɑmɪt) *v.* 嘔吐
roll (rol) *v.* 翻轉；翻身　　　choke (tʃok) *v.* 嗆住；窒息
bring up 嘔吐

5. Be prepared. Determine and verify your Poison Control Center and Fire Department Rescue Squad numbers and keep them near your telephone.

五、要做好準備。查明並確認中毒控制中心與消防隊救護隊的電話號碼，並把這些號碼放在電話附近。

> prepared (prɪ'pɛrd) *adj.* 準備好的
> determine (dɪ'tɝmɪn) *v.* 查明；確定
> verify ('vɛrə‚faɪ) *v.* 確認　　***fire department*** 消防隊

1. (**A**) 誰最常成為中毒的受害者？
   (A) 兒童
   (B) teenager ('tin‚edʒɚ) *n.* 青少年
   (C) adult (ə'dʌlt) *n.* 成人
   (D) 老年人

2. (**D**) 這個資訊最有可能在哪邊找到？
   (A) 在有個人保健相關資訊的廣告中。
   (B) 在有頭暈相關資訊的雜誌裡。
   (C) 在有與良好品質睡眠相關的資訊的書裡。
   (D) 在電話簿扉頁上有關緊急狀況的資訊中。

> * advertisement (‚ædvɚ'taɪzmənt) *n.* 廣告
> contain (kən'ten) *v.* 含有
> personal ('pɝsn̩l) *adj.* 個人的
> hygiene ('haɪdʒin) *n.* 衛生；保健
> dizziness ('dɪzɪnɪs) *n.* 頭暈　　quality ('kwɑlətɪ) *adj.* 優質的
> front (frʌnt) *n.* (書的) 扉頁

3. (**D**) 下列哪一項敘述是正確的？

  (A) 如果受害者是小孩的話，將他或她倒過來抱，有助於讓他吐出來。
  (B) 讓失去意識的受害者喝水，幫助他們恢復意識。
  (C) 如果受害者正在嘔吐，將頭往後仰並施行口對口人工呼吸。
  (D) 萬一中毒，你可以打電話給消防隊救援小組求助。

  * statement (ˈstetmənt) *n.* 敘述　　hold (hold) *v.* 抱著
   upside down 顛倒地　　*throw up* 嘔吐
   come to one's sense 恢復意識　　*in case of* 如果；萬一

4. (**B**) 根據本文，下列哪一個不是家裡可以找到的毒藥？

  (A) 油畫顏料；油漆。
  (B) 木柴。
  (C) 止痛藥。
  (D) Javex 牌漂白劑。

  * firewood (ˈfaɪrˌwʊd) *n.* 木柴
   painkiller (ˈpenˌkɪlɚ) *n.* 止痛藥

5. (**D**) 如果你認為有人已經中毒了，本文建議你 ——————。

  (A) 小心行動並做好準備
  (B) 確認中毒控制中心的電話號碼
  (C) 在緊急救援小組抵達前，不要做任何事
  (D) 馬上聯絡中毒控制中心

  * poison (ˈpɔɪzn̩) *v.* 使中毒　　advise (ədˈvaɪz) *v.* 建議
   cautiously (ˈkɔʃəslɪ) *adv.* 小心地
   contact (ˈkɑntækt) *v.* 聯絡

TEST 24

Read the following passage and choose the best answer for each question.

The "First Thanksgiving" was a harvest festival held in 1621 by the Pilgrims and their Native American neighbors and allies as a token of the gratitude of the former to the latter for helping them get through the difficulties of settling down in a new, hostile environment. Over the years, the celebration of Thanksgiving Day has acquired significance beyond historical facts — it has become a much broader symbol of the entire American experience. Nowadays, apart from taking advantage of the occasion for expressing one's thanks to those who give a helping hand, many people find Thanksgiving a cause for rejoicing.

However, to some Native Americans, the "First Thanksgiving" presents a distorted picture of the history of relations between the European colonists and their descendants and the Native People. It is true that respect and friendship did exist between the Wampanoags and the first generation of Pilgrims in Plymouth; nevertheless, the long history of subsequent violence and discrimination suffered by Native People across America is silenced in American history.

To reveal what really happened to the Native Americans, many Native Americans and their supporters have gathered at the top of Coles Hill, overlooking Plymouth Rock, for the "National Day of Mourning" on every Thanksgiving Day since 1970. They hope that this can serve as a powerful statement of anger at the history of oppression inflicted on the Native People of America, who have suffered the theft of their land and the destruction of their traditional way of life at the hands of the American colonists. 【和平高中】

1. Which of the following is true of the First Thanksgiving?
   (A) It was held before the Pilgrims came to America.
   (B) It took place as a spring festival.
   (C) White people celebrated it together with the Indians.
   (D) Native Americans were thankful to the Pilgrims.

2. For most people in America, Thanksgiving is a time for _____.
   (A) having a good time
   (B) stealing land
   (C) protest
   (D) sailing to a new country

3. Who are the Wampanoags?

  (A) They are descendents of the African-Americans.

  (B) Their ancestors were Spaniards that sailed to America.

  (C) They are descendents of the Pilgrims.

  (D) They are Native Americans.

4. Why did people organize the National Day of Mourning?

  (A) To commemorate a revolution.

  (B) To make public a silenced part of history.

  (C) To distort history as much as possible.

  (D) To mourn those Pilgrims who died during the harsh winter.

5. Which of the following can we infer from the passage?

  (A) The Pilgrims were charitable to the poor Wampanoags.

  (B) Without the Wampanoags, the Pilgrims might have died.

  (C) The Pilgrims stole from the Wampanoags on Thanksgiving.

  (D) The Wampanoags gave land to the Pilgrims to thank them.

TEST 24 詳解

The "First Thanksgiving" was a harvest festival held in 1621 by the Pilgrims and their Native American neighbors and allies as a token of the gratitude shown of the former to the latter for helping them get through the difficulties of settling down in a new, hostile environment.

「第一個感恩節」是在一六二一年時所舉辦的收穫節，那是由新教徒移民者和他們的印第安鄰居兼盟友所舉辦的，那個節日象徵著感謝，因為前者要感謝後者幫助他們，讓他們度過在陌生且不良的環境中定居時，所遭遇到的困境。

Thanksgiving (ˌθæŋks'gɪvɪŋ) *n.* 感恩節
harvest ('hɑrvɪst) *n.* 收穫
festival ('fɛstəvl̩) *n.* 節日；慶典　　hold (hold) *v.* 舉辦
Pilgrim ('pɪlgrɪm) *n.* 新教徒移民（即 1620 年時，搭乘五月花號赴美
　定居的英國清教徒）
native ('netɪv) *adj.* 本地的　　***Native American*** 印第安人
neighbor ('nebɚ) *n.* 鄰居　　ally (ə'laɪ) *n.* 盟友
token ('tokən) *n.* 象徵　　gratitude ('grætəˌtjud) *n.* 感謝
show (ʃo) *v.* 表現；表示　　***the former*** 前者
the latter 後者　　***get through*** 度過
difficulty ('dɪfəˌkʌltɪ) *n.* 困難；困境
settle ('sɛtl̩) *v.* 定居　　***settle down*** 定居
new (nju) *adj.* 新的；陌生的
hostile ('hɑstɪl) *adj.* 敵對的；不良的
environment (ɪn'vaɪrənmənt) *n.* 環境

Over the years, the celebration of Thanksgiving Day has acquired significance beyond historical facts—it has become a much broader symbol of the entire American experience.

多年來，慶祝感恩節這件事，已經具有超出史實的意義 —— 它在**全體美國人**的體驗中，變成了一種更廣泛的象徵。

> *over the years* 多年來　　celebration〔͵sɛlə'breʃən〕*n.* 慶祝
> *Thanksgiving Day* 感恩節　　acquire〔ə'kwaɪr〕*v.* 獲得；開始具有
> significance〔sɪg'nɪfəkəns〕*n.* 意義　　beyond〔bɪ'jɑnd〕*prep.* 超出
> historical〔hɪs'tɔrɪkl̩〕*adj.* 歷史的　　broad〔brɔd〕*adj.* 廣泛的
> symbol〔'sɪmbl̩〕*n.* 象徵　　entire〔ɪn'taɪr〕*adj.* 全體的
> experience〔ɪk'spɪrɪəns〕*n.* 經驗；體驗

Nowadays, apart from taking advantage of the occasion for expressing one's thanks to those who give a helping hand, many people find Thanksgiving a cause for rejoicing.

現在，除了利用這個節日，表達你對幫助你的人的感謝之外，許多人還覺得，這是一個盡情歡樂的正當理由。

> nowadays〔'naʊə͵dez〕*adv.* 現在　　*apart from* 除了⋯之外
> *take advantage of* 利用　　occasion〔ə'keʒən〕*n.* 節日；慶典
> express〔ɪk'sprɛs〕*v.* 表達　　thanks〔θæŋks〕*n.pl.* 感謝
> *give a helping hand* 幫助　　find〔faɪnd〕*v.* 覺得
> cause〔kɔz〕*n.* (正當的) 理由　　rejoicing〔rɪ'dʒɔɪsɪŋ〕*n.* 盡情歡樂

However, to some Native Americans, the "First Thanksgiving" presents a distorted picture of the history of relations between the European colonists and their descendants and the Native People.

但是，對某些印第安人來說，「第一個感恩節」使得歐洲殖民者和其後代，與原住民的關係這段歷史上，呈現了一個扭曲的畫面。

> present〔prɪ'zɛnt〕*v.* 呈現　　distorted〔dɪs'tɔrtɪd〕*adj.* 扭曲的
> picture〔'pɪktʃɚ〕*n.* 畫面　　relation〔rɪ'leʃən〕*n.* 關係
> European〔͵jʊrə'piən〕*adj.* 歐洲的
> colonist〔'kɑlənɪst〕*n.* 殖民地開拓者；移民
> descendant〔dɪ'sɛndənt〕*n.* 子孫；後代

It is true that respect and friendship did exist between the Wampanoags and the first generation of Pilgrims in Plymouth; nevertheless, the long history of subsequent violence and discrimination suffered by Native People across America is silenced in American history.

萬帕諾亞格人和普里茅斯的第一代清教徒移民之間，確實存在著尊重和友誼；然而，之後原住民在美國各地遭受到的暴力和歧視的悠久歷史，在美國歷史上卻被壓制著。

respect (rɪ'spɛkt) *n.* 尊敬；尊重
friendship ('frɛndʃɪp) *n.* 友誼　　exist (ɪg'zɪst) *v.* 存在
Wampanoag *n.* 萬帕諾亞格人（印第安人的一族）
generation (,dʒɛnə'reʃən) *n.* 代
Plymouth ('plɪməθ) *n.* 普里茅斯（美國麻薩諸塞州的海港）
nevertheless (,nɛvəðə'lɛs) *adv.* 然而
subsequent ('sʌbsɪ,kwɛnt) *adj.* 後來的　　violence ('vaɪələns) *n.* 暴力
discrimination (dɪ,skrɪmə'neʃən) *n.* 歧視　　suffer ('sʌfə) *v.* 遭受
across (ə'krɔs) *prep.* 遍及　　silence ('saɪləns) *v.* 壓制

To reveal what really happened to the Native Americans, many Native Americans and their supporters have gathered at the top of Coles Hill, overlooking Plymouth Rock, for the "National Day of Mourning" on every Thanksgiving Day since 1970.

爲了揭露在印第安人身上眞正發生的事，從一九七〇年開始，每到感恩節，許多印第安人和他們的支持者，都會聚集在柯爾斯山上，俯瞰普里茅斯岩石，並將那天視爲「國殤日」。

reveal (rɪ'vil) *v.* 揭露　　supporter (sə'portə) *n.* 支持者
gather ('gæðə) *v.* 聚集　　hill (hɪl) *n.* 山丘
overlook (,ovə'lʊk) *v.* 俯瞰
Plymouth Rock 普里茅斯岩石（位於美國麻薩諸塞州普里茅斯的一塊岩石，用來紀念 1620 年時，新教徒搭乘五月花號，來到美國的一處史蹟。）
mourn (morn) *v.* 悲嘆；哀悼　　***National Day of Mourning*** 國殤日

They hope that this can serve as a powerful statement of anger at the history of oppression inflicted on the Native People of America, who have suffered the theft of their land and the destruction of their traditional way of life at the hands of the American colonists.

他們希望這樣做可以強烈表達出，他們對美國原住民那段受到壓迫的歷史的憤怒，由於美國殖民者的關係，他們的土地被偷走，而且傳統的生活方式也遭到破壞。

> **serve as** 作爲；充當 　　powerful (ˈpaʊɚfəl) *adj.* 強有力的
> statement (ˈstetmənt) *n.* 陳述；聲明 　　anger (ˈæŋgɚ) *n.* 憤怒
> oppression (əˈprɛʃən) *n.* 壓迫；壓制
> inflict (ɪnˈflɪkt) *v.* 施加；使遭受（傷害）
> theft (θɛft) *n.* 偷竊 　　destruction (dɪˈstrʌkʃən) *n.* 破壞
> traditional (trəˈdɪʃənḷ) *adj.* 傳統的
> **at the hands of** 出自…之手；由於…的作用
> colonist (ˈkɑlənɪst) *n.* 殖民地開拓者；殖民地居民

1. (**C**) 以下關於「第一個感恩節」的敘述，何者正確？
   (A) 它早在清教徒移民到達美洲大陸之前就舉辦了。
   (B) 它舉辦的方式就像是春天的節慶。
   (C) <u>白人和印第安人一起慶祝。</u>
   (D) 印第安人很感激清教徒移民者。

   * celebrate (ˈsɛləˌbret) *v.* 慶祝
   　thankful (ˈθæŋkfəl) *adj.* 感謝的

2. (**A**) 對大多數的美國人來說，感恩節是個 _____ 的時刻。
   (A) <u>玩樂</u>　　　　　　　(B) 偷土地
   (C) 抗議　　　　　　　　(D) 航行到新國家

   * **have a good time** 玩得愉快 　　steal (stil) *v.* 偷
   　protest (ˈprotɛst) *n.* 抗議 　　sail (sel) *v.* 航行

3. (**D**)　萬帕諾亞格人是誰？

(A)　他們是非裔美國人的後代。

(B)　他們的祖先是航行到美洲的西班牙人。

(C)　他們是清教徒移民的後代。

(D)　他們是印第安人。

　African-American　非裔美國人

　ancestor ('ænsɛstə) *n.* 祖先

　Spaniard ('spænjəd) *n.* 西班牙人

4. (**B**)　人們為什麼要籌畫國殤日？

(A)　為了要紀念革命。

(B)　為了公開一段被壓制的歷史。

(C)　為了儘可能地扭曲歷史。

(D)　為了哀悼在嚴冬死掉的那些清教徒移民。

　* organize ('ɔrgən,aɪz) *v.* 籌畫；設立

　commemorate (kə'mɛmə,ret) *v.* 紀念

　revolution (,rɛvə'luʃən) *n.* 革命

　public ('pʌblɪk) *adj.* 公開的；眾所周知的

　make public 公開　　distort (dɪs'tɔrt) *v.* 扭曲

　as…as possible 儘可能地　　harsh (hɑrʃ) *adj.* 嚴酷的

　【註】本題有 23% 的同學選 (D)，但根據本文的最後一句話，

　　　　可知應選 (B)。

5. (**B**)　我們可以從本文推論出下列何者？

(A)　清教徒移民對貧窮的萬帕諾亞格人很仁慈。

(B)　要是沒有萬帕諾亞格人，清教徒移民可能會死掉。

(C)　清教徒移民在感恩節那天，偷走了萬帕諾亞格人的東西。

(D)　萬帕諾亞格人為了感謝清教徒移民，而把土地送給他們。

　* infer (ɪn'fɝ) *v.* 推論　　charitable ('tʃærətəbḷ) *adj.* 仁慈的

TEST 25

Read the following passage and choose the best answer for each question.

Scientists have always known that people dance. People in every country of the world and throughout the ages have danced with others as a way of being friendly. There have been religious dances, war dances, political dances, and rain dances. But scientists are now discovering that even tiny infants and some apes know how to dance. A scientist named William Condon has discovered that human infants as young as twenty minutes go through a ritual dance following the speech of an adult. Condon discovered this infant dance by studying slow-motion movies of adults talking to infants. He observed the babies moving their limbs in exact synchrony with the words of the speaker. To him, the baby's movements looked just like a beautiful dance. If infants are in some way not allowed to experience this "dance," they can suffer from learning disabilities. Some new research even suggests that infants begin to dance while still in the womb.

However, human beings are not the only animals that dance. Chimpanzees of the Gombe Forest are known to partake in "rain dances."

The chimps beat rhythmically on their chests and nearby objects. They stamp their feet, clap their hands, and twirl about in circles. Some gorillas have also been seen dancing. These animals move about as if drunk. From all these observations, scientists have concluded that dancing may have something to do with the evolution of man. 【延平中學】

1. What is the best title for this passage?
   (A) "The Dancing Apes of the Gombe Forest"
   (B) "Rain Dance"
   (C) "Scientific Discoveries About Dance"
   (D) "How Infants Dance"

2. What do infants do when they "dance"?
   (A) stamp their feet
   (B) clap their hands
   (C) twirl in circles
   (D) move in rhythm to speech

3. Where do people dance?

    (A) throughout the world

    (B) only in Africa

    (C) in most parts of the world

    (D) only in slow-motion movies

4. Which statement is true about dancing?

    (A) Many animals dance.

    (B) Dance is important in helping infants learn.

    (C) People danced only in the 19th century.

    (D) A few babies can learn to dance.

5. Dancing may help a human infant _____.

    (A) strengthen the leg muscles

    (B) appreciate music

    (C) do leg exercises

    (D) learn to talk

【劉毅老師的話】

    「高三英文閱讀測驗」是專為提昇同學閱測能力而設計的，你一定要持之以恆，做完全部四十回，不可半途而廢。

TEST 25 詳解

Scientists have always known that people dance. People in every country of the world and throughout the ages have danced with others as a way of being friendly.

科學家一直都知道人類會跳舞。世界上各個國家、各個時代的人,都會和別人跳舞,作為友好的表示。

throughout (θru'aut) *prep.* 遍及　　age (edʒ) *n.* 時代
friendly ('frɛndlɪ) *adj.* 友好的

There have been religious dances, war dances, political dances, and rain dances. But scientists are now discovering that even tiny infants and some apes know how to dance.

有宗教舞蹈、戰舞、政治舞,以及祈雨舞。但是,科學家現在發現,甚至連小嬰兒和某些猿類,都知道如何跳舞。

religious (rɪ'lɪdʒəs) *adj.* 宗教的　　***war dance*** 戰舞
political (pə'lɪtɪkl̩) *adj.* 政治的　　***rain dance*** 祈雨舞
tiny ('taɪnɪ) *adj.* 很小的　　infant ('ɪnfənt) *n.* 嬰兒
ape (ep) *n.* 人猿;大猩猩

A scientist named William Condon has discovered that human infants as young as twenty minutes go through a ritual dance following the speech of an adult.

一位名叫威廉・康頓的科學家發現,人類嬰兒最早在出生二十分鐘時,就會跟著大人講的話,做出一些肢體動作。

* as young as twenty minutes 是形容詞片語,用來形容 human infants。

named~ 名叫~　　discover (dɪ'skʌvə) *v.* 發現
go through 經歷;完成　　ritual ('rɪtʃuəl) *adj.* 儀式的
ritual dance 儀式舞蹈 (在此指小嬰兒的動作)　　follow ('falo) *v.* 跟隨
speech (spitʃ) *n.* 說的話　　adult (ə'dʌlt) *n.* 成人

Condon discovered this infant dance by studying slow-motion movies of adults talking to infants. He observed the babies moving their limbs in exact synchrony with the words of the speaker. To him, the baby's movements looked just like a beautiful dance.

康頓藉由研究大人和嬰兒說話的慢動作影片，發現了嬰兒之舞。他觀察到，嬰兒擺動四肢，和說話者所說的話正好同時發生。對他而言，嬰兒的動作看起來就像是美麗的舞蹈。

* of adults talking to infants 是形容詞片語，用來修飾 slow-motion movies。

> slow-motion ('slo'moʃən) *adj.* 慢動作的
> observe (əb'zɝv) *v.* 觀察　　limb (lɪm) *n.* (四) 肢；手；腳
> exact (ɪg'zækt) *adj.* 恰好的；完全的
> synchrony ('sɪŋkrənɪ) *n.* 同時；同步
> ***in synchrony with*** 與～同步
> movement ('muvmənt) *n.* 動作

If infants are in some way not allowed to experience this "dance," they can suffer from learning disabilities. Some new research even suggests that infants begin to dance while still in the womb.

假如嬰兒不知怎樣而無法經歷這場「舞蹈」，他們可能是患有學習障礙。某個新研究甚至認為，嬰兒還在母親的子宮裡時，就開始跳舞了。

> ***in some way*** 以某種方式；不知怎麼地
> allow (ə'laʊ) *v.* 允許；使能夠
> ***suffer from*** 受～之苦；罹患
> disability (,dɪsə'bɪlətɪ) *n.* 無能力；障礙
> research (rɪ'sɝtʃ , 'risɝtʃ) *n.* 研究
> suggest (sə'dʒɛst) *v.* 表明；暗示
> womb (wum) *n.* 子宮

However, human beings are not the only animals that dance.
Chimpanzees of the Gombe Forest are known to partake in "rain
dances."

然而，人類並不是唯一會跳舞的動物。大家都知道，剛貝森林裡的黑猩
猩，就會跳祈雨舞。

chimpanzee〔ˌtʃɪmpænˈzi〕n. 黑猩猩 (= *chimp*)
forest〔ˈfɔrɪst〕n. 森林　　partake〔pɑrˈtek〕v. 參加 < *in* >

The chimps beat rhythmically on their chests and nearby
objects. They stamp their feet, clap their hands, and twirl about
in circles. Some gorillas have also been seen dancing.

這些黑猩猩會有節奏地拍打自己的胸部和附近的東西。牠們會蹈腳、拍手，
還會到處轉圈圈。也有人看過大猩猩在跳舞。

beat〔bit〕v. 打　　rhythmically〔ˈrɪðmɪklɪ〕adv. 有節奏地
chest〔tʃɛst〕n. 胸部　　nearby〔ˈnɪrˌbaɪ〕adj. 附近的
object〔ˈɑbdʒɪkt〕n. 物體；東西　　stamp〔stæmp〕v. 蹈 (腳)
clap〔klæp〕v. 拍 (手)　　twirl〔twɝl〕v. 旋轉
about〔əˈbaʊt〕adv. 到處　　***twirl about*** 到處旋轉
circle〔ˈsɝkl̩〕n. 圓圈　　gorilla〔gəˈrɪlə〕n. 大猩猩

These animals move about as if drunk. From all these observations,
scientists have concluded that dancing may have something to do
with the evolution of man.

這些動物像喝醉酒一樣動來動去。從所有的這些觀察當中，科學家得到的結
論是，跳舞可能與人類的進化有關。

* as if drunk 是 as if ***they were*** drunk 的省略。

move about 動來動去；四處移動　　***as if*** 好像；彷彿
drunk〔drʌŋk〕adj. 喝醉的　　observation〔ˌɑbzɚˈveʃən〕n. 觀察
conclude〔kənˈklud〕v. 下結論　　***have something to do*** 與～有關
evolution〔ˌɛvəˈluʃən〕n. 進化；演化　　man〔mæn〕n. 人類

1.(**C**) 本文的最佳標題爲何？

    (A) 「剛貝森林裡會跳舞的人猿」

    (B) 「祈雨舞」

    (C) <u>「有關舞蹈的科學發現」</u>

    (D) 「嬰兒如何跳舞」

    * title〔'taɪtl̩〕n. 標題　　discovery〔dɪ'skʌvərɪ〕n. 發現

2.(**D**) 當嬰兒「跳舞」時，他們會怎麼做？

    (A) 跺腳　　　　　　　　　(B) 拍手

    (C) 轉圈圈　　　　　　　　(D) <u>跟著說話的節拍移動</u>

    * rhythm〔'rɪðəm〕n. 節奏　　***in rhythm to*** 跟著～的節拍

3.(**A**) 人們會在哪裡跳舞？

    (A) <u>全世界</u>　　　　　　　(B) 只有在非洲

    (C) 在世界上大部分地區　　(D) 只有在慢動作電影裡

4.(**B**) 有關跳舞，下列敘述何者爲眞？

    (A) 許多動物都會跳舞。

    (B) <u>跳舞對於幫助嬰兒學習很重要。</u>

    (C) 人們只有在十九世紀時跳舞。

    (D) 有一些嬰兒可以學會跳舞。

    * statement〔'stetmənt〕n. 敘述

5.(**D**) 跳舞或許可以幫助人類嬰兒 ＿＿＿＿＿＿＿＿＿。

    (A) 鍛鍊腿部肌肉　　　　　(B) 欣賞音樂

    (C) 做腿部運動　　　　　　(D) <u>學習說話</u>

    * strengthen〔'strɛŋθən〕v. 強化；鍛鍊
       muscle〔'mʌsl̩〕n. 肌肉
       appreciate〔ə'priʃɪˌet〕v. 欣賞

TEST 26

Read the following passage and choose the best answer for each question.

Maggots, once used by Australian Aborigines and Native Americans in the days before antibiotics, have been credited with curing three of five severe wounds Dr. Mitsui, a heart surgeon at Okayama University Hospital in western Japan was treating. Two others are still being treated.

"The old therapy is great," said Mitsui. He started the treatment in March, 2004. Under the therapy, maggot larva are placed in the wound, where they dissolve dead infected tissue and produce a substance that disinfects the wound. Mitsui leaves the larva in the wound for a week, and then replaces them with fresh maggots. The process is repeated about three times over two weeks.

Maggot therapy was used in the United States but was largely discontinued with the growing popularity of antibiotics in the 1940s. Mitsui said the therapy is still used in Britain.

Mitsui said the treatment is especially useful for wounds suffered by diabetes patients. Diabetic foot ulcers alone affect about 100,000 people annually in Japan and 10 percent of them have to receive amputations, Mitsui said.

The treatment using maggots now costs about 1 million yen (US$9,300) per patient because all germ-free maggots are currently imported from Australia, Mitsui said. "The cost will be cut to one-fifth that price after similar maggots now being developed at his hospital are available," he said.

Mitsui also said maggot therapy will be applicable in wider areas, not only in diabetes and arterial hardening, but also in arterial ulcers, bed sores and burns. 【南港高中】

1. The passage was most likely published in a _____.
   (A) biography
   (B) medical journal
   (C) financial magazine
   (D) storybook

2. This passage would be of most interest to _____.
   (A) scientists
   (B) psychiatrists
   (C) surgeons
   (D) psychologists

3. Which of the following is NOT true according to the passage?

   (A) Mitsui turned to an unusual remedy that he had never used.

   (B) Maggot larva, placed in the wound, will break up dead infected tissue and produce a substance to clean the wound.

   (C) Because of diabetic foot ulcers, about 10,000 people a year in Japan lose all or part of a foot.

   (D) Maggot therapy is used only in Australia and in the United States.

4. Maggot therapy can be applied in treatment of all of the following EXCEPT _____.

   (A) diabetes   (B) burns

   (C) neurosis   (D) bed sores

5. Which sentence sums up the main idea of the passage?

   (A) Mitsui replaces the dead larva with fresh ones.

   (B) Mitsui's patients are in trouble.

   (C) Amputation is an unavoidable step for the worst diabetic foot ulcers.

   (D) A Japanese doctor revives maggot therapy for diabetic sores.

TEST 26 詳解

Maggots, once used by Australian Aborigines and Native Americans in the days before antibiotics, have been credited with curing three of five severe wounds Dr. Mitsui, a heart surgeon at Okayama University Hospital in western Japan was treating.

在抗生素問世之前，澳洲原住民與印第安人就曾經利用過蛆，因為蛆被認為治癒了三井醫師主治的五個嚴重傷口中的三個，三井醫師是日本西部岡山大學附設醫院的心臟外科醫生。

maggot ('mægət) *n.* 蛆　　once (wʌns) *adv.* 曾經
Australian (ɔ'streljən) *adj.* 澳洲的
aborigine (,æbə'rɪdʒə,ni) *n.* 原住民
Native American 印第安人
antibiotic (,æntɪbaɪ'ɑtɪk) *n.* 抗生素
credit ('krɛdɪt) *v.* 歸功於；認為有（某種優點或成就）< *with* >
cure (kjur) *v.* 治癒　　severe (sə'vɪr) *adj.* 嚴重的
wound (wund) *n.* 傷口　　surgeon ('sɝdʒən) *n.* 外科醫師
treat (trit) *v.* 治療

Two others are still being treated.

"The old therapy is great," said Mitsui. He started the treatment in March, 2004.

另外兩個傷口還在治療中。

「這種古老的療法真是太棒了，」三井說。他在二〇〇四年三月開始使用這種療法。

therapy ('θɛrəpɪ) *n.* 治療法
treatment ('tritmənt) *n.* 治療法

Under the therapy, maggot larva are placed in the wound, where they dissolve dead infected tissue and produce a substance that disinfects the wound.

接受這種治療時，會把蛆的幼蟲放進傷口裡，這些幼蟲會在傷口那裡分解受感染的壞死組織，並產生一種可以消毒傷口的物質。

under ('ʌndɚ) *prep.* 正在接受…；在…之中　　larva ('lɑrvə) *n.* 幼蟲
place (ples) *v.* 放置　　wound (wund) *n.* 傷口
dissolve (dɪ'zɑlv) *v.* 分解
infected (ɪn'fɛktɪd) *adj.* 受感染的　　tissue ('tɪʃʊ) *n.* 組織
substance ('sʌbstəns) *n.* 物質　　disinfect (,dɪsɪn'fɛkt) *v.* 消毒

Mitsui leaves the larva in the wound for a week, and then replaces them with fresh maggots. The process is repeated about three times over two weeks.

三井將幼蟲留在傷口一個星期，然後再換另外一批新的蛆。這樣的過程大約重複三次，歷時兩個星期。

replace (rɪ'ples) *v.* 取代　　fresh (frɛʃ) *adj.* 新的
process ('prɑsɛs) *n.* 過程　　repeat (rɪ'pit) *v.* 重複

Maggot therapy was used in the United States but was largely discontinued with the growing popularity of antibiotics in the 1940s. Mitsui said the therapy is still used in Britain.

美國曾經用過蛆療法，但在一九四〇年代時，由於抗生素愈來愈普遍，就沒什麼人繼續使用蛆療法了。三井說英國還是有在用這種療法。

largely ('lɑrdʒlɪ) *adv.* 大部分地
discontinue (,dɪskən'tɪnju) *v.* 中斷；停止
growing ('groɪŋ) *adj.* 逐漸增加的
popularity (,pɑpjə'lærətɪ) *n.* 普遍；流行
Britain ('brɪtn̩) *n.* 英國

Mitsui said the treatment is especially useful for wounds suffered by diabetes patients.

三井說，這種療法對於糖尿病患者的傷口特別有用。

> especially〔əˋspɛʃəlɪ〕*adv.* 特別地
> useful〔ˋjusfəl〕*adj.* 有用的　　suffer〔ˋsʌfɚ〕*v.* 患（病）
> diabetes〔͵daɪəˋbitɪs〕*n.* 糖尿病　　patient〔ˋpeʃənt〕*n.* 病患

Diabetic foot ulcers alone affect about 100,000 people annually in Japan and 10 percent of them have to receive amputations, Mitsui said.

三井表示，在日本，光是糖尿病足部潰瘍，每年就有大約十萬個人患這種病，而其中百分之十必須接受截肢手術。

> diabetic〔͵daɪəˋbɛtɪk〕*adj.* 糖尿病的
> ulcer〔ˋʌlsɚ〕*n.* 潰瘍　　alone〔əˋlon〕*adj.* 單單；僅僅
> affect〔əˋfɛkt〕*v.* （疾病）侵襲（人）
> annually〔ˋænjuəlɪ〕*adv.* 每年地
> percent〔pɚˋsɛnt〕*n.* 百分之　　receive〔rɪˋsiv〕*v.* 接受
> amputation〔͵æmpjəˋteʃən〕*n.* 截肢（術）

The treatment using maggots now costs about 1 million yen (US$9,300) per patient because all germ-free maggots are currently imported from Australia, Mitsui said.

三井表示，現在每個使用蛆療法的病人，大概要花一百萬日圓（九千三百美元），因為目前所有的無菌蛆，都是從澳洲進口的。

> yen〔jɛn〕*n.* 日圓　　per〔pɚ〕*prep.* 每一
> germ-free〔ˋdʒɝm͵fri〕*adj.* 無菌的
> currently〔ˋkɝəntlɪ〕*adv.* 目前
> import〔ɪmˋport〕*v.* 進口　　Australia〔ɔˋstreljə〕*n.* 澳洲

"The cost will be cut to one-fifth that price after similar maggots now being developed at his hospital are available," he said.

「等到現在在他醫院裡培育的那些同類的蛆能夠使用之後，費用將會降到原價的五分之一，」他說。

> cut (kʌt) v. 削減；降低　　similar ('sɪmələ) adj. 同類的；類似的
> develop (dɪ'vɛləp) v. 培育
> available (ə'veləbḷ) adj. 可用的；可獲得的

Mitsui also said maggot therapy will be applicable in wider areas, not only in diabetes and arterial hardening, but also in arterial ulcers, bed sores and burns.

三井還說，蛆療法將會被應用在更廣泛的領域，不只是糖尿病與動脈硬化，它還可用在動脈潰瘍、褥瘡與燒燙傷。

> applicable ('æplɪkəbḷ) adj. 適用的　　wide (waɪd) adj. 廣泛的
> area ('ɛrɪə) n. 領域　　***not only…but also*** ~ 不僅…而且~
> arterial (ɑr'tɪrɪəl) adj. 動脈的　　hardening ('hɑrdn̩ɪŋ) n. 硬化
> sore (sor) n. (身體上的) 瘡；潰瘍
> ***bed sore*** 褥瘡　　burn (bɝn) n. 燒燙傷

1. (**B**) 本文最有可能刊登在 ——————————— 。

　　(A) 傳記　　　(B) 醫學期刊　　(C) 財經雜誌　　(D) 故事書

　　* publish ('pʌblɪʃ) v. 出版；刊登　　biography (baɪ'ɑgrəfɪ) n. 傳記
　　medical ('mɛdɪkḷ) adj. 醫學的　　journal ('dʒɝnḷ) n. 期刊
　　financial (fə'nænʃəl) adj. 財務的；金融的
　　storybook ('storɪ,bʊk) n. 故事書

2. (**C**) 會對本文最有興趣的是 ——————————— 。

　　(A) 科學家　　　(B) psychiatrist (saɪ'kaɪətrɪst) n. 精神病醫師
　　(C) 外科醫師　　(D) psychologist (saɪ'kɑlədʒɪst) n. 心理學家

3.(**D**) 根據本文，下列何者不是事實？

(A) 三井改用一種他從來沒用過的特殊療法。

(B) 放在傷口中的蛆幼蟲會分解感染的壞死組織，並產生一種可以消毒傷口的物質。

(C) 日本每年大約有一萬人，因為糖尿病足部潰瘍，而失去整隻腳或腳的某部位。

(D) <u>只有澳洲與美國在使用蛆療法。</u>

　* ***turn to*** 求助於；轉向

　unusual (ʌn'juʒʊəl) *adj.* 不尋常的；特殊的

　remedy ('rɛmədɪ) *n.* 治療法　　***break up*** 分解

　clean (klin) *v.* 消毒；洗淨

　　【註】 本題有很多同學選 (B) 和 (C)，但注意，本題是選錯誤的選項，所以要選 (D)。

4.(**C**) 蛆療法可以被運用在疾病治療，除了 ＿＿＿＿＿＿＿＿ 。

(A) 糖尿病　　　　　　　　(B) 燒燙傷

(C) ***neurosis*** (njʊ'rosɪs) *n.* 神經病

(D) 褥瘡

　* apply (ə'plaɪ) *v.* 應用　　except (ɪk'sɛpt) *prep.* 除了…之外

5.(**D**) 哪一句話能概述本文的主題？

(A) 三井把死掉的幼蟲換成新的。

(B) 三井的病人有麻煩。

(C) 對病情最嚴重的糖尿病足潰瘍患者來說，截肢是不可避免的。

(D) <u>一位日本醫生恢復使用蛆療法來治療糖尿病潰瘍。</u>

　* sum (sʌm) *v.* 概略地敘述 <*up*>　　***be in trouble*** 有麻煩

　unavoidable (ˌʌnə'vɔɪdəbl) *adj.* 不可避免的

　step (stɛp) *n.* 步驟

　revive (rɪ'vaɪv) *v.* 使恢復；使再流行

　　【註】 本題有 1/3 的同學選 (C)，但因為本文是問最適合的主題，所以要選一個能個概述整篇文章的選項，故選 (D)。

TEST 27

Read the following passage, and choose the best answer for each question.

When you turn on the television news, nearly half
of everything you see is murder, crime, violence and
disaster. There are rarely stories about people helping
others, about new scientific discoveries or even about
the environment. Instead of highlighting the academic
achievements of the local high school students, viewers
are more likely to see a report of a schoolboy attacking
others with a knife. Experts say it causes an emotional
response in the viewer and that being stimulated by a
thrilling sensation is very similar to taking drugs. Intense
and graphic images of pain and violence cause our
adrenaline to pump and our hearts to beat faster. In this
situation, we experience a rush, very close to what we
feel after taking drugs or doing extreme sports.

Unfortunately, it creates a <u>vicious</u> circle of wanting
more and more violence, just like a drug addiction.
The more bloodshed people watch, the more normal it
becomes, and then they need to see even more violence
to feel satisfied. While these images satisfy a craving
for excitement, they also make people afraid of their

neighbors and the world outside the house. Who among us want to live in fear for the rest of our lives, seeing the violence in our minds and in our nightmares? The only solution is for the news media to become more responsible and look not just at their checkbooks, but also at the health of our nation. 【明倫高中】

1. The passage is mainly about _____.
   (A) how to avoid producing TV programs of poor quality
   (B) why television news is so important in this modern world
   (C) the negative effect of watching too much violence on TV
   (D) why there are so many people who enjoy listening to music

2. According to the passage, why do people like to see more and more violence?
   (A) The viewers feel calm and peaceful while watching scenes of bloodshed.
   (B) The viewing experience resembles a drug addiction.
   (C) People in general enjoy having their hearts beating extremely fast.
   (D) Both teenagers and adults can't resist the temptation of being scared.

3. Which of the following physical responses might be
caused by watching violent images?

(A) Slowing of the heart rate.

(B) The dullness of sensation.

(C) Relaxation of muscles.

(D) Increase of adrenaline secretion.

4. Which of the following can replace the word
"vicious" in this passage?

(A) wicked

(B) conventional

(C) beneficial

(D) contradictory

5. What should the news media do?

(A) Be responsible for their checkbooks.

(B) Be responsible for their own health.

(C) Not be responsible for anything.

(D) Be more responsible for the health of our
nation.

TEST 27 詳解

When you turn on the television news, nearly half of everything you see is murder, crime, violence and disaster.

當你打開電視新聞時，你所看到的幾乎有一半是謀殺案、犯罪、暴力，和災難。

> nearly ('nɪrlɪ) *adv.* 幾乎　　murder ('mɜdə) *n.* 謀殺案
> crime (kraɪm) *n.* 犯罪　　violence ('vaɪələns) *n.* 暴力
> disaster (dɪz'æstə) *n.* 災難

There are rarely stories about people helping others, about new scientific discoveries or even about the environment.

很少有和助人、科學新發現，或甚至是和環境有關的新聞報導。

> rarely ('rɛrlɪ) *adv.* 很少　　story ('storɪ) *n.* 新聞報導
> scientific (,saɪən'tɪfɪk) *adj.* 科學的
> discovery (dɪ'skʌvərɪ) *n.* 發現
> environment (ɪn'vaɪrənmənt) *n.* 環境

Instead of highlighting the academic achievements of the local high school students, viewers are more likely to see a report of a schoolboy attacking others with a knife.

觀眾的注意力不會集中在當地高中生的學術成就，他們反而比較有可能去看男學生用刀子攻擊別人的報導。

> ***instead of*** 不⋯而~　　highlight ('haɪ,laɪt) *v.* 強調；使注意力集中於
> academic (,ækə'dɛmɪk) *adj.* 學術的
> achievements (ə'tʃivmənts) *n. pl.* 成就　　local ('lokḷ) *adj.* 當地的
> viewer ('vjuə) *n.* 觀眾
> report (rɪ'port) *n.* 報導　　schoolboy ('skul,bɔɪ) *n.* 男學生
> attack (ə'tæk) *v.* 攻擊　　knife (naɪf) *n.* 刀子

Experts say it causes an emotional response in the viewer, and that being stimulated by a thrilling sensation is very similar to taking drugs.

專家說，這會引發觀衆的情緒反應，而且被令人震撼的感覺所刺激，和吸毒很像。

expert (ˈɛkspɜt) *n.* 專家　　cause (kɔz) *v.* 導致；造成
emotional (ɪˈmoʃənḷ) *adj.* 情緒的
response (rɪˈspɑns) *n.* 反應　　stimulate (ˈstɪmjə,let) *v.* 刺激
thrilling (ˈθrɪlɪŋ) *adj.* 令人震撼的；充滿刺激的
sensation (sɛnˈseʃən) *n.* 感覺　　similar (ˈsɪmələ) *adj.* 類似的
drug (drʌg) *n.* 毒品　　*take drugs* 吸毒

Intense and graphic images of pain and violence cause our adrenaline to pump and our hearts to beat faster.

痛苦和暴力強烈又逼眞的影像，會使我們的腎上腺素釋出，而且會使我們的心臟跳得更快。

intense (ɪnˈtɛns) *adj.* 強烈的
graphic (ˈgræfɪk) *adj.* 逼眞的　　image (ˈɪmɪdʒ) *n.* 影像
adrenaline (ædˈrɛnḷɪn) *n.* 腎上腺素
pump (pʌmp) *v.* 釋出；間歇地噴出　　beat (bit) *v.* 跳動

In this situation, we experience a rush, very close to what we feel after taking drugs or doing extreme sports.

在這種情況下，我們會經歷一陣快感，那和我們吸毒，或是做極限運動後的感覺很類似。

experience (ɪkˈspɪrɪəns) *v.* 經歷
rush (rʌʃ) *n.* （感情的）一陣激動；（吸毒後產生的）異常快感
close (klos) *adj.* 接近的　　extreme (ɪkˈstrim) *adj.* 極限的

Unfortunately, it creates a <u>vicious</u> circle of wanting more and more violence, just like a drug addiction.

不幸的是，它會引起一種需要愈來愈多暴力的惡性循環，就像是毒品上癮一樣。

> unfortunately (ʌn'fɔrtʃənɪtlɪ) *adv.* 不幸地
> create (krɪ'et) *v.* 產生；引起
> vicious ('vɪʃəs) *adj.* 惡性的
> circle ('s3kḷ) *n.* 循環　　addiction (ə'dɪkʃən) *n.* 上癮

The more bloodshed people watch, the more normal it becomes, and then they need to see even more violence to feel satisfied.

人們看了愈多的流血事件，它就變得愈普通，然後他們就需要看更多的暴力事件，才會感到滿足。

> * 「the + 比較級…the + 比較級」表「愈…就愈～」。

> bloodshed ('blʌd,ʃɛd) *n.* 流血事件
> normal ('nɔrmḷ) *adj.* 正常的；普通的

While these images satisfy a craving for excitement, they also make people afraid of their neighbors and the world outside the house. Who among us want to live in fear for the rest of our lives, seeing the violence in our minds and in our nightmares?

雖然這些影像滿足了對刺激的渴望，但它們也讓人們害怕自己的鄰居，以及屋外的世界。我們有誰想要在往後的日子當中，過著擔心受怕的日子，並在腦中和惡夢中看著這些暴力影像？

> while (hwaɪl) *conj.* 雖然　　satisfy ('sætɪs,faɪ) *v.* 滿足
> craving ('krevɪŋ) *n.* 渴望　　excitement (ɪk'saɪtmənt) *n.* 刺激
> fear (fɪr) *n.* 害怕；恐懼　　rest (rɛst) *n.* 其餘部分
> nightmare ('naɪt,mɛr) *n.* 惡夢

The only solution is for the news media to become more
responsible and look not just at their checkbooks, but also at the
health of our nation.

唯一的解決之道就是，新聞媒體要變得更有責任心，不要只注意到自己的支
票簿，也要注意全體國民的身心健全。

solution (sə'luʃən) n. 解決之道   media ('midɪə) n. pl. 媒體
responsible (rɪ'spɑnsəbḷ) adj. 負責任的
checkbook ('tʃɛk͵bʊk) n. 支票簿
health (hɛlθ) n. (身心的) 健全；健康
nation ('neʃən) n. (全體) 國民

1. (**C**) 這篇文章主要是關於 _____。
   (A) 如何避免製作品質差的電視節目
   (B) 電視新聞在現代世界會如此重要的原因
   (C) 在電視上看到太多暴力事件的負面影響
   (D) 爲什麼會有這麼多人喜歡聽音樂的原因

   * mainly ('menlɪ) adv. 主要地
     avoid (ə'vɔɪd) v. 避免   produce (prə'djus) v. 製作
     poor (pʊr) adj. 差的   quality ('kwɑlətɪ) n. 品質
     negative ('nɛgətɪv) adj. 負面的   effect (ɪ'fɛkt) n. 影響

2. (**B**) 根據本文，爲什麼人們喜歡看愈來愈多的暴力事件？
   (A) 當觀衆看到流血事件的景象時，會感到十分平靜。
   (B) 看電視的經驗像是毒品上癮。
   (C) 一般人喜歡讓自己的心跳得非常快。
   (D) 青少年及成年人都無法抗拒恐懼的誘惑。

   * calm (kɑm) adj. 平靜的   peaceful ('pisfəl) adj. 平靜的
     scene (sin) n. 景象   resemble (rɪ'zɛmbḷ) v. 像
     people in general 一般人
     extremely (ɪk'strimlɪ) adv. 極度地；非常
     resist (rɪ'zɪst) v. 抗拒   temptation (tɛmp'teʃən) n. 誘惑
     scared (skɛrd) adj. 恐懼的

3. (**D**) 下列哪一種身體反應，可能是因爲看到暴力影像所引起的？

(A) 心跳的速度減慢。

(B) 感覺遲鈍。

(C) 肌肉放鬆。

(D) 腎上腺素分泌增加。

* physical〔'fɪzɪkl̩〕*adj.* 身體的   response〔rɪ'spɑns〕*n.* 反應
rate〔ret〕*n.* 速度   dullness〔'dʌlnɪs〕*n.* 遲鈍
relaxation〔ˌrilæks'eʃən〕*n.* 放鬆   muscle〔'mʌsl̩〕*n.* 肌肉
increase〔'ɪnkris〕*n.* 增加   secretion〔sɪ'kriʃən〕*n.* 分泌

4. (**A**) 下列哪一個字可以代替本文中的 "vicious"？

(A) ***wicked***〔'wɪkɪd〕*adj.* 邪惡的

(B) conventional〔kən'vɛnʃənl̩〕*adj.* 傳統的

(C) beneficial〔ˌbɛnə'fɪʃəl〕*adj.* 有益的

(D) contradictory〔ˌkɑntrə'dɪktərɪ〕*adj.* 矛盾的

* replace〔rɪ'ples〕*v.* 代替

【註】 本題有不少同學選錯，要注意，做閱讀測驗時，如果題目問
到看不懂的字，一定要根據上下文，仔細推敲字義。在本文
中，講到痛苦和暴力會引起一種需要愈來愈多暴力的循環，
所以同學們大概可以猜到，一定是不好的循環，因此，答案
就應該選 (A)。

5. (**D**) 新聞媒體應該做什麼？

(A) 爲他們的支票簿負責。

(B) 爲他們自己的健康負責。

(C) 不要爲任何事負責。

(D) 對於我們全體國民的身心健全要更有責任心。

TEST 28

Read the following passage and choose the best answer for each question.

Jane was in the middle of the highway when her car stopped all of a sudden. She had no idea what was wrong with her car, and she did not know what to do. She was late for her new job. She hated the idea of being late. It was making her nervous. No one wants to be late for work on their first day, especially for their dream job. Desperate, Jane stopped a passing motorist. She asked him to call a mechanic from the nearest service station. At that moment, it started to rain. Jane could not believe this was happening to her on such an important day.

Finally, a big chubby fellow arrived in his truck. It was the mechanic, and apparently he was not very pleased to be out in the rain. He took a quick look under the hood. All he did was lightly twist a small device inside, and the engine started to work.

"That's great!" said Jane contentedly, as she had not expected the automobile to be repaired so quickly. "I still have a chance to get to the office on time. Tell me, how much do I owe you?"

"8 dollars and 20 cents," answered her savior.

"That much?" protested Jane. "I'm not stingy, but you only turned a small screw."

"That's easy," snapped the mechanic impatiently. "I charge 20 cents for turning the small screw, and the other 8 dollars for knowing exactly which screw to turn."

【南湖高中】

1. The best title of the passage would be _____.
   (A) A Greedy Mechanic
   (B) An Accident
   (C) The Value of a Small Screw
   (D) The Price of Know-how

2. The mechanic got the engine to start by _____.
   (A) repairing the hood
   (B) removing a small device
   (C) turning a small screw
   (D) changing a battery

3. We can conclude that _____.

   (A) Jane was happy to pay the mechanic
   (B) Jane was deceived by the mechanic
   (C) the mechanic charged mostly for his knowledge
   (D) the service that the mechanic performed required difficult skills

4. When her car broke down, Jane was on her way to _____.

   (A) a job interview
   (B) a repair shop
   (C) a service station
   (D) her new job

5. The "hood" of a car is _____.

   (A) inside the car, near the driver
   (B) at the front of the car, over the engine
   (C) under the car, near the rear
   (D) under the engine

TEST 28 詳解

Jane was in the middle of the highway when her car stopped
all of a sudden. She had no idea what was wrong with her car,
and she did not know what to do.

珍的車子突然在公路中間停下來。她不知道她的車是哪邊故障了，也不
知道該怎麼辦。

> *in the middle of* 在…中間　　highway (ˈhaɪˌwe) *n.* 公路
> *all of a sudden* 突然地 (= *suddenly*)　　*have no idea* 不知道
> wrong (rɔŋ) *adj.* 故障的

She was late for her new job. She hated the idea of being late. It
was making her nervous. No one wants to be late for work on their
first day, especially for their dream job.

她新工作上班要遲到了。她討厭遲到這個想法。那會讓她緊張。沒有人想在
第一天上班就遲到，特別是自己夢寐以求的工作。

> nervous (ˈnɝvəs) *adj.* 緊張的　　especially (əˈspɛʃəlɪ) *adv.* 特別是
> dream (drim) *adj.* 理想的

Desperate, Jane stopped a passing motorist. She asked him to call
a mechanic from the nearest service station.

珍不顧一切攔下一位路過的汽車駕駛人。並請他從最近的維修站叫個技工來。

> * Desperate, Jane stopped a passing motorist. 爲分詞構句，由 *Because
> Jane was* desperate, Jane stopped…轉化而來。
>
> > desperate (ˈdɛspərɪt) *adj.* 不顧一切的　　stop (stap) *v.* 攔下
> > passing (ˈpæsɪŋ) *adj.* 路過的
> > motorist (ˈmotərɪst) *n.* 汽車駕駛人
> > mechanic (məˈkænɪk) *n.* 技工；維護員　　*service station* 維修站

At that moment, it started to rain. Jane could not believe this was happening to her on such an important day.

那時候開始下起雨了。珍無法相信在這麼重要的日子，這種事竟然會發生在她身上。

　　at that moment 在那時候

Finally, a big chubby fellow arrived in his truck. It was the mechanic, and apparently he was not very pleased to be out in the rain.

　　最後，一個高大圓胖的男人開著他的卡車過來了。他是位技工，而且顯然他不喜歡在下雨天還外出。

　　chubby (ˈtʃʌbɪ) adj. 圓胖的　　fellow (ˈfɛlo) n. 男人
　　truck (trʌk) n. 卡車
　　apparently (əˈpɛrəntlɪ) adv. 顯然　　pleased (plizd) adj. 高興的

He took a quick look under the hood. All he did was lightly twist a small device inside, and the engine started to work.

他很快看了一下引擎蓋下面。他只是輕輕轉了一下裡面的一個小裝置，引擎就開始運轉了。

　　take a look 看一眼　　quick (kwɪk) adj. 很快的
　　hood (hʊd) n. 引擎蓋　　lightly (ˈlaɪtlɪ) adv. 輕輕地
　　twist (twɪst) v. 扭轉　　device (dɪˈvaɪs) n. 裝置
　　inside (ɪnˈsaɪd) adv. 在裡面　　engine (ˈɛndʒən) n. 引擎
　　work (wɝk) v. (機器) 運轉

"That's great!" said Jane contentedly, as she had not expected the automobile to be repaired so quickly. "I still have a chance to get to the office on time. Tell me, how much do I owe you?"

　　「太好了！」珍很滿意地說。因為她沒想到車子這麼快就修好了。「我還有機會準時上班。告訴我，我要給你多少錢？」

contentedly (kən'tɛntɪdlɪ) *adv.* 滿意地　　expect (ɪk'spɛkt) *v.* 預期
automobile (,ɔtə'mobɪl) *n.* 汽車　　repair (rɪ'pɛr) *v.* 修理
on time 準時　　owe (o) *v.* 欠

"8 dollars and 20 cents," answered her savior.

"That much?" protested Jane. "I'm not stingy, but you only turned a small screw."

　　「八塊二角，」她的救星回答。

　　「這麼貴？」珍抗議說。「我不是小氣，但是你只不過是轉個小螺絲而已。」

cent (sɛnt) *n.* 一分錢　　savior ('sevjɚ) *n.* 救星
protest (prə'tɛst) *v.* 抗議　　stingy ('stɪndʒɪ) *adj.* 小氣的
turn (tɝn) *v.* 轉動　　screw (skru) *n.* 螺絲

"That's easy," snapped the mechanic impatiently. "I charge 20 cents for turning the small screw, and the other 8 dollars for knowing exactly which screw to turn."

　　「那簡單，」技師不耐煩地大聲說。「我收兩角是因為轉了一個小螺絲，而其他的八塊，是因為我確切地知道要轉哪一個螺絲。」

snap (snæp) *v.* 大聲地說　　impatiently (ɪm'peʃəntlɪ) *adv.* 不耐煩地
charge (tʃɑrdʒ) *v.* 收（費）　　exactly (ɪg'zæktlɪ) *adv.* 確切地

1. (**D**) 本文最好的標題是 ＿＿＿＿＿＿＿＿ 。

(A) 一位貪心的技師　　　　(B) 一場意外
(C) 一個小螺絲的價值　　　(D) <u>專業知識的價格</u>

* title ('taɪtl̩) *n.* 題目　　greedy ('gridɪ) *adj.* 貪婪的
accident ('æksədənt) *n.* 意外　　value ('vælju) *n.* 價值
know-how ('no,haʊ) *n.* 專門知識；技術

【註】本題有不少同學選(A)，但根據文章內容，其實並沒有說技師
很貪心，或許同學們讀完文章，會覺得技師貪心，但是和(A)
相較之下，(D)是更好的答案。

2.(**C**) 技師發動引擎的方法是 _____。

   (A) 修引擎蓋　　　　　　　(B) 拿掉一個小裝置

   (C) **轉一個小螺絲**　　　　(D) 換電池

    * remove (rɪ'muv) *v.* 除去　　change (tʃendʒ) *v.* 更換

     battery ('bætərɪ) *n.* 電池

3.(**C**) 我們可以斷定 _____。

   (A) 珍很高興付錢給技師　　(B) 珍被技工騙了

   (C) 技工收取的費用，大部分都是因為他的知識

   (D) 技師所提供的服務需要艱深的技術

    * conclude (kən'klud) *v.* 下結論；斷定

     deceive (dɪ'siv) *v.* 欺騙

     perform (pɚ'fɔrm) *v.* 進行；提供（服務）

     require (rɪ'kwaɪr) *v.* 需要

     difficult ('dɪfəˌkʌlt) *adj.* 艱深的；困難的

4.(**D**) 珍的車子拋錨時，她正要去 _____ 的途中。

   (A) 工作面試　　　　　　　(B) 修理廠

   (C) 維修站　　　　　　　　(D) **做她的新工作**

    * *break down* 拋錨　　*on one's way to* 在去～的途中

     interview ('ɪntɚˌvju) *n.* 面試　　*repair shop* 修理廠

5.(**B**) 車子的 "hood" 是在 _____。

   (A) 車內接近駕駛人的地方

   (B) **車子前半部的引擎上**

   (C) 車子底部靠近車尾的地方

   (D) 在引擎下面

    * front (frʌnt) *n.* 前面　　rear (rɪr) *n.* 尾部；後面

TEST 29

Read the following passage, and choose the best answer for each question.

He got the most applause at the closing ceremony of the 28th Olympics in Athens. But he was not a gold medallist, nor did he win a silver medal. He only won bronze. Why, then, did he earn the most applause? It was because he exemplified the Olympic spirit and Olympic values. He **exuded** friendliness, magnanimity and goodwill.

His name is Vanderlei de Lima, a Brazilian marathon runner. This wiry, 35-year-old would have won gold if he had not been attacked unexpectedly by a crazy spectator who grabbed him when he was the frontrunner and only five kilometers from the stadium.

By the time he finally broke free from his attacker's grip, he had been overtaken by Italian runner Stefano Baldini, who went on to take the gold medal, and American Mebrahtom Keflezighi, who took silver.

With a third-place medal in his hand, the Brazilian showed extraordinary grace. He ran into the stadium with a great smile on his face. How could he smile when he should be angry? "My dream was to win an Olympic medal," he said.

The international Olympic Committee bestowed upon him a special medal named after the founder of the modern Olympic movement, Baron Pierre de Coubertin.

The medal of sportsmanship was given to him in recognition of his "exceptional demonstration of fair play and Olympic values." 【麗山高中】

1. Which is the best title for the article?
   (A) True Olympic Marathon
   (B) True Olympic Loser
   (C) True Olympic Champion
   (D) True Olympic Value

2. What does **exude** mean in this article?
   (A) give up   (B) give off
   (C) give away   (D) give in

3. Why didn't Vanderlei de Lima win the gold medal?

(A) Someone hit him.

(B) Someone insulted him.

(C) Someone attacked him.

(D) Someone blackmailed him.

4. Who is Baron Pierre de Coubertin?

(A) The host of the closing ceremony of the 28th Olympics.

(B) A member of the international Olympic Committee.

(C) The designer of the medal of sportsmanship.

(D) The founder of the modern Olympic movement.

5. When did the event happen?

(A) in 2004

(B) in 2000

(C) in 1996

(D) in 1992

TEST 29 詳解

He got the most applause at the closing ceremony of the 28th
Olympics in Athens. But he was not a gold medallist, nor did he
win a silver medal.

他在第二十八屆雅典奧運的閉幕典禮中，得到最多掌聲。不過他旣不是
金牌得主，也不是銀牌得主。

applause〔ə'plɔz〕*n.* 鼓掌；稱讚
closing〔'klozɪŋ〕*adj.* 閉幕的　　ceremony〔'sɛrə,monɪ〕*n.* 典禮
Olympics〔o'lɪmpɪks〕*n.* 奧運會（= *Olympic Games*）
Athens〔'æθənz〕*n.* 雅典（希臘首都）
gold〔gold〕*adj.* 金的　*n.* 金牌
medallist〔'mɛdḷɪst〕*n.* 獲得獎牌者　　silver〔'sɪlvɚ〕*adj.* 銀的
medal〔'mɛdḷ〕*n.* 獎牌

He only won bronze. Why, then, did he earn the most applause?
It was because he exemplified the Olympic spirit and Olympic
values. He **exuded** friendliness, magnanimity and goodwill.

他只拿到銅牌而已。那麼他爲什麼得到最多掌聲呢？因爲他是奧運精神與價
值的楷模。他表現出友好、寬宏大量與善意。

bronze〔branz〕*n.* 銅牌　　earn〔ɝn〕*v.* 獲得
exemplify〔ɪg'zɛmplə,faɪ〕*v.* 作爲例證
Olympic〔o'lɪmpɪk〕*adj.* 奧運會的
spirit〔'spɪrɪt〕*n.* 精神
values〔'væljʊz〕*n. pl.* 價值觀
exude〔ɪg'zud〕*v.* 散發；表現
friendliness〔'frɛndlɪnɪs〕*n.* 友好；友誼
magnanimity〔,mægnə'nɪmətɪ〕*n.* 寬宏大量；大度量
goodwill〔'gʊd,wɪl〕*n.* 善意

His name is Vanderlei de Lima, a Brazilian marathon runner.

他的名字是萬得雷・得利馬，他是巴西的馬拉松跑者。

Brazilian〔brə'zɪljən〕*adj.* 巴西的
marathon〔'mærə,θɑn〕*adj.* 馬拉松的

This wiry, 35-year-old would have won gold if he had not been attacked unexpectedly by a crazy spectator who grabbed him when he was the frontrunner and only five kilometers from the stadium.

這名三十五歲的結實男子，如果沒有突然被瘋狂觀衆攻擊的話，他就會贏得金牌，當時他一路領先，而且距離體育場只有五公里遠。

wiry〔'waɪrɪ〕*adj.* (人、身體等) 肌肉結實的
attack〔ə'tæk〕*v.* 攻擊
unexpectedly〔,ʌnɪk'spɛktɪdlɪ〕*adv.* 突然；意外地
crazy〔'krezɪ〕*adj.* 瘋狂的　　spectator〔spɛk'tetɚ〕*n.* 觀衆
grab〔græb〕*v.* 抓住
frontrunner〔'frʌnt'rʌnɚ〕*n.* (比賽中) 領先者
kilometer〔'kɪlə,mitɚ〕*n.* 公里
stadium〔'stedɪəm〕*n.* (戶外) 體育場

By the time he finally broke free from his attacker's grip, he had been overtaken by Italian runner Stefano Baldini, who went on to take the gold medal, and American Mebrahtom Keflezighi, who took silver.

當他終於掙脫攻擊者的控制時，他已經被後來拿到金牌的義大利跑者斯蒂法諾・巴狄尼，還有拿到銀牌的美國跑者梅布拉托・凱佛茲奇給追過了。

by the time 到了…的時候　　*break free from* 掙脫；逃離
attacker〔ə'tækɚ〕*n.* 攻擊者　　grip〔grɪp〕*n.* (緊) 抓；控制
overtake〔,ovɚ'tek〕*v.* 追過 (某人)
Italian〔ɪ'tæljən〕*adj.* 義大利的
go on 接續；繼續　　take〔tek〕*v.* 獲得 (獎賞等)

With a third-place medal in his hand, the Brazilian showed
extraordinary grace.　He ran into the stadium with a great smile on
his face.

　　手中握著第三名的獎牌，這名巴西人表現得非常優雅。他跑進體育場時，
臉上還笑得很開心。

　　　　third-place *adj.* 第三名的
　　　　extraordinary (ɪkˈstrɔrdṇ͵ɛrɪ) *adj.* 格外的；非常的
　　　　grace (gres) *n.* 優雅

How could he smile when he should be angry?　"My dream was to
win an Olympic medal," he said.

當他應該生氣的時候，怎麼笑得出來？「我的夢想是贏得一面奧運獎牌，」
他說。

　　The international Olympic Committee bestowed upon him a
special medal named after the founder of the modern Olympic
movement, Baron Pierre de Coubertin.

　　國際奧運委員會頒發了一枚特別的獎牌給他，那個獎牌是以現代奧運創
始人，巴龍・皮耶・德・古柏丁的名字命名的。

　　　　committee (kəˈmɪtɪ) *n.* 委員會
　　　　bestow (bɪˈsto) *v.* 授與；頒發
　　　　be named after 以…的名字命名
　　　　founder (ˈfaʊndɚ) *n.* 創立者
　　　　movement (ˈmuvmənt) *n.* 運動

　　The medal of sportsmanship was given to him in recognition
of his "exceptional demonstration of fair play and Olympic
values."

　　頒發代表運動家精神的獎牌給他，是要表彰他「對公平競賽與奧運價值的優秀示範」。

> sportsmanship (ˈsportsmənˌʃɪp) *n.* 運動家精神
> recognition (ˌrɛkəgˈnɪʃən) *n.* 表彰；褒揚
> *in recognition of* 褒獎；表彰
> exceptional (ɪkˈsɛpʃənḷ) *adj.* 特別的；優秀的
> demonstration (ˌdɛmənˈstreʃən) *n.* 示範
> fair (fɛr) *adj.* 公平的　　play (ple) *n.* 競賽

1. (**C**) 何者是最適合本文的標題？
    (A) 眞正的奧運馬拉松
    (B) 眞正的奧運輸家
    (C) 眞正的奧運冠軍
    (D) 眞正的奧運價值

　　* title (ˈtaɪtḷ) *n.* 標題　　article (ˈɑrtɪkḷ) *n.* 文章
　　　champion (ˈtʃæmpɪən) *n.* 冠軍

> 【註】　本題有超過一半的同學選 (D)，但是仔細看本文，從頭到尾
> 　　　　講的都是有關萬得雷・得利馬的事，故應選 (C)。

2. (**B**) 這篇文章中的 "exude" 的意思是什麼？
    (A) give up 放棄
    (B) *give off* 散發出
    (C) give away 贈送
    (D) give in 屈服；讓步

> 【註】　本題有不少同學選 (D)，應該是因為看不懂這個字。同學們要
> 　　　　注意，碰到考生字時，最好的辦法，就是用刪去法，把不可
> 　　　　能的選項都刪除，那麼猜中正確答案的可能性就很大。

3. (**C**) 為什麼萬得雷・得利馬沒有贏得金牌？

    (A) 有人打他。   (B) 有人侮辱他。

    (C) <u>有人攻擊他。</u>   (D) 有人勒索他。

    * hit (hɪt) v. 毆打   insult (ɪn'sʌlt) v. 侮辱

    blackmail ('blæk,mel) v. 敲詐；勒索

4. (**D**) 巴龍・皮耶・德・古柏丁是誰？

    (A) 第二十八屆奧運閉幕典禮的主持人。

    (B) 國際奧委會的委員。

    (C) 運動家精神獎牌的設計者。

    (D) <u>現代奧運的創始人。</u>

    * host (host) n. 主持人   member ('mɛmbɚ) n. 會員

    designer (dɪ'zaɪnɚ) n. 設計者

    【註】 這題也有超過一半的同學選錯，但是答案明明在文章中説
            得很清楚，像這樣的題目，沒有拿到分數是非常可惜的。

5. (**A**) 這件事發生在何時？

    (A) <u>在二〇〇四年</u>

    (B) 在二〇〇〇年

    (C) 在一九九六年

    (D) 在一九九二年

    * event (ɪ'vɛnt) n. 事件

TEST 30

Read the following passage and choose the best answer for each question.

Each object tells a story. Even the most ordinary objects can present to us powerful images. Sometimes it is the ordinary nature of these objects that actually makes them so extraordinary. Such is the case with an old leather shoe in a museum in Alaska. At first glance it does not look like much. It is a woman's shoe of a style popular in the 1890s. But what is unique about this shoe is where it was found. It was discovered on the Chilkoot Pass, the famous trail used by the people seeking gold in Alaska. Who it belonged to or why it was left there is not known. Was it perhaps dropped by accident as the woman climbed up the 1,500 stairs carved out of ice? Or did she throw away goods that she didn't need in order to travel lighter?

Over 100,000 people with "gold fever" made this trip hoping to become millionaires. Few of them understood that on their way they would have to cross a harsh wilderness. Unprepared for such a dangerous journey, many died of starvation and exposure to the cold weather. The Canadian government finally started requiring the gold seekers to bring one ton of supplies with them. This was thought to be enough for a person to survive for one year. They would carry their supplies in backpacks each weighing up to fifty pounds; it usually took at least 40 trips to get everything to the top and over the pass.

Whoever dropped the shoe must have been a brave and determined woman. Perhaps she was successful and made it to Alaska. Perhaps she had to turn back in defeat. No one will ever know for sure, but what we know is that she took part in one of the greatest adventures of the 19th century.

【南湖高中】

1. Why is the woman's ordinary leather shoe so unusual?
   (A) Because it belonged to a very famous woman at one time.
   (B) Because it was found near a famous trail.
   (C) Because it reflects the lifestyle of the past.
   (D) Because its style was fashionable.

2. The Canadian government made gold seekers bring one year's supplies with them so that _____.
   (A) they could have weapons to fight with enemies
   (B) they could have things to trade with each other
   (C) they would not die of hunger and cold
   (D) they would lead a rich and comfortable life

3. According to this passage, most people who went to Alaska _____.

   (A) made a big fortune from gold
   (B) had a bitter fight with their enemies
   (C) lost their shoes on the way
   (D) were not properly equipped

4. No matter what happened to the woman who owned the shoe, _____.

   (A) she didn't have good taste in shoes
   (B) she was brave and adventurous
   (C) she dropped the shoe on the trail on purpose
   (D) her other shoe was dropped in the gold mine

5. The author of this passage implies that _____.

   (A) simple objects can stimulate our imagination
   (B) "gold fever" was the worst disaster ever recorded in history
   (C) Alaska was not an ideal place for making shoes
   (D) museums are the best places to go if you'd like to know about gold fever

TEST 30 詳解

Each object tells a story. Even the most ordinary objects can present to us powerful images. Sometimes it is the ordinary nature of these objects that actually makes them so extraordinary.

每個物品都有一個故事。即使是最平凡的東西,也能呈現給我們動人的影像。有時候,實際上讓這些東西如此不平凡的,就是它們平凡的本質。

object ('ɑbdʒɪkt) *n.* 物品;東西
ordinary ('ɔrdn̩,ɛrɪ) *adj.* 平凡的
present (prɪ'zɛnt) *v.* 呈現
powerful ('pauəfəl) *adj.* 有力的;動人的
image ('ɪmɪdʒ) *n.* 影像　　nature ('netʃə) *n.* 本質
actually ('æktʃuəlɪ) *adv.* 實際上
extraordinary (ɪk'trɔrdn̩,ɛrɪ) *adj.* 不尋常的;非凡的

Such is the case with an old leather shoe in a museum in Alaska. At first glance it does not look like much. It is a woman's shoe of a style popular in the 1890s. But what is unique about this shoe is where it was found.

阿拉斯加一間博物館裡的一隻舊皮鞋就是這樣。它第一眼看起來沒什麼特別。這是一八九〇年代一款流行的女鞋。不過這隻鞋的獨特之處,是在於它被發現的地方。

case (kes) *n.* 事實　　leather ('lɛðə) *adj.* 皮製的
Alaska (ə'læskə) *n.* 阿拉斯加 (美國西北部之一州)
glance (glæns) *n.* 一瞥;看一眼
much (mʌtʃ) *n.* 重要之物
style (staɪl) *n.* 式樣　　unique (ju'nik) *adj.* 獨特的

It was discovered on the Chilkoot Pass, the famous trail used by the people seeking gold in Alaska. Who it belonged to or why it was left there is not known.

它是在奇爾庫山隘上發現的,那是以前的阿拉斯加淘金客所走的著名小路。沒有人知道這隻鞋是誰的,或是它為何被留在那裡。

> discover (dɪ'skʌvɚ) v. 發現　　pass (pæs) n. 山隘;關口
> trail (trel) n. 小徑　　seek (sik) v. 尋找　　*belong to* 屬於

Was it perhaps dropped by accident as the woman climbed up the 1,500 stairs carved out of ice? Or did she throw away goods that she didn't need in order to travel lighter?

是不是那位女士在爬一千五百級冰階時,意外掉下來的呢?還是她為了能更輕便地旅行,才把不需要的東西丟掉呢?

> drop (drɑp) v. 使掉落　　*by accident* 意外地
> climb (klaɪm) v. 攀爬　　stair (stɛr) n. 階梯
> carve (kɑrv) v. 切割　　*out of* 用…;由…
> *throw away* 丟掉　　goods (gʊdz) n. pl. 物品
> light (laɪt) adv. 輕便地　　*travel light* 帶很少行李旅行

Over 100,000 people with "gold fever" made this trip hoping to become millionaires. Few of them understood that on their way they would have to cross a harsh wilderness.

有超過十萬個懷著「淘金熱」的人,踏上了這段旅程,希望變成百萬富翁。其中很少有人了解,這趟路程要穿越令人不舒服的荒野。

> fever ('fivɚ) n. 狂熱　　*gold fever* 淘金熱
> millionaire (ˌmɪljən'ɛr) n. 百萬富翁　　*on one's way* 在途中
> cross (krɔs) v. 穿越
> harsh (hɑrʃ) adj. 嚴酷的;令人不舒服的
> wilderness ('wɪldɚnɪs) n. 荒野

Unprepared for such a dangerous journey, many died of starvation and exposure to the cold weather.

很多人沒有準備好，就踏上這趟危險的旅途，所以他們不是餓死，就是因為暴露在寒冷的氣候下而冷死。

> unprepared (ˏʌnprɪˈpɛrd) *adj.* 未準備的
> journey (ˈdʒɝnɪ) *n.* 旅程
> *die of* 因…而死
> starvation (stɑrˈveʃən) *n.* 飢餓
> exposure (ɪkˈspoʒɚ) *n.* 暴露；接觸 < *to* >

The Canadian government finally started requiring the gold seekers to bring one ton of supplies with them. This was thought to be enough for a person to survive for one year.

加拿大政府最後開始規定，淘金客必須隨身攜帶一噸重的補給物資。那些物資被認為夠一個人活一年。

> Canadian (kəˈnedɪən) *adj.* 加拿大的
> government (ˈgʌvɚnmənt) *n.* 政府
> finally (ˈfaɪnlɪ) *adv.* 最後
> require (rɪˈkwaɪr) *v.* 要求；規定
> *gold seeker* 淘金客　ton (tʌn) *n.* 噸
> supplies (səˈplaɪz) *n. pl.* 補給物資
> survive (səˈvaɪv) *v.* 存活

They would carry their supplies in backpacks each weighing up to fifty pounds; it usually took at least 40 trips to get everything to the top and over the pass.

他們將補給物資裝在背包裡，每個背包都重達五十磅；通常至少要走四十趟，
才能把所有東西都帶上山頂並穿越山隘。

> carry ('kærɪ) v. 攜帶
> backpack ('bæk,pæk) n. 背包
> weigh (we) v. 重~   ***up to*** 高達
> pound (paʊnd) n. 磅   ***at least*** 至少
> trip (trɪp) n. 走一趟   top (tɑp) n. 山頂

Whoever dropped the shoe must have been a brave and
determined woman. Perhaps she was successful and made it to
Alaska. Perhaps she had to turn back in defeat.

不管這隻鞋是誰掉的，她一定是個勇敢又堅決的女人。也許她已經成功
抵達阿拉斯加。也許她必須無功而返。

> brave (brev) adj. 勇敢的
> determined (dɪ'tɜmɪnd) adj. 堅決的
> ***make it to*** ~ 成功到達~   ***turn back*** 返回
> defeat (dɪ'fit) n. 失敗

No one will ever know for sure, but what we know is that she took
part in one of the greatest adventures of the 19th century.

沒有人能確切知道，不過我們所知道的是，她參加了十九世紀最偉大的探險
之一。

> ***for sure*** 確定   ***take part in*** 參加
> adventure (əd'vɛntʃə) n. 探險；冒險
> century ('sɛntʃərɪ) n. 世紀

1. (**B**) 爲何這位女士的平凡皮鞋這麼不平凡？

(A) 因爲它屬於從前一位非常有名的女士。

(B) 因爲它是在一條有名的小路上被發現的。

(C) 因爲它反映了以前的生活型態。

(D) 因爲它的款式很流行。

* unusual〔ʌnˈjuʒuəl〕*adj.* 不平凡的　　*at one time* 曾經；一度
reflect〔rɪˈflɛkt〕*v.* 反映　　past〔pæst〕*n.* 過去
fashionable〔ˈfæʃənəbḷ〕*adj.* 流行的；時髦的

2. (**C**) 加拿大政府要淘金客隨身帶一年的補給物資，所以 ＿＿＿＿＿＿＿。

(A) 他們才會有武器跟敵人戰鬥

(B) 他們才能有東西可以彼此交易

(C) 他們才不會餓死和凍死

(D) 他們才會著過富裕而舒適的生活

* *so that* 以便於（表目的）　　weapon〔ˈwɛpən〕*n.* 武器
enemy〔ˈɛnəmɪ〕*n.* 敵人　　trade〔tred〕*v.* 做買賣；進行交易
lead a…life 過著…的生活

3. (**D**) 根據本文，大多數到阿拉斯加去的人 ＿＿＿＿＿＿＿。

(A) 都因爲黃金而致富

(B) 都與敵人進行一場激烈的戰鬥

(C) 都在路上遺失了鞋子

(D) 沒有適當的裝備

* fortune〔ˈfɔrtʃən〕*n.* 一大筆錢　　*make a fortune* 發財；致富
bitter〔ˈbɪtɚ〕*adj.* 激烈的　　fight〔faɪt〕*n.* 戰鬥
lose〔luz〕*v.* 遺失　　*on the way* 在路上
properly〔ˈprɑpɚlɪ〕*adv.* 適當地　　equip〔ɪˈkwɪp〕*v.* 裝備

【註】　本題有不少同學選 (A)，但根據文章內容，並沒有說每個去淘
金的人都致富，只說很多人因爲沒有準備好而餓死或冷死，
所以應該選 (D)。

4. (**B**) 無論擁有這隻鞋的女人發生了什麼事，＿＿＿＿＿＿＿。

    (A) 她對鞋子的品味並不高

    (B) <u>她既勇敢又愛冒險</u>

    (C) 她故意把這隻鞋丟在小路上

    (D) 她的另一隻鞋掉在金礦裡

    * ***no matter what*** 無論什麼   own (on) *v.* 擁有

    taste (test) *n.* 品味

    adventurous (əd'vɛntʃərəs) *adj.* 愛冒險的

    on purpose 故意地   ***gold mine*** 金礦

5. (**A**) 本文的作者暗示＿＿＿＿＿＿＿。

    (A) <u>簡單的東西能激發我們的想像力</u>

    (B) 「淘金熱」是有史以來最大的災難

    (C) 阿拉斯加不是個製鞋的好地方

    (D) 如果你想了解淘金熱的話，博物館是最好的地方

    * imply (ɪm'plaɪ) *v.* 暗示   simple ('sɪmpl̩) *adj.* 簡單的

    stimulate ('stɪmjə,let) *v.* 刺激

    imagination (ɪ,mædʒə'neʃən) *n.* 想像力

    disaster (dɪz'æstɚ) *n.* 災難   record (rɪ'kɔrd) *v.* 記錄

    ideal (aɪ'diəl) *adj.* 理想的

【劉毅老師的話】

    學測和指考都會考閱讀測驗，按照歷年的出題方式來看，每篇閱測的作答時間大概只有 8~10 分鐘，同學們平時練習時，最好是計時答題，訓練自己的作答速度。

TEST 31

Read the following passage and choose the best answer for each question.

If you're planning a family holiday in the States, take note. U.S. airlines' practice of allowing a toddler to fly seated on an adult's lap was criticized in early August when the country's National Transportation Safety Board recommended that kids under two years old be restrained in their own seats while in the air. So far, the U.S. Federal Aviation Administration (FAA) has declined to make that mandatory, citing a 1995 study that concluded the cost of buying another ticket might force more families to drive — and risk roadway accidents. Still, the FAA advises that a child weighing less than 18kg fly in a safety or car seat buckled into his own seat on the plane. If you're flying on a U.S. carrier and decide to get your toddler a seat, ask the airline whether it gives discounts on tickets for children under age 2; many airlines offer up to half off. Rules vary for other national carriers. Icelandair and Lufthansa, for example, don't allow the use of safety seats during takeoff and landing, while Alitalia bans them altogether and charges an extra fee for lap riders.

—— By Lisa McLaughlin 【景美女中】

1. What is the opinion of the National Transportation Safety Board?

   (A) Babies under age 2 had better not take long journeys.
   (B) It's illegal to restrain kids of any age in their seats.
   (C) Children should be bought their own seats.
   (D) It doesn't make sense that airlines charge the same for children and adults.

2. According to the FAA, American families _____.

   (A) care about their safety more than the ticket price
   (B) risk their lives more on the roads than in the air
   (C) are likely to decline the bargain offers of airlines
   (D) are likely to criticize the government's policy on transportation safety

3. According to the FAA, what is the best way for a child under 18kg to travel?

   (A) At half price.
   (B) In its own child safety seat.
   (C) The child should travel in a car, not a plane.
   (D) As a lap rider.

4. Something "mandatory" is a _____.

   (A) must   (B) danger
   (C) debate   (D) fantasy

5. On which airline can you use a child safety seat during the flight, but not during landing?

   (A) Alitalia.   (B) Lufthansa.
   (C) U.S. Airways.   (D) Any American airline.

TEST 31 詳解

If you're planning a family holiday in the States, take note.

如果你在計畫全家到美國旅行，請注意。

> holiday ('holə,de) *n.* 旅行；渡假
> *the States* 美國　　*take note* 注意

U.S. airlines' practice of allowing a toddler to fly seated on an adult's lap was criticized in early August when the country's National Transportation Safety Board recommended that kids under two years old be restrained in their own seats while in the air.

美國航空公司允許學步幼童搭飛機時，坐在成人大腿上的慣例，在八月初受到批評，因爲該國的全國運輸安全委員會建議，兩歲以下的孩童，在飛行時要被限制在自己的座位上。

> airline ('ɛr,laɪn) *n.* 航空公司
> practice ('præktɪs) *n.* 慣例　　allow (ə'laʊ) *v.* 允許
> toddler ('tɑdlɚ) *n.* 學步幼童　　fly (flaɪ) *v.* 搭飛機
> seat (sit) *v.* 使就座　*n.* 座位；座椅　　adult (ə'dʌlt) *n.* 成人
> lap (læp) *n.* 大腿　　criticize ('krɪtə,saɪz) *v.* 批評
> transportation (,trænspɚ'teʃən) *n.* 運輸
> board (bɔrd) *n.* 委員會
> recommend (,rɛkə'mɛnd) *n.* 建議　　kid (kɪd) *n.* 小孩
> restrain (rɪ'stren) *v.* 限制　　*in the air* 在空中

So far, the U.S. Federal Aviation Administration (FAA) has declined to make that mandatory, citing a 1995 study that concluded the cost of buying another ticket might force more families to drive — and risk roadway accidents.

到目前爲止，美國聯邦航空局（FAA）已經拒絕把這項規定強制化，並引用一個 1995 年的研究，結論是多買一張票的成本，可能會迫使更多家庭開車——並冒著車禍的危險。

> ***so far*** 到目前爲止；至今
> federal (ˈfɛdərəl) *adj.* 聯邦的
> aviation (ˌevɪˈeʃən) *n.* 航空；飛行
> administration (ədˌmɪnəˈstreʃən) *n.* 行政部門；局
> ***Federal Aviation Administration*** 美國聯邦航空管理局
> （簡稱爲 FAA）
> decline (dɪˈklaɪn) *v.* 拒絕
> mandatory (ˈmændəˌtorɪ) *adj.* 強制的
> cite (saɪt) *v.* 引用　　conclude (kənˈklud) *v.* 下結論；斷定
> force (fɔrs) *v.* 迫使　　risk (rɪsk) *v.* 冒～險
> roadway (ˈrodˌwe) *n.* 公路
> accident (ˈæksədənt) *n.* 意外；車禍

Still, the FAA advises that a child weighing less than 18kg fly in a safety or car seat buckled into his own seat on the plane.

但是，美國聯邦航空局建議，體重不到十八公斤的小朋友，飛行時應坐在安全椅上，或坐在汽車安全座位中，並用安全帶把座位繫在飛機的座椅上。

> still (stɪl) *adv.* 不過；然而
> advise (ədˈvaɪz) *v.* 建議　　weigh (we) *v.* 重～
> safety (ˈseftɪ) *n.* 安全裝置　　buckle (ˈbʌkl̩) *v.* 扣住

If you're flying on a U.S. carrier and decided to get your toddler a seat, ask the airline whether it gives discounts on tickets for children under age 2; many airlines offer up to half off. Rules vary for other national carriers.

如果你要搭乘美國的飛機，並決定給學步幼童一個座位時，問問航空公司，
是否能給兩歲以下幼童的機票打個折扣；許多航空公司會給高達一半的折扣。
其他國家班機的規定則各不相同。

> carrier (ˈkærɪə) *n.* 飛機　　discount (ˈdɪskaʊnt) *n.* 折扣
> offer (ˈɔfə) *v.* 提供　　*up to* 多達
> off (ɔf) *prep.* 打折扣；減價　　vary (ˈvɛrɪ) *v.* 不同

Icelandair and Lufthansa, for example, don't allow the use of
safety seats during takeoff and landing, while Alitalia bans them
altogether and charges an extra fee for lap riders.

> —— By Lisa McLaughlin

舉例來說，冰島航空及德國航空，就不允許在起飛及降落時，使用安全坐椅，
但是，義大利航空就完全禁止安全座椅，並對坐在腿上的幼童，收取一筆額
外費用。

> —— 麗莎·麥克勞夫倫

> takeoff (ˈtekˌɔf) *n.* 起飛　　landing (ˈlændɪŋ) *n.* 降落
> while (hwaɪl) *conj.* 然而　　ban (bæn) *v.* 禁止
> altogether (ˌɔltəˈgɛðə) *adv.* 完全地
> charge (tʃɑrdʒ) *v.* 收 (費)　　extra (ˈɛkstrə) *adj.* 額外的
> fee (fi) *n.* 費用　　rider (ˈraɪdə) *n.* 騎士；乘坐的人

1. (**C**) 全國運輸安全委員會的看法爲何？

    (A) 兩歲以下的嬰兒最好不要長途旅行。

    (B) 限制任何年紀的兒童要坐在座位上是違法的。

    (C) <u>應該付錢讓小孩有自己的座位。</u>

    (D) 航空公司對小孩和大人都收一樣的費用是不合理的。

> * opinion (əˈpɪnjən) *n.* 意見；看法　　*had better* 最好
> *take a journey* 旅行　　illegal (ɪˈligl̩) *adj.* 違法的
> *make sense* 合理　　charge (tʃɑrdʒ) *v.* 收 (費)

2. (**B**) 根據 FAA 的看法，美國家庭 ＿＿＿＿＿＿＿＿。

    (A) 關心安全勝過票價

    (B) <u>開車比搭飛機還要冒著生命危險</u>

    (C) 可能會拒絕航空公司的優待票

    (D) 可能會批評政府的運輸安全政策

     * *be likely to V.* 可能～

     bargain ('bɑrgɪn) *n.* 廉價；特惠   offer ('ɔfɚ) *n.* 提供

     policy ('pɑləsɪ) *n.* 政策

     【註】 本題有 1/4 的同學選 (A)，但根據本文第 9-10 行可知，正確

         答案應為 (B)。

3. (**B**) 根據 FAA 的說法，不到十八公斤的孩童旅行時，最好的方式是什麼？

    (A) 半價。

    (B) <u>坐在他自己的兒童安全座椅上。</u>

    (C) 小孩應該要搭車而不是飛機。

    (D) 坐在別人大腿上。

4. (**A**) 「強制性」的事是 ＿＿＿＿＿＿＿＿。

    (A) *must* (mʌst) *n.* 必須做的事

    (B) 危險

    (C) debate (dɪ'bet) *n.* 辯論

    (D) fantasy ('fæntəsɪ) *n.* 幻想

     【註】 本題有不少同學選錯，但根據文章內容，然後使用刪去法

         去掉不可能的答案，應該可以找出正確答案為 (A)。

5. (**B**) 哪一家航空公司在飛行時可使用兒童安全座椅，但是在降落時不行？

    (A) 義大利航空公司。   (B) <u>德國航空公司。</u>

    (C) 美利堅航空公司。   (D) 任何美國航空公司。

     * airways ('ɛr,wez) *n.* 航空公司

     【註】 本題有不少同學選錯，但根據文章倒數 3-4 行，可知正確答

         案應為冰島航空和德國航空，故選 (B)。

TEST 32

Read the following passage and choose the best answer for each question.

For a few days in January, a young rhesus monkey called ANDi became one of the most famous animals on the planet, his endearing features plastered across countless newspapers. Created by a team at the Oregon Regional Primate Research Center near Portland so that each of his cells carries a gene for a glowing green protein, ANDi is the world's first transgenic primate. His name derives from "inserted DNA" spelt backwards.

Some reports suggested that ANDi is just one step removed from "designer" human babies. But if anything, he shows that transgenic people are still far from a practical reality. ANDi gives out not even the faintest green glow —— the introduced gene taken from a jellyfish was alive in two other fetuses that died spontaneously, but in ANDi it seems to be silent. Nor did ANDi's creators hope to develop a method to use in people. Rather, they are interested in creating genetically modified monkeys for use in medical research. "We discourage any extrapolations to people," says Gerald Schatten, the team's leader.

But many other experts, when asked to look a decade or more into the future, believe that "germline" gene therapy, which aims to produce babies carrying modified genes that will be inherited by future generations, might become part of mainstream medicine.

In March 1998, a conference was held in Los Angeles that threw a spotlight on human germline gene manipulation, then considered a taboo subject. At the meeting, leading scientists spoke in favor of the idea, arguing that excessive regulation could <u>hamper</u> research of medical value. Last year, a report from the American Association for the Advancement of Science (AAAS) dampened the enthusiasm, calling for a temporary suspension on such research. 【成功高中】

1. What is so special about ANDi?
   (A) He is the most endearing primate on the planet.
   (B) He is the world's first genetically modified primate.
   (C) He can produce a greenish glow in the dark.
   (D) He derives his name from "inserted DNA" spelt backwards.

2. Which statement about ANDi's creators is TRUE?

(A) They are eager to apply their knowledge to humans.

(B) They believe that germline gene therapy might become part of mainstream medicine in decades.

(C) They introduced a jellyfish gene into three monkey fetuses, and ANDi was the only survivor.

(D) They suggest that ANDi is just one step removed from "designer" human babies.

3. What does the word "hamper" in the last paragraph possibly mean?

(A) adopt   (B) conduct

(C) encourage   (D) restrict

4. What attitude did AAAS hold toward human germline manipulation in a report published last year?

(A) careful   (B) enthusiastic

(C) totally against (D) strongly in favor of

5. Where would this passage most likely appear?

(A) ANDi's diary

(B) a science magazine

(C) a medical case report

(D) an doctor's instruction handbook

TEST 32 詳解

For a few days in January, a young rhesus monkey called
ANDi became one of the most famous animals on the planet, his
endearing features plastered across countless newspapers.

一月份有幾天，一隻叫做安迪的年輕恆河獼猴，變成了地球上最有名的
動物，他以可愛的樣子佔據了無數報紙的版面。

> rhesus (ˈrisəs) *n.* 恆河獼猴 (= *rhesus monkey*) (產於印度北部的
> 一種短尾猴；體小，毛長而呈棕黃色；供醫學實驗用)
> planet (ˈplænɪt) *n.* 地球；行星
> endearing (ɪnˈdɪrɪŋ) *adj.* 令人喜愛的　　features (ˈfitʃəz) *n. pl.* 容貌
> plaster (ˈplæstɚ) *v.* 塗抹；貼滿　　across (əˈkrɔs) *prep.* 遍及
> countless (ˈkauntlɪs) *adj.* 無數的

Created by a team at the Oregon Regional Primate Research Center
near Portland so that each of his cells carries a gene for a glowing
green protein, ANDi is the world's first transgenic primate.

安迪是一個波特蘭附近的奧勒岡州地區靈長類研究中心的小組所創造出來的，
所以牠的每個細胞都有一個綠色螢光蛋白基因，安迪是全球第一隻基因轉殖
的靈長類動物。

> create (krɪˈet) *v.* 創造　　team (tim) *n.* 小組
> Oregon (ˈɔrɪˌgɑn) *n.* 奧勒岡州 (美國西部的一州)
> regional (ˈridʒənḷ) *adj.* 區域性的　　primate (ˈpraɪmɪt) *n.* 靈長類
> research (ˈrisɝtʃ) *n.* 研究
> Portland (ˈportlənd) *n.* 波特蘭 (美國奧勒岡州西北部之一城市)
> so that 所以 (表目的)　　cell (sɛl) *n.* 細胞
> carry (ˈkærɪ) *v.* 帶有　　gene (dʒin) *n.* 基因
> glowing (ˈgloɪŋ) *adj.* 發光的　　protein (ˈprotin) *n.* 蛋白質
> transgenic (trænsˈdʒɛnɪk) *adj.* 基因轉殖的【因遺傳物質之人工轉換
> (即俗稱的「遺傳工程」) 而有異種基因存在其中的，或因而產生的】

His name derives from "inserted DNA" spelt backwards.

他的名字是來自於「嵌入去氧核糖核酸」倒過來拼。

derive〔dəˊraɪv〕v. 源自   inserted〔ɪnˊsɝtɪd〕adj. 插入的；嵌入的
DNA 去氧核糖核酸（= *Deoxyribonucleic Acid*）
spell〔spɛl〕v. 拼字   backwards〔ˊbækwɚdz〕adv. 倒；逆

Some reports suggested that ANDi is just one step removed from "designer" human babies. But if anything, he shows that transgenic people are still far from a practical reality.

有些報導指出，安迪與「訂做」人類寶寶只有一步之遙。但是說起來，牠也證明了基因轉殖人類和現實還有一大段距離。

suggest〔səgˊdʒɛst〕v. 指出
remove〔rɪˊmuv〕v. 移動；離去 < *from* >
designer〔dɪˊzaɪnɚ〕adj.（產品）由設計師專門設計的
if anything 說起來   show〔ʃo〕v. 證明；說明
far from 遠離   practical〔ˊpræktɪkḷ〕adj. 實際的
reality〔rɪˊælətɪ〕n. 現實

ANDi gives out not even the faintest green glow —— the introduced gene taken from a jellyfish was alive in two other fetuses that died spontaneously, but in ANDi it seems to be silent.

安迪甚至連最微弱的綠光都發不出來 —— 那是從水母身上抽出來的基因，在植入其他兩隻後來自然死亡的猴子胎兒內時，都還會繼續活動。但在安迪體內的基因，卻似乎毫無動靜。

give out 散發出   faint〔fent〕adj. 微弱的
glow〔glo〕n. 光輝   introduced〔ˌɪntrəˊdjust〕adj. 植入的
jellyfish〔ˊdʒɛlɪˌfɪʃ〕n. 水母   alive〔əˊlaɪv〕adj. 活的；繼續活動的
fetus〔ˊfitəs〕n. 胎兒   spontaneously〔spɑnˊtenɪəslɪ〕adv. 自然地
silent〔ˊsaɪlənt〕adj. 靜止的；不活動的

Nor did ANDi's creators hope to develop a method to use in people. Rather, they are interested in creating genetically modified monkeys for use in medical research.

安迪的創造者也不希望研發出能應用在人類身上的方法。更確切地說，他們的興趣是在於創造出能應用在醫學研究上的基因改造猴。

creator (krɪ'etɚ) *n.* 創造者　　develop (dɪ'vɛləp) *v.* 發展
method ('mɛθəd) *n.* 方法　　rather ('ræðɚ) *adv.* 更確切地說
genetically (dʒə'nɛtɪklɪ) *adv.* 基因上　　modify ('mɑdə,faɪ) *v.* 修改
genetically modified 基因改造的　　medical ('mɛdɪkl) *adj.* 醫學的

"We discourage any extrapolations to people," says Gerald Schatten, the team's leader.

該小組的領導人吉偌‧夏頓說：「我們反對任何推斷到人類身上的做法。」

discourage (dɪs'kɝɪdʒ) *v.* 反對
extrapolation (ɛk,stræpo'leʃən) *n.* 推斷；外推
leader ('lidɚ) *n.* 領導人

But many other experts, when asked to look a decade or more into the future, believe that "germline" gene therapy, which aims to produce babies carrying modified genes that will be inherited by future generations, might become part of mainstream medicine.

不過很多其他專家，在被問到對於十年或更久之後的未來展望時，都認為「生殖系」基因治療法，其目的在於製造出帶有改造基因的嬰兒，並使那個基因遺傳給後代，可能會成為主流醫學的一部份。

expert ('ɛkspɝt) *n.* 專家　　decade ('dɛked) *n.* 十年
look into 觀察　　germline ('dʒɝm,laɪn) *n.* 生殖系
therapy ('θɛrəpɪ) *n.* 治療法　　aim (em) *v.* 目的在於
inherit (ɪn'hɛrɪt) *v.* 繼承；遺傳而得
generation (,dʒɛnə'reʃən) *n.* 世代
mainstream ('men,strim) *adj.* 主流的　　medicine ('mɛdəsṇ) *n.* 醫學

In March 1998, a conference was held in Los Angeles that
threw a spotlight on human germline gene manipulation, then
considered a taboo subject.

一九八八年三月，在洛杉磯舉行了一場會議，其焦點都集中於操縱人類
生殖基因，這在當時被視為是禁忌話題。

> conference（'kɑnfərəns）*n.* 會議　　　 hold（hold）*v.* 舉辦
> spotlight（'spɑt,laɪt）*n.* 衆人注目的焦點
> manipulation（mə,nɪpju'leʃən）*n.* 操縱
> consider（kən'sɪdə）*v.* 視為　　　 taboo（tə'bu）*adj.* 禁忌的
> subject（'sʌbdʒɪkt）*n.* 主題；題目

At the meeting, leading scientists spoke in favor of the idea, arguing
that excessive regulation could <u>hamper</u> research of medical value.

在這場會議中，卓越的科學家表示贊成這個觀念，並認為過度管制可能會阻
礙具有醫學價值的研究。

> leading（'lidɪŋ）*adj.* 第一流的；卓越的　　 *in favor of* 贊成
> argue（'ɑrgju）*v.* 主張　　 excessive（ɪk'sɛsɪv）*adj.* 過度的
> regulation（,rɛgjə'leʃən）*n.* 管制　　 hamper（'hæmpə）*v.* 阻礙
> value（'vælju）*n.* 價值　　 *of medical value* 具有醫學價值的

Last year, a report from the American Association for the
Advancement of Science (AAAS) dampened the enthusiasm,
calling for a temporary suspension on such research.

去年，一篇來自美國科學促進會（AAAS）的報告，要求要暫時中止這方面
的研究，才使得熱情降溫。

> association（ə,sosɪ'eʃən）*n.* 協會；學會
> advancement（əd'vænsmənt）*n.* 促進
> dampen（'dæmpən）*v.* 降低；減少
> enthusiasm（ɪn'θjuzɪ,æzəm）*n.* 熱情　　 *call for* 要求
> temporary（'tɛmpə,rɛrɪ）*adj.* 暫時的
> suspension（sə'spɛnʃən）*n.*（暫時）中止；中斷

1. (**B**) 安迪爲什麼這麼特別？
  (A) 他是地球上最可愛的靈長類。
  (B) <u>他是世界上第一隻經過基因改造的靈長類。</u>
  (C) 他在黑暗中會發出淺綠色的光。
  (D) 他的名字來自於「嵌入去氧核糖核酸」倒過來拼。

  * greenish〔'ɡrinɪʃ〕*adj.* 淺綠色的

2. (**C**) 關於安迪的創造者，下列哪一個的敘述是**眞的**？
  (A) 他們渴望將他們的知識應用在人類身上。
  (B) 他們相信生殖系基因療法在數十年後，會變成主流醫學的一部份。
  (C) <u>他們將水母的基因植入三隻猴子胎兒體內，而安迪是唯一存活下來的。</u>
  (D) 他們指出安迪離「訂做」人類寶寶只有一步之遙。

  * statement〔'stetmənt〕*n.* 敘述　　eager〔'iɡɚ〕*adj.* 渴望的
  apply〔ə'plaɪ〕*v.* 應用 < to >　　survivor〔sə'vaɪvɚ〕*n.* 生還者

  【註】 本題只有 1/3 的同學選對，這題考得非常細，乍看之下，(B)
  　　　(C)(D) 好像都是對的，但是要特別注意，題目是問「安迪的
  　　　創造者」，而 (B) 是其他專家的看法，(D) 是有些報導的內容，
  　　　這兩項都不是安迪的創造者說的，故不選。

3. (**D**) 在最後一段中出現的 "hamper"，意思可能是什麼？
  (A) adopt〔ə'dɑpt〕*v.* 採用
  (B) conduct〔kən'dʌkt〕*v.* 做；進行
  (C) encourage〔ɪn'kɝɪdʒ〕*v.* 鼓勵
  (D) *restrict*〔rɪ'strɪkt〕*v.* 限制

  【註】 本題有非常多同學選錯，根據文章內容，的確不太容易猜出
  　　　正確的意思，所以這題算是考同學的英文程度。閱讀測驗要
  　　　答得好，除了應試時沉著冷靜之外，識字率的多寡也是非常
  　　　重要的。建議同學考前一定要背「電腦統計常考字彙」和
  　　　「考前必背字彙」，充實自己的字庫。

4. (**A**) 去年美國科學促進會（AAAS）所發表的報告，對於人類生殖系操
縱抱持何種態度？

(A) 很小心的
(B) 非常熱中的
(C) 完全反對
(D) 強烈贊成

　* publish〔'pʌblɪʃ〕v. 發表
　　enthusiastic〔ɪn‚θjuzɪ'æstɪk〕adj. 狂熱的；熱中的
　　totally〔'totḷɪ〕adv. 完全　　against〔ə'gɛnst〕prep. 反對
　　strongly〔'strɔŋlɪ〕adv. 強烈地

　　【註】 本題有 36%的同學選 (B)，但根據文章倒數 2-3 行，可知 (B)
　　　　　是錯的。

5. (**B**) 這篇文章最有可能出現在哪裡？

(A) 安迪的日記
(B) 科學雜誌
(C) 醫學病例報告
(D) 醫師的指導手冊

　* appear〔ə'pɪr〕v. 出現　　diary〔'daɪərɪ〕n. 日記
　　case〔kes〕n. 病例
　　instruction〔ɪn'strʌkʃən〕n. 指導
　　handbook〔'hænd‚bʊk〕n. 手冊

TEST 33

Read the following passage and choose the best answer for each question.

One of the ways that poets create powerful images is to combine contradictory ideas. For example, a poet might combine the ideas of heat and cold, or love and hate. In just such a way Donald Hall combined contradictory ideas in the following short poem, titled *My Son, the Executioner*:

> My son, my executioner,
> I take you in my arms,
> Quiet and small and just astir,
> And whom my body warms.
>
> We twenty-five and twenty-two,
> Who seemed to live forever,
> Observe enduring life in you
> And start to die together.

【大同高中】

1. Who is speaking in this poem?
   (A) A father.　　(B) A newborn boy.
   (C) An executioner.　　(D) An immortal person.

2. What does "twenty-five and twenty- two" mean?

(A) That is how many children the parents have had.

(B) The boy's parents are twenty-five and twenty-two years old.

(C) That is how old the parents were when their boy killed them.

(D) That is how old the parents were when they stopped having more children.

3. Why does the speaker say that the parents will now "start to die together"?

(A) Giving birth to a baby causes people to die.

(B) The baby will begin trying to kill his parents.

(C) Having a baby makes the parents feel older and closer to death.

(D) The parents are so sick of taking care of their baby that they feel like they are dying.

4. The word "Executioner" is similar in meaning to:

_____.

(A) Creator   (B) Healer

(C) Killer   (D) Performer

5. What are the two contradictory ideas in this poem?

(A) Childhood and adulthood.

(B) Killing and love.

(C) Birth and death.

(D) Motherhood and fatherhood.

TEST 33 詳解

One of the ways that poets create powerful images is to
combine contradictory ideas. For example, a poet might combine
the ideas of heat and cold, or love and hate.

詩人創造強烈意象的方式之一，就是將對立的概念結合在一起。舉例來
說，詩人可以結合冷和熱或愛與恨的概念。

> poet (ˈpo·ɪt) *n.* 詩人　　powerful (ˈpaʊəfəl) *adj.* 強烈的
> image (ˈɪmɪdʒ) *n.* 意象　　combine (kəmˈbaɪn) *v.* 結合
> contradictory (ˌkɑntrəˈdɪktərɪ) *adj.* 對立的
> cold (kold) *n.* 冷　　hate (het) *n.* 憎恨

In just such a way Donald Hall combined contradictory ideas in
the following short poem, titled *My Son, the Executioner*:

多納·霍爾就是以這樣的方式，將對立的概念結合在下面這首短詩中，這首
詩的標題是「我兒，我的劊子手」。

> poem (ˈpo·ɪm) *n.* 詩　　title (ˈtaɪtḷ) *v.* 稱為；加標題於
> *titled* ~　標題為　　executioner (ˌɛksɪˈkjuʃənɚ) *n.* 劊子手

My son, my executioner,
I take you in my arms,
Quiet and small and just astir,
And whom my body warms.

我兒，我的劊子手，
我把你抱在懷裡，
安靜嬌小又很有活力，
我用我的身體溫暖你。

arm〔ɑrm〕*n.* 手臂　　***in one's arms*** 在某人懷中
just〔dʒʌst〕*adv.* 很；非常
astir〔ə'stɝ〕*adj.* 活動起來的；充滿活力的
warm〔wɔrm〕*v.* 使溫暖

We twenty-five and twenty-two,
Who seemed to live forever,
Observe enduring life in you
And start to die together.

我們是二十五歲和二十二歲，
好像會永遠活著，
看著你永恆的生命，
然後就開始一起死掉。

observe〔əb'zɝv〕*v.* 觀察；注意看
enduring〔ɪn'djʊrɪŋ〕*adj.* 持久的；永恆的

1. (**A**) 在這首詩中，說話的人是誰？

(A) 一位父親。　　　　　(B) 一個新生兒。
(C) 一個劊子手。　　　　(D) 一個長生不死的人。

　* newborn〔'nju'bɔrn〕*adj.* 剛出生的
　 immortal〔ɪ'mɔrtl̩〕*adj.* 不死的；永恆的

2. (**B**) 「二十五與二十二」的意思是什麼？

(A) 那是這對父母所擁有的小孩數目。
(B) 男孩的父母是二十五歲與二十二歲。
(C) 那是這對父母被孩子殺掉時的年齡。
(D) 那是這對父母不再繼續生小孩時的年齡。

3. (**C**) 爲何說話者說這對父母現在將要「開始一起死去」？

(A) 生小孩會使人死掉。

(B) 這個嬰兒會開始試著殺掉父母。

(C) 有小孩讓父母覺得自己更老，而且更接近死亡。

(D) 這對父母非常厭倦照顧小孩，所以他們覺得自己快死了。

　　* *give birth to* 生（孩子）　　cause (kɔz) v. 導致；使

　　sick (sɪk) adj. 厭倦的 <*of*>　　dying ('daɪɪŋ) adj. 快要死的

4. (**C**) 與 "Executioner" 這個字意思相近的是：＿＿＿＿＿。

(A) creator (krɪ'etə) n. 創造者

(B) healer ('hilə) n. 治療者

(C) *killer* ('kɪlə) v. 殺手

(D) performer (pə'fɔrmə) n. 表演者

5. (**C**) 在這首詩中的兩個對立概念爲何？

(A) 童年與成年。

(B) 殺戮與愛。

(C) 生與死。

(D) 母親與父親的角色。

　　* childhood ('tʃaɪld,hʊd) n. 童年時代

　　adulthood (ə'dʌlt,hʊd) n. 成年時期

　　killing ('kɪlɪŋ) n. 殺害

　　motherhood ('mʌðə,hʊd) n. 母性；母親的身份

　　fatherhood ('faðə,hʊd) n. 父性；父親的身份

TEST 34

Read the following passage and choose the best answer for each question.

There are more than 50 different kinds of kangaroos in the world today. The smallest ones are only five centimeters tall but the biggest are more than two meters. Kangaroos cannot walk or run. They just jump. The best time to see kangaroos in action is the evening and early morning. They spend the daytime **snoozing** in the shade. Straight after they are born, the joeys (baby kangaroos), which are only about two-and-a-half centimeters long, have to drag themselves to their mother's pouch. They find their way there by following the pattern of their mother's hairs. They stay in the pouch until they are eight months old. After that, they leave home for good. Sometimes the joeys aren't too keen on making their way in the big wide world. A 50 pound joey, for example, was once found still living in its mother's pouch. Have you ever wondered why these animals are called "kangaroos"? Well, according to one story, when Captain Cook landed in Australia and heard the aborigines calling these amazing animals "Kangooroo," he wrote the name down as " kangaroo." That's how this animal got its name. 【復興高中】

1. An appropriate description of the theme of the passage is _____.

   (A) how joeys are brought up
   (B) the joey's growth
   (C) how joeys learn to jump
   (D) the reason why joeys stay in the pouch

2. When is the best time to see kangaroos moving around?

   (A) early in the morning   (B) at noon
   (C) at nighttime   (D) in the afternoon

3. According to the article, which of the following statements is true?

   (A) The biggest kangaroo is taller than the average person.
   (B) Straight after the joeys are born, they can jump into the pouch by themselves.
   (C) From the time the joeys are eight months old they stay in the pouch.
   (D) All joeys enjoy making their way in the big wide world.

4. As used in this passage, the word "snoozing" means

   (A) posing.   (B) varying.
   (C) raising.   (D) sleeping.

5. The word "kangaroo" comes from _____.

   (A) the noise the animals make
   (B) the aborigine word for this animal
   (C) Captain Cook's pet
   (D) the Australian government

TEST 34 詳解

There are more than 50 different kinds of kangaroos in the world today. The smallest ones are only five centimeters tall but the biggest are more than two meters.

現在世界上有超過五十種不同的袋鼠。最小的只有五公分高，但是最大的卻超過兩公尺。

kangaroo〔͵kæŋɡə′ru〕*n.* 袋鼠
centimeter〔′sɛntə͵mitɚ〕*n.* 公分
meter〔′mitɚ〕*n.* 公尺

Kangaroos cannot walk or run. They just jump. The best time to see kangaroos in action is the evening and early morning. They spend the daytime **snoozing** in the shade.

袋鼠不會走路或跑步。牠們只會跳。看袋鼠活動的最好時間是傍晚或一大清早。牠們白天都在樹蔭下打瞌睡。

jump〔dʒʌmp〕*v.* 跳　　　*in action* 活動中
daytime〔′de͵taɪm〕*n.* 白天　　snooze〔snuz〕*v.* 打瞌睡
shade〔ʃed〕*n.* 樹蔭　　*in the shade* 在樹蔭下

Straight after they are born, the joeys (baby kangaroos), which are only about two-and-a-half centimeters long, have to drag themselves to their mother's pouch.

小袋鼠（袋鼠寶寶）大約只有 2.5 公分長，牠們一出生就必須要費力地走到媽媽的育兒袋中。

straight〔stret〕*adv.* 立刻　　joey〔dʒɔɪ〕*n.* 幼獸；小袋鼠
drag〔dræg〕*v.* 費力地走　　pouch〔pautʃ〕*n.* 育兒袋；腹袋

They find their way there by following the pattern of their
mother's hairs. They stay in the pouch until they are eight months
old. After that, they leave home for good.

牠們順著媽媽的毛路,來找到通往育兒袋的路。牠們待在育兒袋中,直到八
個月大。之後牠們就會永遠離開家。

> follow ('falo) v. 順著 (道路等) 前進
> pattern ('pætən) n. 圖案;形式　　hair (hɛr) n. 毛髮
> *for good* 永遠 (= *forever*)
>
> 【註】 小袋鼠出生時全身光溜溜的,這時袋鼠媽媽會用牠的舌頭舔自
> 　　　 己的毛,從生殖口一直舔到育兒袋的口邊,而小袋鼠就順著這
> 　　　 一條濕潤的毛路用前爪爬到袋鼠媽媽的育兒袋中,並含住袋中
> 　　　 四個乳頭之一,吸收養分長大。

Sometimes the joeys aren't too keen on making their way in the
big wide world. A 50 pound joey, for example, was once found
still living in its mother's pouch.

有時候,小袋鼠對於在廣闊的世界中自食其力,並不是太熱衷。舉例來說,
就曾經發現一隻 50 磅重的小袋鼠,仍然生活在媽媽的育兒袋中。

> keen (kin) adj. 熱衷的;敏銳的
> *make one's way* 靠自己;自食其力
> wide (waɪd) adj. 寬廣的
> pound (paʊnd) n. 磅 (重量單位)

Have you ever wondered why these animals are called "kangaroos"?
Well, according to one story, when Captain Cook landed in
Australia and heard the aborigines calling these amazing animals
"Kangooroo," he wrote the name down as " kangaroo." That's
how this animal got its name.

你是否曾經想知道，為什麼這些動物叫作 "kangaroos" 呢？嗯，根據某個故事的說法，當庫克船長登陸澳洲時，聽到原住民叫這些令人驚訝的動物 "Kangooroo"，他把這個名字寫下來，並寫成 "kangaroo"。那就是這種動物命名的由來。

> wonder〔ˈwʌndɚ〕v. 想知道
> captain〔ˈkæptn̩〕n. 船長
> land〔lænd〕v. 登陸；抵達
> aborigine〔ˌæbəˈrɪdʒəni〕n. 原住民
> amazing〔əˈmezɪŋ〕adj. 驚人的　　　***write down*** 寫下來

1. (**B**) 對於本文主題的適當敘述是 _____ 。
　　(A) 如何撫養小袋鼠長大
　　(B) 小袋鼠的成長
　　(C) 小袋鼠如何學習跳躍
　　(D) 小袋鼠待在育兒袋的理由

　　* appropriate〔əˈpropriɪt〕adj. 適當的
　　　description〔dɪˈskrɪpʃən〕n. 敘述
　　　theme〔θim〕n. 主題
　　　bring up 撫養長大　　　growth〔groθ〕n. 成長

2. (**A**) 何時是看袋鼠四處活動的最佳時間？
　　(A) 一大清早　　　　　　(B) 正午
　　(C) 晚上　　　　　　　　(D) 下午

　　* ***move around*** 四處活動
　　　nighttime〔ˈnaɪtˌtaɪm〕n. 夜晚

3.(**A**) 根據本文，下列哪一個敘述是正確的？

(A) 最大的袋鼠比普通人還高。

(B) 小袋鼠一出生，就會自己跳到育兒袋中。

(C) 從小袋鼠八個月大開始，牠們就會待在育兒袋中。

(D) 所有的小袋鼠都喜歡在廣闊的世界中自食其力。

* average〔'ævərɪdʒ〕*adj.* 普通的

the average person 普通人

4.(**D**) 本文中所使用的 "snoozing" 這個字，意思是 _____。

(A) 擺姿勢

(B) 改變

(C) 養育

(D) 睡覺

* pose〔poz〕*v.* 擺姿勢　　vary〔'vɛrɪ〕*v.* 改變

raise〔rez〕*v.* 養育；提高

5.(**B**) "kangaroo" 這個字是源自 _____。

(A) 那些動物所發出的聲音

(B) 代表這種動物的原住民單字

(C) 庫克船長的寵物

(D) 澳洲政府

* noise〔nɔɪz〕*n.* 噪音；聲音　　pet〔pɛt〕*n.* 寵物

TEST 35

Read the following passage, and choose the best answer for each question.

What is the secret of writing a good letter? Here are two main ones. Don't try to be fancy. Don't try to impress your reader. You'll be successful if you follow these seven Cs.

Clear. Use short direct sentences. Make them easy to understand. Communicate as if the reader were right there with you.

Correct. Make sure what you say is correct. Don't guess, even with spelling. Flip open your dictionary. If you need to, check reference books, too. Use them as much as you need to.

Complete. Don't scatter your points. Finish one point completely before going on to the next. This is good organization, too.

Courteous. Be friendly rather than **flippant**. Present your information nicely even if you are complaining about something. In all letters, treat others as you want them to treat you.

Concise. Make each point as clearly and briefly as you can.

Conversational. This is really the secret of good writing. Just "talk" to the person. Such a letter has a natural, friendly tone. Let your personality come through naturally.

Considerate. Think of the reader's point of view as you write. Write about what you believe the reader needs or wants to know. Try to be helpful. This will build good feeling toward you.

The seven Cs are about writing letters. But how about school papers? Use the seven Cs, too. Write as if you are talking to your teacher or professor. You'll be surprised. You'll almost instantly become a good writer. And you might even enjoy writing from now on. 【和平高中】

1. This selection is about _____.
   (A) doing well in school
   (B) the seven Cs of writing
   (C) being yourself
   (D) enjoying writing

2. According to this passage, one secret to good writing is to _____.

(A) "talk" to the reader
(B) try to sound impressive
(C) include long sentences
(D) have a strong introduction

3. Based on this passage, we can assume _____.

(A) letter writing is more important than other types of writing
(B) writing should not be taken too seriously
(C) the seven Cs are all you need to know to be a great writer
(D) good letter writers can write papers well, too

4. In this passage, the writer presents information in _____.

(A) chronological order
(B) a list
(C) a series of comparisons
(D) a description

5. The word "**flippant**" in the 5th paragraph means _____.

(A) happy
(B) intelligent
(C) overly casual
(D) speedy

TEST 35 詳解

What is the secret of writing a good letter? Here are two main ones. Don't try to be fancy. Don't try to impress your reader. You'll be successful if you follow these seven C's.

把一封信寫好的秘訣是什麼？主要有兩點。不要想寫得很華麗。不要想打動讀者。如果你遵循下面七個 C，那麼你就會成功。

> secret ('sikrıt) *n.* 秘訣　　fancy ('fænsı) *adj.* 華麗的
> impress (ım'prɛs) *v.* 使印象深刻；打動 (人心)
> follow ('falo) *v.* 遵守

Clear. Use short direct sentences. Make them easy to understand. Communicate as if the reader were right there with you.

清楚。使用簡短而直接的句子。讓這些句子容易瞭解。好像讀者就在你身邊那樣跟他們溝通。

> direct (də'rɛkt) *adj.* 直接的
> communicate (kə'mjunə,ket) *v.* 溝通；傳達　　*as if* 好像

Correct. Make sure what you say is correct. Don't guess, even with spelling. Flip open your dictionary. If you need to, check reference books, too. Use them as much as you need to.

正確。要確定你所說的是正確的。就算是拼字，也不要亂猜。很快地翻一下字典。如果有需要的話，也去查查參考書。有需要就儘量使用這些參考書。

guess〔gɛs〕*v.* 猜；推測
spelling〔'spɛlɪŋ〕*n.* 拼字
flip〔flɪp〕*v.* 快速翻（書頁等）　　check〔tʃɛk〕*v.* 查對
reference〔'rɛfərəns〕*adj.* 參考的

Complete. Don't scatter your points. Finish one point completely before going on to the next. This is good organization, too.

完整。不要分散你的重點。把一個重點完整地說完，才繼續下一個重點。這樣也會有條有理。

scatter〔'skætɚ〕*v.* 散播；把…散放
point〔pɔɪnt〕*n.* 重點　　**go on** 繼續
organization〔ˌɔrgənə'zeʃən〕*n.* 組織；條理

Courteous. Be friendly rather than **flippant**. Present your information nicely even if you are complaining about something. In all letters, treat others as you want them to treat you.

有禮貌。要友善，不要無禮。把你要傳達的資訊好好說出來，即使你是在抱怨某件事。在所有的信件中，你希望對別人怎麼對你，你就要怎麼對他們。

courteous〔'kɝtɪəs〕*adj.* 有禮貌的
rather than 而不是
flippant〔'flɪpənt〕*adj.* 輕率的；無禮的
present〔prɪ'zɛnt〕*v.* 提出；表達　　***even if*** 即使
complain〔kəm'plen〕*v.* 抱怨　　treat〔trit〕*v.* 對待

Concise. Make each point as clearly and briefly as you can.

簡潔。儘量讓每個重點都簡短而清楚。

> concise (kən'saɪs) *adj.* 簡潔的；簡明的
> *as ~ as one can* 儘可能地~
> briefly ('briflɪ) *adv.* 簡短地

Conversational. This is really the secret of good writing. Just "talk" to the person. Such a letter has a natural, friendly tone. Let your personality come through naturally.

口語化。這是寫得好的真正秘訣。就對那個人「說話」。這樣信就會有自然而友善的語氣。讓你的個性自然地表現出來。

> conversational (,kɑnvə'seʃənl) *adj.* 口語的；會話的
> tone (ton) *n.* 語調；語氣
> personality (,pɜsn'ælətɪ) *n.* 個性；性格
> *come through* 表現

Considerate. Think of the reader's point of view as you write. Write about what you believe the reader needs or wants to know. Try to be helpful. This will build good feeling toward you.

體貼。當你在寫的時候，要考慮到讀者的觀點。寫一些你認為讀者需要或想知道的東西。試著幫助讀者。這會建立讀者對你的好感。

> considerate (kən'sɪdərɪt) *adj.* 體貼的
> *point of view* 觀點
> helpful ('hɛlpfəl) *adj.* 有幫助的；主動幫忙的
> toward (tə'word) *prep.* 對於

The seven Cs are about writing letters. But how about school papers? Use the seven Cs, too. Write as if you are talking to your teacher or professor.

這就是關於寫信的七個 C。但是寫學校報告的時候怎麼辦呢？也可以用這七個 C。就像在對老師或教授講話那樣寫。

paper ('pepɚ) *n.* 報告　　professor (prə'fɛsɚ) *n.* 教授

You'll be surprised. You'll almost instantly become a good writer. And you might even enjoy writing from now on.

你會很驚訝。你幾乎會立刻成為寫作高手，而且你甚至會從現在開始愛上寫作。

instantly ('ɪnstəntlɪ) *adv.* 立刻地　　*from now on* 從現在開始

1. (**B**) 這篇選文是關於 _____ 。
　(A) 在學校的表現良好　　　(B) 寫作的七個 C
　(C) 做自己　　　　　　　(D) 喜歡寫作
　* selection (sə'lɛkʃən) *n.* 選文　　do (du) *v.* 表現

2. (**A**) 根據本文，寫得好的一個秘訣是 _____ 。
　(A) 和讀者「說話」
　(B) 試著讓人聽起來印象深刻
　(C) 包含長的句子
　(D) 有強而有力的引言
　* impressive (ɪm'prɛsɪv) *adj.* 令人印象深刻的
　　include (ɪn'klud) *v.* 包括
　　introduction (ˌɪntrə'dʌkʃən) *n.* 引言；序言

3. (**D**) 根據這篇文章，我們可以斷定 _____ 。

(A) 寫信比其他類型的寫作重要

(B) 不應該把寫作看得太認眞

(C) 要成爲一個好作家，這七個 C 是你所必須知道的

(D) 會寫信的人，報告也寫得好

 * *based on* 根據 (= *according to*)
 assume〔ə'sjum〕*v.* 認爲；斷定
 take ~ seriously 把~看得很認眞

【註】本題有 43% 的同學選 (C)，但根據文章內容，只說知道這
七個 C 可以寫好信件和報告，可以成爲寫作高手，可是
並沒有說要成爲好作家，必須要知道這七個 C。

4. (**D**) 在本文中，作者 _____ 來傳達資訊。

(A) 依年代順序 (B) 列表

(C) 做一系列的比較 (D) 用描述

 * chronological〔ˌkrɑnə'lɑdʒɪkl̩〕*adj.* 按年代順序的
 list〔lɪst〕*n.* 表　　*a series of* 一系列的；一連串的
 comparison〔kəm'pærəsn̩〕*n.* 比較
 description〔dɪ'skrɪpʃən〕*n.* 敘述；描寫

【註】本題有 27% 的同學選 (C)，但根據文章內容，應選 (D)。

5. (**C**) 第五段的 "flippant" 的意思是 _____ 。

(A) 快樂的 (B) 聰明的

(C) 非常隨便的 (D) 快速的

 * intelligent〔ɪn'tɛlədʒənt〕*adj.* 聰明的
 overly〔'ovəlɪ〕*adv.* 過分地；非常
 casual〔'kæʒuəl〕*adj.* 隨便的；非正式的
 speedy〔'spidɪ〕*adj.* 快速的

TEST 36

Read the following passage and choose the best answer for each question.

Like so many other things in this modern world, television technology has progressed tremendously in the past one or two decades. For example, we used to have only three channels to choose from in Taiwan, but today the choices are overwhelming, with nearly one hundred cable and satellite channels. People often ask whether this kind of progress is good or bad for us. Certainly there are advantages — educationally, politically and socially. It provides up-to-date news about important events. It expands our horizons by exposing us to other countries and cultures. It helps us to become more aware of our own communities, through public service advertisements. It helps democracy to thrive, by providing a place where different political voices can be heard.

What then are the disadvantages? While television may have informational and educational potential, it certainly cannot replace conventional schooling or the value of opening up a book to study and learn on one's own. As every parent and every child knows, television can indeed be a distraction from studying and learning. Some research has shown that television, with its wealth of violent programming, may bring about more aggressive behavior among adolescents and adults alike, or at least desensitize people to the horrors of crime and violence. Other studies have shown that television dampens our creativity, making us more passive and less able to think for ourselves. Although none of these findings have been fully confirmed, there is no doubt that it can easily turn us into overweight, out-of-shape couch potatoes. With less television in our lives, we will have more time not only for studying, but also for family, friends, hobbies and sports. We'll be better off both psychologically and physically. 【復興高中】

1. What is the main idea of this article?

(A) The role of conventional schooling cannot be replaced by TV.

(B) We should use our judgment to make the best use of television.

(C) Watching TV takes up so much of our time that many of us depend on TV as our only source of entertainment.

(D) Parents should be held responsible for their children's violent behavior if they don't help their children choose good TV programs.

2. How many television channels did we have before we had cable and satellite TV?

  (A) One.   (B) Two.

  (C) Three.   (D) Nearly one hundred.

3. What is the political advantage of TV mentioned in this article?

  (A) It provides up-to-date news about important events.
  (B) It expands our horizons by exposing us to other countries and cultures.
  (C) It helps us to become more aware of our own communities.
  (D) It helps democracy to thrive.

4. Which of the following is NOT a possible result of watching less TV?

  (A) We might become psychologically abnormal.
  (B) We might have more time to cultivate our hobbies.
  (C) We might have more time to study.
  (D) We might have better health.

5. What do you think the meaning of the phrase "couch potato" is?

  (A) a certain flavor of potato chips
  (B) a plant which is similar to a potato
  (C) a person who spends lots of time watching TV and gets little exercise
  (D) a couch decorated with many potatoes

TEST 36 詳解

Like so many other things in this modern world, television technology has progressed tremendously in the past one or two decades.

就像現代世界的許多其他事物一樣，電視科技在過去這一、二十年間，有很大的進展。

> **modern** ('modən) *adj.* 現代的
> **technology** (tɛk'nɑlədʒɪ) *n.* 科技
> **progress** (prə'grɛs) *v.* 進步
> **tremendously** (trɪ'mɛndəslɪ) *adv.* 極大地
> **decade** ('dɛked) *n.* 十年

For example, we used to have only three channels to choose from in Taiwan, but today the choices are overwhelming, with nearly one hundred cable and satellite channels.

例如，我們以前在台灣只有三個頻道可以選，但是現在有超多選擇，有將近一百個有線電視及衛星頻道。

> ***used to*** 以前　　**channel** ('tʃænl) *n.* 頻道
> **overwhelming** (,ovə'hwɛlmɪŋ) *adj.* 壓倒性的；數量極多的
> **nearly** ('nɪrlɪ) *adv.* 幾乎
> **cable** ('kebl) *n.* 有線電視
> **satellite** ('sætl,aɪt) *n.* 人造衛星

People often ask whether this kind of progress is good or bad for us. Certainly there are advantages—educationally, politically and socially. It provides up-to-date news about important events.

人們常問，這樣的進步對我們而言是好是壞。當然會有好處——在教育、政治與社會方面都有。它提供了我們重大事件的最新消息。

progress (ˈprɑgrɛs) *n.* 進步　　certainly (ˈsɝtn̩lɪ) *adv.* 當然；一定
advantage (ədˈvæntɪdʒ) *n.* 優點；好處
educationally (ˌɛdʒəˈkeʃənl̩ɪ) *adv.* 教育上
politically (pəˈlɪtɪkl̩ɪ) *adv.* 政治上
socially (ˈsoʃəlɪ) *adv.* 社會上
provide (prəˈvaɪd) *v.* 提供　　up-to-date (ˈʌptəˈdet) *adj.* 最新的
news (njuz) *n.* 消息　　event (ɪˈvɛnt) *n.* 事件

It expands our horizons by exposing us to other countries and cultures. It helps us to become more aware of our own communities, through public service advertisements.

它以讓我們接觸其他國家與文化的方式，來拓展我們的視野。它透過公益廣告，幫助我們更注意我們自己的社會。

expand (ɪkˈspænd) *v.* 拓展
horizons (həˈraɪzn̩z) *n. pl.* 視野；知識範圍
expose (ɪkˈspoz) *v.* 使接觸 < *to* >
aware (əˈwɛr) *adj.* 知道的；注意的 < *of* >
community (kəˈmjunətɪ) *n.* 社會　　*public service* 公益服務
advertisement (ˌædvəˈtaɪzmənt) *n.* 廣告

It helps democracy to thrive, by providing a place where different political voices can be heard.

　　What then are the disadvantages?

它有助於民主政治的蓬勃發展，它提供場所，讓不同的政治意見都能被聽見。
　　那麼有什麼壞處呢？

democracy (dəˈmɑkrəsɪ) *n.* 民主政治　　thrive (θraɪv) *v.* 蓬勃發展
political (pəˈlɪtɪkl̩) *adj.* 政治的　　voice (vɔɪs) *n.* 意見
disadvantage (ˌdɪsədˈvæntɪdʒ) *n.* 缺點；壞處

While television may have informational and educational potential, it certainly cannot replace conventional schooling or the value of opening up a book to study and learn on one's own.

儘管電視可能有知識與教育方面的潛力，但是它一定無法取代傳統的學校教育，或是自己打開書本研讀與學習的重要性。

> while〔hwaɪl〕*conj.* 儘管
> informational〔͵ɪnfɚˈmeʃən̩〕*adj.* 知識的
> educational〔͵ɛdʒəˈkeʃən̩〕*adj.* 教育的
> potential〔pəˈtɛnʃəl〕*n.* 潛力   replace〔rɪˈples〕*v.* 取代
> conventional〔kənˈvɛnʃən̩〕*adj.* 傳統的
> schooling〔ˈskulɪŋ〕*n.* 學校教育
> value〔ˈvæljʊ〕*n.* 價值；重要性
> *on one's own* 靠自己

As every parent and every child knows, television can indeed be a distraction from studying and learning.

就如每個父母與兒童所知道的，電視確實會讓人無法專心唸書與學習。

> *as one knows* 正如某人所知
> indeed〔ɪnˈdid〕*adv.* 的確
> distraction〔dɪˈstrækʃən〕*n.* 使人分心的事物

Some research has shown that television, with its wealth of violent programming, may bring about more aggressive behavior among adolescents and adults alike, or at least desensitize people to the horrors of crime and violence.

有些研究指出，電視上有大量的暴力節目，可能會造成青少年與成人都出現更多攻擊性的行為，或著至少會讓人們對於犯罪與暴力的恐怖變得不敏感。

research ('risʒtʃ) *n.* 研究 (= *study*)　　show (ʃo) *v.* 顯示；指出
wealth (wɛlθ) *n.* 大量 < *of* >　　violent ('vaɪələnt) *adj.* 暴力的
programming ('progræmɪŋ) *n.* 節目　　***bring about*** 導致；造成
aggressive (ə'grɛsɪv) *adj.* 攻擊性的
behavior (bɪ'hevjə) *n.* 行為　　adolescent (,ædḷ'ɛsn̩t) *n.* 青少年
adult (ə'dʌlt) *n.* 成人　　alike (ə'laɪk) *adv.* 同樣地
A *and* B *alike* A 和 B 都一樣　　***at least*** 至少
desensitize (di'sɛnsə,taɪz) *v.* 使遲鈍；使變得不敏感
horror ('hɔrə) *n.* 恐怖　　crime (kraɪm) *n.* 犯罪
violence ('vaɪələns) *n.* 暴力

Other studies have shown that television dampens our creativity,
making us more passive and less able to think for ourselves.

其他研究指出，電視會使我們的創造力下降，而且會讓我們比較被動，還有
比較沒辦法獨立思考。

study ('stʌdɪ) *n.* 研究　　dampen ('dæmpən) *v.* 抑制；降低
creativity (,krie'tɪvətɪ) *n.* 創造力
passive ('pæsɪv) *adj.* 消極的；被動的　　able ('ebḷ) *adj.* 能夠的
for oneself 獨自地；靠自己

Although none of these findings have been fully confirmed, there
is no doubt that it can easily turn us into overweight, out-of-shape
couch potatoes.

雖然這些研究結果沒有一個被充分證實，但是毫無疑問地，電視很容易就能
讓我們變成體重過重、身材走樣的沙發馬鈴薯。

none (nʌn) *pron.* 全無；沒有一個
findings ('faɪndɪŋz) *n. pl.* 研究的結果　　fully ('fulɪ) *adv.* 充分地
confirm (kən'fʒm) *v.* 證實　　***there is no doubt that*** 無疑地，~
turn A *into* B 使 A 變成 B　　overweight ('ovə'wet) *adj.* 過重的
out-of-shape ('autəv'ʃep) *adj.* 身材走樣的　　couch (kautʃ) *n.* 長沙發
couch potato 沙發馬鈴薯（指整天坐在沙發上看電視的人）

With less television in our lives, we will have more time not only for studying, but also for family, friends, hobbies and sports. We'll be better off both psychologically and physically.

在我們的生活中，愈少看電視，就會有愈多時間，不僅可以唸書，還可以陪家人、朋友、培養嗜好與運動。我們在身心兩方面都會更健康。

> ***not only…but also~*** 不僅…而且~
> hobby ('hɑbɪ) *n.* 嗜好　　***better off*** 情況較好
> psychologically (ˌsaɪkə'lɑdʒɪklɪ) *adv.* 心理上
> physically ('fɪzɪklɪ) *adv.* 身體上

1. (**B**) 本文的主旨為何？
   (A) 傳統學校教育的角色無法被電視取代。
   (B) 我們應該運用自己的判斷力，來好好利用電視。
   (C) 看電視佔用了我們這麼多時間，我們很多人都仰賴電視，作為唯一的娛樂來源。
   (D) 如果父母親不幫小孩選擇好的電視節目，他們就應該為小孩的暴力行為負責。

   > * role (rol) *n.* 角色　　judgment ('dʒʌdʒmənt) *n.* 判斷力
   > ***take up*** 佔用 (時間、地方等)
   > depend (dɪ'pɛnd) *v.* 依賴 < *on* >　　source (sors) *n.* 來源
   > entertainment (ˌɛntə'tenmənt) *n.* 娛樂
   > ***hold responsible for*** 為…負責　　program ('progræm) *n.* 節目

   【註】 本題有 1/3 的同學選 (C)，根據文章內容，並沒有提到說很多人都把電視當成唯一的娛樂來源，所以這個答案是錯的。

2. (**C**) 在我們擁有有線電視與衛星電視之前，我們有幾個電視頻道？
   (A) 一個。　　　　　　　　(B) 兩個。
   (C) 三個。　　　　　　　　(D) 將近一百個。

3. (**D**) 本文中提到，電視所帶來的政治利益爲何？

(A) 它提供重大事件的最新消息。

(B) 它讓我們接觸到其他國家與文化，拓展了我們的視野。

(C) 它幫助我們更加注意我們自己的社會。

(D) 它幫助民主政治蓬勃發展。

* mention ('mɛnʃən) v. 提到　article ('ɑrtɪkl) n. 文章

4. (**A**) 下列哪一個不是少看電視可能的結果？

(A) 我們也許會變得心理不正常。

(B) 我們也許會有更多時間培養嗜好。

(C) 我們也許會有更多時間唸書。

(D) 我們也許會更健康。

* abnormal (æb'nɔrml) adj. 不正常的
cultivate ('kʌltə,vet) v. 培養　health (hɛlθ) n. 健康

5. (**C**) 你認爲 "couch potato" 這個片語是什麼意思？

(A) 某種洋芋片的口味

(B) 一種與馬鈴薯相似的植物

(C) 一個花很多時間看電視而不太做運動的人

(D) 一個用很多馬鈴薯裝飾的長沙發

* phrase (frez) n. 片語　certain ('sɜtṇ) adj. 某種
flavor ('flevɚ) n. 口味
potato chips 洋芋片　plant (plænt) n. 植物
similar ('sɪmələ) adj. 相似的
decorate ('dɛkə,ret) v. 裝飾

TEST 37

Read the following passage, and choose the best answer for each question.

Where there is a will, there is a way. That is to say, when we make up our mind to do something, however difficult it may be, we can find a way to make it come true.

The real reason why we do not try to do certain things, or fail to do them when we try, is often that we are in fact unwilling to do them. When we are reluctant to do something, we set to work to find all kinds of strange excuses, and make mountains out of molehills. Every difficulty is exaggerated, and we fill our mind with obstacles, which cause us to think it is impossible for our dreams to become realities. Our desire is like a thin, feeble stream of water that is turned aside or blocked by every small obstacle. But a rushing current simply sweeps rocks, trees, and banks out of its way and forces itself through or over every obstruction. In a similar way, aggressive desire and strong determination will overcome the difficulties we face. If we have these, then we will discover the royal road to success. 【陽明高中】

1. Every plan is doomed to fail if we _____.

   (A) exaggerate every obstacle

   (B) study extremely hard

   (C) keep on fighting to the end

   (D) work very hard

2. If a person has strong determination to do things, he or she will _____.

   (A) do things with reluctance

   (B) do things without hesitation

   (C) be afraid of difficulties

   (D) be able to find a way to escape

3. To "make mountains out of molehills" means to _____.

   (A) find excuses   (B) exaggerate

   (C) succeed   (D) be aggressive

4. Which of the following is a simile?

   (A) Where there is a will, there is a way.

   (B) Make a mountain out of a molehill.

   (C) Our desire is like a thin, feeble stream of water.

   (D) But a rushing current simply sweeps rocks, trees, and banks out of its way.

5. What is a rushing current compared with?

   (A) An obstruction.

   (B) Aggressive desire.

   (C) The royal road to success.

   (D) A molehill.

TEST 37 詳解

Where there is a will, there is a way. That is to say, when we make up our mind to do something, however difficult it may be, we can find a way to make it come true.

有志者，事竟成。也就是說，當我們下定決心要做某件事時，不論有多困難，我們都可以找到實現它的方法。

> will〔wɪl〕 *n.* 意志　　***that is to say*** 也就是說
> however〔haʊ'ɛvɚ〕 *adv.* 無論多麼地 (= *no matter how*)
> ***make up*** one's ***mind*** 下定決心　　***come true*** 實現

The real reason why we do not try to do certain things, or fail to do them when we try, is often that we are in fact unwilling to do them.

我們不試著去做某些事情，或是試了卻做不到，真正的理由常是我們其實不願意去做。

> certain〔'sɝtn̩〕 *adj.* 某些　　***fail to*** *V.* 無法～
> ***in fact*** 事實上　　unwilling〔ʌn'wɪlɪŋ〕 *adj.* 不願意的

When we are reluctant to do something, we set to work to find all kinds of strange excuses, and make mountains out of molehills.

當我們不情願去做某件事時，我們會開始找各種奇怪的藉口，然後小題大作。

> reluctant〔rɪ'lʌktənt〕 *adj.* 不情願的
> ***set to work*** 開始；著手進行
> excuse〔ɪk'skjus〕 *n.* 藉口　　molehill〔'mol,hɪl〕 *n.* 鼴鼠丘
> ***make mountains out of molehills*** 言過其實；小題大作
> (= ***make a mountain out of a molehill***)

Every difficulty is exaggerated, and we fill our mind with obstacles, which cause us to think it is impossible for our dreams to become realities.

每個困難都被誇大,我們讓自己的心充滿阻礙,這樣就會使我們覺得,要實現自己的夢想是不可能的。

exaggerate (ɪgˈzædʒəˌret) v. 誇大;誇張
fill (fɪl) v. 使充滿　　obstacle (ˈɑbstəkl̩) n. 阻礙
reality (rɪˈælətɪ) n. 事實

Our desire is like a thin, feeble stream of water that is turned aside or blocked by every small obstacle.

我們的願望就像一道細長而微弱的水流,這道水流會因爲每一個小阻礙而轉變方向,或是被堵住。

desire (dɪˈzaɪr) n. 慾望;願望　　thin (θɪn) adj. 細長的
feeble (ˈfibl̩) adj. 微弱的　　stream (strim) n. 溪流;水流
aside (əˈsaɪd) adv. 向一邊　　*turn aside* 使轉變方向
block (blɑk) v. 堵塞

But a rushing current simply sweeps rocks, trees, and banks out of its way and forces itself through or over every obstruction.

但是急流就可以輕易地將石頭、樹木,以及堤防沖離它的路徑,而且可以強行通過或跨越每一道障礙。

rushing (ˈrʌʃɪŋ) adj. 急速的　　current (ˈkɜənt) n. 水流
simply (ˈsɪmplɪ) adv. 輕易地　　sweep (swip) v. 沖走
bank (bæŋk) n. 堤防;河岸
out of one's way 不在預期的路線(或軌道)上
force (fors) v. 強迫　　through (θru) prep. 通過
obstruction (əbˈstrʌkʃən) n. 障礙

In a similar way, aggressive desire and strong determination will overcome the difficulties we face. If we have these, then we will discover the royal road to success.

同樣地，積極的慾望和強烈的決心，會克服我們所面臨的困難。如果我們擁有這些東西，那麼我們就會發現成功的捷徑。

> similar ('sɪmələ) *adj.* 相似的；類似的
> *in a similar way* 同樣地
> aggressive (ə'grɛsɪv) *adj.* 積極的
> determination (dɪ,tɜ˞mə'neʃən) *n.* 決心
> overcome (,ovə˞'kʌm) *v.* 克服
> discover (dɪ'skʌvə˞) *v.* 發現
> royal ('rɔɪəl) *adj.* 皇家的   *royal road* 捷徑

1. (**A**) 每個計畫都註定會失敗，如果我們 ＿＿＿＿＿＿。
   (A) 誇大每個阻礙
   (B) 非常用功唸書
   (C) 持續奮鬥到最後
   (D) 非常努力

   > * doom (dum) *v.* 註定
   >   extremely (ɪk'strimlɪ) *adv.* 非常地
   >   *keep on* 繼續   fight (faɪt) *v.* 奮鬥

2. (**B**) 如果一個人做事有強烈的決心去做事，他或她將會 ＿＿＿＿＿＿。
   (A) 不情願地做事
   (B) 毫不猶豫地做事
   (C) 害怕困難
   (D) 能找到逃避的方法

   > * reluctance (rɪ'lʌktəns) *n.* 不情願
   >   hesitation (,hɛzə'teʃən) *n.* 猶豫
   >   escape (ə'skep) *v.* 逃避

3. (**B**) "make mountains out of molehills" 的意思是 ＿＿＿＿＿＿＿。

    (A) 找藉口   (B) 誇大

    (C) 成功   (D) 積極

【註】 本題有 28% 的同學選 (C)，但根據上下文判斷，我們不情願做某件事，而開始找奇怪的藉口，如此一來，成功的機率就很小，所以不可能是這個答案。

4. (**C**) 下列何者是明喻？

    (A) 有志者，事竟成。

    (B) 言過其實；小題大作。

    (C) 我們的願望就像一道細長而微弱的水流。

    (D) 但是急流可以輕易地將石頭，樹木，以及堤防沖離它的路徑。

    * simile ('sıməˌli) *n.* 明喻【就是句中有 as 或 like 出現時】

5. (**B**) 急流被拿來和什麼做比較？

    (A) 障礙。   (B) 積極的慾望。

    (C) 成功的捷徑。   (D) 鼴鼠丘。

【註】 本題有 30% 的同學選 (C)，但根據文章內容，應該要選 (B)。

【劉毅老師的話】

    成為閱測答題高手並不難，只要你有決心、有毅力，就沒有任何事能阻礙你。

TEST 38

Read the following passage and choose the best answer for each question.

Paris has long been one of Europe's most popular destinations with its famous history, culture, and art. If you ask any French person which building stands out as an example of these three characteristics, they will probably answer, "The Louvre, of course!"

In its 800-year history, the building has served many purposes, including acting as a home for some of France's greatest kings. But in 1793, after the French Revolution, the Louvre was turned into a public museum, allowing valuable and important works of art to be enjoyed by everyone. Since then, many more pieces of art have been collected by the Louvre. If you wanted to look at each of the 300,000 pieces for just a few seconds, it would take you five weeks to see them all.

The Louvre is home to many well-known paintings, but its most famous and most visited "resident" is Leonardo da Vinci's "Mona Lisa." It was painted almost 400 years ago, and is believed to be one of the world's greatest works of art. Each year over 3 million people flock to the Louvre. Many come to see this great masterpiece and study the Mona Lisa's strange smile. Some people say that she looks happy, while others say she looks sad. People also say that she looks sad one day and then happy the next. Everybody reads her differently, and her enigmatic smile is a large part of her popularity. There are many things to see in Paris, but no visit to France's capital would be complete without getting lost in this great building, or in the smile of this most famous lady.

【南湖高中】

1. The Louvre _____.
   (A) was Leonardo da Vinci's residence
   (B) is the capital of France
   (C) has been one of Europe's least popular destinations
   (D) was once a home for French kings

2. Paris is NOT famous for _____.
   (A) high technology   (B) history
   (C) art   (D) culture

3. Which of the following statements is NOT correct?

(A) The Louvre is about 800 years old.

(B) In 1973, the Louvre became a public museum.

(C) There are 300,000 works of art in the Louvre's collection.

(D) The Louvre attracts more than 3 million tourists each year.

4. Why is the "Mona Lisa" so popular?

(A) She smiles happily.

(B) She looks sad.

(C) It's hard to understand her mysterious smile.

(D) Her smile grows bigger and bigger.

5. Which of the following is NOT true?

(A) The Louvre is believed to be one of the world's greatest works of art.

(B) It would take you several weeks to take a look at all the treasures in the Louvre.

(C) Many people interpret the Mona Lisa's facial expression differently.

(D) The French Revolution happened in the 18th century.

TEST 38 詳解

Paris has long been one of Europe's most popular destinations
with its famous history, culture, and art.

巴黎有著名的歷史、文化與藝術，使其長久以來，一直都是歐洲最受歡
迎的旅遊目的地之一。

culture (ˈkʌltʃɚ) *n.* 文化
destination (ˌdɛstəˈneʃən) *n.* (旅遊) 目的地

If you ask any French person which building stands out as an
example of these three characteristics, they will probably answer,
"The Louvre, of course!"

如果你問任何一個法國人，哪一棟建築物，是最能突顯這三個特質的實例，
他們可能會回答：「當然是羅浮宮！」

stand out 突出
characteristic (ˌkærɪktəˈrɪstɪk) *n.* 特質
probably (ˈprɑbəblɪ) *adv.* 可能
Louvre (ˈluvɚ) *n.* 羅浮宮 (坐落在巴黎的國家藝術博物館)

In its 800-year history, the building has served many purposes,
including acting as a home for some of France's greatest kings.

在這座建築物的八百年歷史當中，它曾有許多種用途，包括作爲某些法
國偉大君主的家。

serve (sɜv) *v.* 適合 (特定用途或目的)
purpose (ˈpɜpəs) *n.* 用途
including (ɪnˈkludɪŋ) *prep.* 包括　　***act as*** 充當

But in 1793, after the French Revolution, the Louvre was turned into a public museum, allowing valuable and important works of art to be enjoyed by everyone.

不過在一七九三年，也就是法國大革命之後，羅浮宮變成了一座公共博物館，所有的人都可以欣賞到珍貴且重要的藝術品。

revolution〔͵rɛvə'luʃən〕*n.* 革命
French Revolution 法國大革命（1789 年）
turn into 變成   museum〔mju'ziəm〕*n.* 博物館
allow〔ə'lau〕*v.* 允許；讓
valuable〔'væljuəbḷ〕*adj.* 珍貴的
work of art 藝術品   enjoy〔ɪn'dʒɔɪ〕*v.* 欣賞

Since then, many more pieces of art have been collected by the Louvre. If you wanted to look at each of the 300,000 pieces for just a few seconds, it would take you five weeks to see them all.

從那時起，就有更多更多的藝術品被收藏在羅浮宮裡。如果你想把那三十萬件作品，每件都花幾秒鐘看一下，那麼你要花五個星期才能看完。

many more 更多更多的   piece〔pis〕*n.* 一件
art〔ɑrt〕*n.* 藝術作品   collect〔kə'lɛkt〕*v.* 收集；收藏
second〔'sɛkənd〕*n.* 秒

The Louvre is home to many well-known paintings, but its most famous and most visited "resident" is Leonardo da Vinci's "Mona Lisa."

羅浮宮是很多著名畫作的家，不過最有名且最多人參訪的「居民」是李奧納多‧達文西的「蒙娜麗莎」。

be home to~ 是~的所在地

well-known (ˈwɛlˈnon) *adj.* 著名的

painting (ˈpentɪŋ) *n.* 畫　　**most** (most) *adv.* 最多

visit (ˈvɪzɪt) *v.* 參觀　　**resident** (ˈrɛzədənt) *n.* 居民

Leonardo da Vinci 李奧納多‧達文西 (1452-1519；義大利畫家、
建築家、科學家)

Mona Lisa 蒙娜麗莎 (達文西之畫作)

It was painted almost 400 years ago, and is believed to be one of
the world's greatest works of art. Each year over 3 million people
flock to the Louvre.

這幅畫差不多是在四百年前畫的，而且它被認為是全世界最偉大的藝術品之
一。每年有超過三百萬人成群進入羅浮宮。

　　paint (pent) *v.* 畫　　**almost** (ˈɔlˌmost) *adv.* 差不多

　　flock (flɑk) *v.* 成群而來 (或去)

Many come to see this great masterpiece and study the Mona
Lisa's strange smile. Some people say that she looks happy, while
others say she looks sad.

很多人是來看這件偉大的傑作，然後研究一下蒙娜麗莎奇特的笑容。有人說
她看起來很快樂，然而也有人說她看起來很憂傷。

　　masterpiece (ˈmæstəˌpis) *n.* 傑作

　　study (ˈstʌdɪ) *v.* 研究

　　strange (strendʒ) *adj.* 奇特的　　**while** (ˌhwaɪl) *conj.* 然而

People also say that she looks sad one day and then happy the
next. Everybody reads her differently, and her enigmatic smile is
a large part of her popularity.

人們還說她某一天看起來很憂傷，而隔天看起來很快樂。每個人對她的解讀都不一樣，她的神祕的笑容就是她受歡迎的主因。

> read (rid) *v.* 解讀
> enigmatic (ˌɛnɪgˋmætɪk) *adj.* 神祕的
> popularity (ˌpɑpjəˋlærətɪ) *n.* 受歡迎

There are many things to see in Paris, but no visit to France's capital would be complete without getting lost in this great building, or in the smile of this most famous lady.

巴黎有很多東西可以看，不過如果沒有迷失在這棟偉大的建築物裡，或是在這位最著名的女士的笑容裡，那麼你的法國首都之旅就不算完整。

> visit (ˋvɪzɪt) *n.* 參觀；遊覽；觀光（旅行）
> capital (ˋkæpət!) *n.* 首都
> complete (kəmˋplit) *adj.* 完整的　　***get lost*** 迷失

1. (**D**) 羅浮宮 _____。
   (A) 曾經是李奧納多‧達文西的住所
   (B) 是法國的首都
   (C) 是全歐洲最不受歡迎的旅遊目的地之一
   (D) 曾經是法國國王的家
    * residence (ˋrɛzədəns) *n.* 住宅；宅邸　　least (list) *adj.* 最少的
    【註】 本題有 26% 的同學選 (C)，但根據文章內容，羅浮宮是歐洲最受歡迎的旅遊目的地之一，因此這個選項是錯誤的。

2. (**A**) 巴黎有名的不是 _____。
   (A) 高科技　　(B) 歷史　　(C) 藝術　　(D) 文化
    * technology (tɛkˋnɑlədʒɪ) *n.* 科技

3. (**B**) 下列哪一項敘述不正確？

  (A) 羅浮宮已經有八百年歷史了。

  (B) <u>在一九七三年時，羅浮宮變成了公共博物館。</u>

  (C) 羅浮宮收藏了三十萬件藝術品。

  (D) 羅浮宮每年吸引超過三百萬名遊客。

   * tourist ('tʊrɪst) *n.* 遊客　　attract (ə'trækt) *v.* 吸引

   【註】 本題有 27% 的同學選 (C)，但注意，本題是選錯誤的選項，
     故應選 (B)。

4. (**C**) 爲何「蒙娜麗莎」這麼受歡迎？

  (A) 她笑得很快樂。

  (B) 她看起來很憂傷。

  (C) <u>很難理解她的神祕笑容。</u>

  (D) 她愈笑愈開懷。

   * mysterious (mɪs'tɪrɪəs) *adj.* 神祕的　　grow (gro) *v.* 變得

5. (**A**) 下列哪一個不是事實？

  (A) <u>羅浮宮被認爲是世界上最偉大的藝術品之一。</u>

  (B) 要把羅浮宮的所有珍藏品看完，要花好幾個星期。

  (C) 許多人對蒙娜麗莎的臉部表情有不同的解釋。

  (D) 法國大革命發生在十八世紀。

   * showroom ('ʃo,rum) *n.* 展覽室

   treasure ('trɛʒɚ) *n.* 寶藏；珍藏品

   interpret (ɪn'tɜprɪt) *v.* 解釋

   facial ('feʃəl) *adj.* 臉部的

   expression (ɪk'sprɛʃən) *n.* 表情

TEST 39

Read the following passage and choose the best answer for each question.

"Have a talk with your dog and call me in the morning."

That's what doctors might say after reading new studies about people and their pets. Studies are showing that pets are good for your health. It does not seem to matter whether your pet is a dog or a goldfish. Pets may do more for you than you will ever do for them.

For example, the blood pressure of some people who were studied stayed the same — or went down — when they spoke to animals. Normal blood pressure is important to good health. And doctors say blood pressure often goes up when people talk to people.

Animals also seem to help people who are sick or lonely. People in nursing homes showed great joy when pets were brought to them. They liked to touch the animals and talk to them. And they liked to talk to one another about the animals.

One man had suffered a stroke and had not spoken for a long time. A puppy was placed on his wheelchair tray. Suddenly the man was laughing softly. "Puppy," he whispered.

Patients at a mental hospital were given small animals, such as white mice, birds, and guinea pigs. Caring for the pets gave these patients a reason to talk and work together. Many became calmer and more hopeful.

In France, a veterinarian found that pets helped children who would not communicate with other people. The children first touched and played with the pets and then began speaking with adults.

Do animals have the "magic" power to help people? Scientists think the magic is simply love and trust. Pets are likely to welcome people and show them affection. They give people something to care about. They make people feel wanted and needed. The studies seem to show that animals are "good medicine." Maybe the animals have known that all along. 〔建國中學〕

1. The theory that pets are good for your health is
   _____.

   (A) supported by experiments
   (B) supported by the author's experience
   (C) supported by opinions only
   (D) not supported at all

2. After reading this article, you can conclude that

   _____.

   (A) people with pets never get sick
   (B) pets seem to promote good health
   (C) pets should replace medicine
   (D) everyone should have a pet

3. Which is the best title for this article?

   (A) The Magic Touch of Animals
   (B) Animals Are Amazing and Healthy
   (C) Pets are better than medicine
   (D) Pets Bring Healthy Benefits

4. Choose the FALSE statement.

   (A) Older people enjoyed both talking to the pets and talking about them.
   (B) Pets were shown to reduce blood pressure in young children.
   (C) Scientists believe that love and trust are beneficial to health.
   (D) Taking care of pets gave mental patients a sense of purpose.

5. Which of these is an opinion?

   (A) Normal blood pressure is a sign of good health.
   (B) A sick man responded to a puppy.
   (C) Animals know when people are ill.
   (D) Goldfish and lizards are kinds of pets.

TEST 39 詳解

"Have a talk with your dog and call me in the morning."
「和你的狗說說話，然後早上打個電話給我。」

That's what doctors might say after reading new studies about people and their pets. Studies are showing that pets are good for your health.
　這是醫生看過關於人們和其寵物的最新研究之後，可能會說的話。研究顯示，寵物有益健康。

　　　pet (pɛt) *n.* 寵物　　study ('stʌdɪ) *n.* 研究

It does not seem to matter whether your pet is a dog or a goldfish. Pets may do more for you than you will ever do for them.
你的寵物是狗或金魚，似乎並不重要。寵物為你做的，可能多於你為牠們所做的。

　　　matter ('mætɚ) *v.* 重要　　goldfish ('gold,fɪʃ) *n.* 金魚
　　　ever ('ɛvɚ) *adv.* 在任何時候；始終 (加強語氣)

For example, the blood pressure of some people who were studied stayed the same — or went down — when they spoke to animals.
　　舉例來說，當某些研究對象在對動物說話時，他們的血壓會持平或是下降。

　　　pressure ('prɛʃɚ) *n.* 壓力　　*blood pressure* 血壓
　　　stay (ste) *v.* 保持　　*go down* 下降

Normal blood pressure is important to good health. And doctors say blood pressure often goes up when people talk to people.

血壓正常對健康來說很重要。醫生說，當人和人交談時，血壓常常會上升。

normal ('nɔrml̩) adj. 正常的　　**go up** 上升

Animals also seem to help people who are sick or lonely. People in nursing homes showed great joy when pets were brought to them.

動物似乎也能幫助生病或寂寞的人。當寵物被帶到待在養老院的人身邊時，那些人都顯得非常開心。

lonely ('lonlɪ) adj. 寂寞的　　**nursing home** 養老院
joy (dʒɔɪ) n. 歡樂

They liked to touch the animals and talk to them. And they liked to talk to one another about the animals.

他們喜歡撫摸動物，然後跟牠們說話。而且他們也喜歡互相談論動物的事。

one another 互相

One man had suffered a stroke and had not spoken for a long time. A puppy was placed on his wheelchair tray. Suddenly the man was laughing softly. "Puppy," he whispered.

有個中風的人，已經很久沒開口說話。有隻小狗被放在他的輪椅桌墊。突然間，那個人輕輕地笑了。「小狗，」他低聲地說著。

suffer ('sʌfɚ) v. 罹患　　stroke (strok) n. 中風
puppy ('pʌpɪ) n. 小狗　　place (ples) v. 放置
wheelchair ('hwil'tʃɛr) n. 輪椅　　tray (tre) n. 托盤；淺盤
wheelchair tray 輪椅桌墊　　suddenly ('sʌdn̩lɪ) adv. 突然地
softly ('sɔftlɪ) adv. (聲音) 輕輕地　　whisper ('hwɪspɚ) v. 低語

Patients at a mental hospital were given small animals, such as white mice, birds, and guinea pigs.

有人給精神病院的患者一些小動物，像是小白鼠、小鳥，還有天竺鼠。

> patient〔'peʃənt〕*n.* 病人
> mental〔'mɛntḷ〕*adj.* 精神病的
> mice〔maɪs〕*n. pl.* 老鼠（單數為 mouse〔maʊs〕）
> ***guinea pig*** 天竺鼠

Caring for the pets gave these patients a reason to talk and work together. Many became calmer and more hopeful.

照顧這些寵物，給了這些病患一起說話和工作的理由。很多人都變得比較平靜和樂觀。

> calm〔kɑm〕*adj.* 平靜的
> hopeful〔'hopfəl〕*adj.* 抱著希望的；樂觀的

In France, a veterinarian found that pets helped children who would not communicate with other people.

在法國，有位獸醫發現，寵物對於無法和別人溝通的小孩，也有幫助。

> veterinarian〔ˌvɛtərə'nɛrɪən〕*n.* 獸醫（= *vet*）
> communicate〔kə'mjunəˌket〕*v.* 溝通

The children first touched and played with the pets and then began speaking with adults.

小孩一開始會摸摸寵物，還有跟牠們玩，後來就會開始跟大人說話了。

> first〔fɝst〕*adv.* 最初　　adult〔ə'dʌlt〕*n.* 成人

Do animals have the "magic" power to help people?
Scientists think the magic is simply love and trust.

動物有幫助人類的「神奇」力量嗎？科學家認為，這個神奇的力量只不過是愛和信任而已。

> scientist ('saɪəntɪst) *n.* 科學家　　magic ('mædʒɪk) *adj.* 神奇的
> simply ('sɪmplɪ) *adv.* 只不過；僅僅　　trust (trʌst) *n.* 信任

Pets are likely to welcome people and show them affection.
They give people something to care about. They make people
feel wanted and needed.

寵物可能會歡迎人類，並對他們表達情感。牠們會讓人們有事情可以關心。牠們讓人們有被需要的感覺。

> ***be likely to V.*** 可能～　　welcome ('wɛlkəm) *v.* 歡迎
> affection (ə'fɛkʃən) *n.* 情感　　***care about*** 關心

The studies seem to show that animals are "good medicine."
Maybe the animals have known that all along.

這些研究似乎是顯示，動物是「良藥」。或許動物們一直都知道這件事。

> medicine ('mɛdəsṇ) *n.* 藥　　***all along*** 一直

1. (**A**) 動物有益健康的理論是 ＿＿＿＿＿＿＿。

    (A) 經實驗證明的

    (B) 經作者的經驗證實的

    (C) 只經過一般人的意見證實

    (D) 完全沒有經過證實的

> * theory ('θiərɪ) *n.* 理論　　support (sə'port) *v.* 證明；證實
> experiment (ɪk'spɛrəmənt) *n.* 實驗　　author ('ɔθɚ) *n.* 作者
> experience (ɪk'spɪrɪəns) *n.* 經驗
> opinion (ə'pɪnjən) *n.* 意見；看法　　***not…at all*** 一點也不

2. (**B**) 看完本文以後，你可以推論出 ＿＿＿＿＿＿＿＿＿＿ 。

(A) 有養寵物的人永遠不會生病

(B) 寵物似乎可以促進健康

(C) 寵物應該取代藥物

(D) 每個人都應該養寵物

* conclude (kən'klud) v. 推論出；斷定
promote (prə'mot) v. 促進　replace (rɪ'ples) v. 取代

3. (**D**) 本文最好的題目是？

(A) 動物魔術般的觸摸　　(B) 動物是令人驚奇和有益健康的

(C) 寵物比藥物好　　　　(D) 寵物帶來健康上的好處

4. (**B**) 選出錯誤的敘述。

(A) 老人家喜歡對寵物說話和討論牠們。

(B) 寵物被證明可以降低幼童的血壓。

(C) 科學家相信愛與信任有益健康。

(D) 照顧寵物使精神病患者有使命感。

* statement ('stetmənt) n. 敘述　show (ʃo) v. 證明
reduce (rɪ'djus) v. 降低　beneficial (,bɛnə'fɪʃəl) adj. 有益的
sense (sɛns) n. 感覺　purpose ('pɜpəs) n. 目標

5. (**C**) 下列何者是一般人的意見？

(A) 血壓正常表示很健康。

(B) 生病的人會對小狗有反應。

(C) 動物們知道人類是不是生病了。

(D) 金魚跟蜥蜴是寵物。

* opinion (ə'pɪnjən) n. 意見；看法
sign (saɪn) n. 表示；徵兆
respond (rɪ'spand) v. 反應　lizard ('lɪzəd) n. 蜥蜴

【註】 本題有不少同學選錯，題目的意思是，要選出意見，也就
是文中沒有提到，是讀者自行推想出來的觀念或看法，所
以最好的答案是 (C)。

TEST 40

Read the following passage and choose the best answer for each question.

In Japanese legend, Kaguya was a beautiful princess who came from the moon and was born inside a bamboo stalk. Today, at the Tokyo University of Agriculture, her namesake is a 14-month-old mouse. She was created by scientists using two eggs and no sperm. She is the first mouse born by parthenogenesis (from the Greek for virgin birth), a reproductive method seen in insects and reptiles but never before in mammals.

For the moment, Kaguya's creation is a brilliant piece of science with little or no application to humans. The process is so technically difficult—not to mention ethically charged—that it is hard to see how it could be attempted with human beings. In theory, the technique might be used to create stem cells, but even this scenario is farfetched. What the experiment offers, however, is a glimpse into one of the central mysteries of mammalian biology: Why do we need genes from both a mother and a father in order to be born?

The answer, most scientists suspect, has to do with a peculiar process called parental or genomic imprinting, which seems to occur only in mammals. Biologists have discovered subtle changes that are made to about 100 genes that make a mammalian DNA molecule male or female. How does a cell know which form to imprint on its DNA? The cell checks out the surrounding microscopic environment to see if the environment seems more male or female.

All other things being equal, an embryo must have both a maternal genomic imprint (usually from an egg) and a páternal genomic imprint (usually from a sperm), or it won't grow properly. If it has two paternal imprints, the placenta grows but not the embryo. If it has two maternal imprints, the embryo grows but not the supporting placenta.

Scientists now have a better understanding of procreation. "In spite of all the differences between men and women — our fights, arguments and seeming incompatibility — we still need a set of male and female genes for the species to go on," says Tomohiro Kono, who is the leader of the research team at the Tokyo University of Agriculture.

【北一女中】

1. In Japanese legend, Kaguya was probably _____.
   (A) a fair lady from the moon
   (B) a Japanese warrior
   (C) a 14-month-old girl who liked to eat bamboo shoots
   (D) a college student who studied the moon

2. The mouse Kaguya's birth is fantastic because _____.
   (A) she was born inside a bamboo stalk
   (B) she has no biological father
   (C) she was kept at the Tokyo University of Agriculture
   (D) she was reproduced from the eggs of insects and reptiles

3. We can infer from the 2nd paragraph that _____.
   (A) the technique by which the mouse was produced is simple
   (B) the technique can be applied to humans but it will raise ethical problems
   (C) the technique has been applied to creating stem cells
   (D) the experiment gives us a chance to understand why we need genes from both sexes

4. Which of the following is true?
   (A) Genomic imprinting seems to occur only in humans and mice.
   (B) About 100 molecules change greatly to make a mammal male or female.
   (C) A cell does not know which form to imprint on its DNA.
   (D) In a natural environment, an embryo needs the genomic imprints from both its parents to develop properly.

5. The word "scenario" in the 2nd paragraph means _____.
   (A) a person with great knowledge of a subject
   (B) a picture formed in the mind
   (C) a description of a possible course of events
   (D) an animal with sharp long front teeth

TEST 40 詳解

In Japanese legend, Kaguya was a beautiful princess who came from the moon and was born inside a bamboo stalk. Today, at the Tokyo University of Agriculture, her namesake is a 14-month-old mouse.

在日本的傳說中，Kaguya 是一位來自月亮的美麗公主，她在竹子裡出生。現在在東京農業大學，有一隻跟她同名的十四個月大的老鼠。

* who came from…stalk 是形容詞子句，修飾先行詞 princess。

legend (ˈlɛdʒənd) *n.* 傳奇　　princess (ˈprɪnsɪs) *n.* 公主
bamboo (bæmˈbu) *n.* 竹子　　stalk (stɔk) *n.* 莖；幹
agriculture (ˈægrɪˌkʌltʃɚ) *n.* 農業
namesake (ˈnemˌsek) *n.* 同名的人或物　　mouse (maʊs) *n.* 老鼠

She was created by scientists using two eggs and no sperm. She is the first mouse born by parthenogenesis (from the Greek for virgin birth), a reproductive method seen in insects and reptiles but never before in mammals.

她是科學家用兩顆卵子創造出來的，沒有用到精子。她是第一隻以單性繁殖（這各字是來自希臘，意指處女生育）生出來的老鼠，這種繁殖方法常見於昆蟲和爬蟲類，但是以前從來沒有發生在哺乳類動物身上。

* a reproductive…mammals 是前句 parthenogenesis 的同位語。

create (krɪˈet) *v.* 創造　　egg (ɛg) *n.* 卵子
sperm (spɝm) *n.* 精子
parthenogenesis (ˌparθənoˈdʒɛnəsɪs) *n.* 單性繁殖
Greek (grik) *n.* 希臘文　　for (fɔr) *prep.* 代表
virgin (ˈvɝdʒən) *n.* 處女　　reproductive (ˌriprəˈdʌktɪv) *adj.* 繁殖的
insect (ˈɪnsɛkt) *n.* 昆蟲　　reptile (ˈrɛptl) *n.* 爬蟲類
mammal (ˈmæml) *n.* 哺乳類動物

For the moment, Kaguya's creation is a brilliant piece of science with little or no application to humans.

目前，Kaguya 的誕生是科學上輝煌的成就，但幾乎不適用於人類。

for the moment 目前　　creation〔krɪ'eʃən〕*n.* 創造；產生
brilliant〔'brɪljənt〕*adj.* 輝煌的　　piece〔pis〕*n.* 作品
little or no 幾乎沒有　　application〔͵æplə'keʃən〕*n.* 適用；用途

The process is so technically difficult — not to mention ethically charged — that it is hard to see how it could be attempted with human beings.

這個過程的技術非常困難 —— 更別提道德上的譴責 —— 所以很難看出要如何在人類身上嘗試。

process〔'prɑsɛs〕*n.* 過程　　technically〔'tɛknɪk!ɪ〕*adv.* 技術上地
not to mention 更別提　　ethically〔'ɛθɪk!ɪ〕*adv.* 道德上；倫理上
charge〔tʃɑrdʒ〕*v.* 譴責　　attempt〔ə'tɛmpt〕*v.* 嘗試
human beings 人類

In theory, the technique might be used to create stem cells, but even this scenario is farfetched.

理論上，這項技術可以被用來製造幹細胞，但即使是設想這樣的情況，也太過牽強。

in theory 理論上　　technique〔tɛk'nik〕*n.* 技術
stem〔stɛm〕*n.*（草木的）莖　　cell〔sɛl〕*n.* 細胞
stem cell 幹細胞　　scenario〔sɪ'nɛrɪ͵o〕*n.* 設想的情況；局面
farfetched〔'fɑr'fɛtʃt〕*adj.* 牽強的；勉強的；不自然的

What the experiment offers, however, is a glimpse into one of the central mysteries of mammalian biology: Why do we need genes from both a mother and a father in order to be born?

然而，這項實驗所提供的，是讓我們看一下哺乳類生物學的主要奧秘之一：
為什麼我們同時需要來自父親和母親的基因，才能被生出來？

experiment (ɪk'spɛrəmənt) *n.* 實驗　　offer ('ɔfə) *v.* 提供
glimpse (glɪmps) *n.* 一瞥；一看　　central ('sɛntrəl) *adj.* 主要的
mystery ('mɪstərɪ) *n.* 奧秘；謎
mammalian (mæ'mɛlɪən) *adj.* 哺乳類動物的
biology (baɪ'ɑlədʒɪ) *n.* 生物學　　gene (dʒin) *n.* 基因
in order to V. 為了要～；以便於～

The answer, most scientists suspect, has to do with a peculiar
process called parental or genomic imprinting, which seems to
occur only in mammals.

大部分科學家懷疑，這個答案可能與一個獨特的過程有關，這個過程被
稱為親代印記或遺傳印記，它似乎只發生在哺乳類動物身上。

suspect (sə'spɛkt) *v.* 懷疑　　　*have to do with* 與～有關
peculiar (pɪ'kjuljə) *adj.* 獨特的
parental (pə'rɛntḷ) *adj.* 父母的；親代的
genomic (dʒə'nomɪk) *adj.* 染色體組的；遺傳的
imprinting (ɪm'prɪntɪŋ) *n.* 刻印；印記

Biologists have discovered subtle changes that are made to about
100 genes that make a mammalian DNA molecule male or female.
How does a cell know which form to imprint on its DNA?

生物學家已經發現，大約有一百組基因會發生細微的變化，而使得哺乳類動物
的 DNA 分子變成男性或女性。細胞是如何知道要將哪一種形式印記在 DNA
上呢？

biologist (baɪ'ɑlədʒɪst) *n.* 生物學家　　subtle ('sʌtḷ) *adj.* 細微的
DNA 去氧核糖核酸　　molecule ('mɑlə,kjul) *n.* 分子
male (mel) *adj.* 男性的　　female ('fimel) *adj.* 女性的
form (fɔrm) *n.* 形式　　imprint (ɪm'prɪnt) *v.* 印記

The cell checks out the surrounding microscopic environment to
see if the environment seems more male or female.

細胞會查看周遭的細微環境，看看這個環境看起來比較像男性還是女性。

> ***check out*** 檢查
> surrounding（ sə'raʊndɪŋ) *adj.* 周圍的
> microscopic (ˌmaɪkrə'skɑpɪk) *adj.* 非常微小的
> environment（ ɪn'vaɪrənmənt) *n.* 環境

　　All other things being equal, an embryo must have both a
maternal genomic imprint (usually from an egg) and a paternal
genomic imprint (usually from a sperm), or it won't grow properly.

　　在其他條件都相同的情況下，胚胎必須同時有母親的遺傳印記（通常來
自卵子），和父親的遺傳印記（通常來自精子），否則它就無法適當地成長。

　　* All other things being equal…是由 When all other things are equal,…
　　轉化而來的分詞構句。

> equal（'ikwəl) *adj.* 同樣的　　embryo（'ɛmbrɪ,o) *n.* 胚胎
> maternal（ mə'tɜnḷ) *adj.* 母親的
> paternal（ pə'tɜnḷ) *adj.* 父親的
> properly（'prɑpəlɪ) *adv.* 適當地

If it has two paternal imprints, the placenta grows but not the
embryo. If it has two maternal imprints, the embryo grows but not
the supporting placenta.

如果有兩個父親的印記，胎盤會成長，但胚胎不會。如果有兩個母親的印記，
胚胎會成長，但支持的胎盤不會。

> placenta（ plə'sɛntə) *n.* 胎盤
> supporting（ sə'portɪŋ) *adj.* 支持的

Scientists now have a better understanding of procreation. "In spite of all the differences between men and women — our fights, arguments and seeming incompatibility—we still need a set of male and female genes for the species to go on," says Tomohiro Kono, who is the leader of the research team at the Tokyo University of Agriculture.

科學家現在對於繁殖有更深入的了解。「儘管男女之間有這麼多差異 —— 我們的爭論、爭執，還有外表上的不一致 —— 我們還是需要一組男性和女性的基因，才能讓人類繼續繁殖，」東京農業大學研究小組的領導人 Tomohiro Kono 先生說。

procreation〔͵prokrɪˈeʃən〕*n.* 生殖；繁殖　　*in spite of* 儘管
fight〔faɪt〕*n.* 爭論　　argument〔ˈɑrgjəmənt〕*n.* 爭論
seeming〔ˈsimɪŋ〕*adj.* 外表上的
incompatibility〔͵ɪnkəm͵pætəˈbɪlətɪ〕*n.* 相反；性格的不一致
set〔sɛt〕*n.* 一組　　species〔ˈspiʃɪz〕*n.* 物種
the species 人類　　*go on* 繼續

1.(**A**) 在日本的傳說中，Kaguya 可能是 ＿＿＿＿＿＿＿＿。

(A) 一位來自月亮的美女　　(B) 一名日本勇士

(C) 一名十四個月大的女孩，她喜歡吃竹筍

(D) 一名研究月球的大學生

* fair〔fɛr〕*adj.* 美麗的　　warrior〔ˈwɔrɪɚ〕*n.* 戰士
shoot〔ʃut〕*n.* 嫩芽　　*bamboo shoot* 竹筍

2.(**B**) 老鼠 Kaguya 的誕生非常奇妙，因為 ＿＿＿＿＿＿＿＿。

(A) 她在竹子裡出生　　(B) 她沒有親生父親

(C) 她被飼養在東京農業大學

(D) 她是由昆蟲和爬蟲類的卵子繁殖出來的

* fantastic〔fænˈtæstɪk〕*adj.* 奇妙的
biological〔͵baɪəˈlɑdʒɪkl̩〕*adj.* 生物的
biological father 生父　　keep〔kip〕*v.* 飼養

3. (**D**) 我們可以從第二段推論出 ＿＿＿＿＿＿＿。

(A) 製造出這隻老鼠的技術非常簡單

(B) 這項技術可以應用在人類身上，但會產生道德上的問題

(C) 這項技術已經被用來製造幹細胞

(D) 這個實驗使我們有機會了解，爲什麼我們同時需要兩種性別的基因

* infer (ɪnˈfɝ) v. 推論　　apply (əˈplaɪ) v. 應用
raise (rez) v. 引起；使產生　　ethical (ˈεθɪkl̩) adj. 道德上的

【註】本題有 32% 的同學選 (C)，但根據文章內容，只說理論上可以用來製造幹細胞，所以這個選項是錯誤的。

4. (**D**) 下列何者爲眞？

(A) 遺傳印記似乎只發生在人類和老鼠身上。

(B) 約一百組分子產生巨大的改變，使哺乳類動物變成男性或女性。

(C) 細胞不知道要將何種形式印記在 DNA 上。

(D) 在自然的環境中，胚胎需要來自父母雙方的遺傳印記，才能夠適當地發育。

* mice (maɪs) n. pl. 老鼠 (mouse 的複數)

【註】本題有 1/5 的同學選 (B)，但根據文章內容，那一百組分子是產生細微的變化，故不選 (B)；另外，還有 1/5 的同學選 (C)，同樣根據內文，細胞會查看週遭的細微環境，來決定要將哪一種形式印記在 DNA 上，所以這個選項也是錯誤的。

5. (**C**) 第二段中的 "scenario" 的意思是 ＿＿＿＿＿＿＿。

(A) 一個專精某科目的人

(B) 在心中形成的一個影像

(C) 對事件的可能發展所做的描述

(D) 一隻門牙又利又長的動物

* description (dɪˈskrɪpʃən) n. 描述　　course (kors) n. 過程；發展
event (ɪˈvεnt) n. 事件　　sharp (ʃɑrp) adj. 銳利的
front tooth 前齒；門牙

本書答題錯誤率分析表

本資料經過「劉毅英文家教班」閱讀測驗大賽 400 多位同學實際考試過，經過電腦統計分析，錯誤率如下：

測　驗	題號	正確選項	錯誤率	最多人選的錯誤選項	測　驗	題號	正確選項	錯誤率	最多人選的錯誤選項
Test 1	1	A	25 %	C	Test 10	1	C	37 %	D
	2	D	12 %	B		2	D	8 %	A
	3	C	46 %	D		3	D	10 %	A / B
	4	B	27 %	A		4	D	28 %	C
	5	C	26 %	B		5	D	24 %	C
Test 2	1	C	12 %	A	Test 11	1	A	30 %	C
	2	C	41 %	A		2	A	66 %	B
	3	B	19 %	C		3	C	43 %	B
	4	C	37 %	D		4	C	32 %	A
	5	C	17 %	A		5	B	29 %	A
Test 3	1	D	3 %	C	Test 12	1	A	42 %	C
	2	B	10 %	A		2	A	70 %	C
	3	B	45 %	C		3	B	34 %	D
	4	D	29 %	B		4	D	45 %	B
	5	D	44 %	B		5	B	60 %	D
Test 4	1	C	23 %	B	Test 13	1	B	35 %	A
	2	B	33 %	C		2	D	58 %	B / C
	3	C	35 %	B		3	D	30 %	A
	4	D	36 %	A		4	C	54 %	A / D
	5	A	36 %	B		5	B	31 %	B
Test 5	1	C	16 %	A	Test 14	1	C	39 %	D
	2	D	55 %	C		2	B	18 %	A / C
	3	B	44 %	A		3	B	36 %	A
	4	A	21 %	B		4	D	23 %	B
	5	C	51 %	B		5	D	21 %	B
Test 6	1	D	6 %	A	Test 15	1	C	6 %	A / B
	2	A	7 %	D		2	A	26 %	D
	3	D	17 %	C		3	B	54 %	D
	4	D	29 %	A		4	A	13 %	D
	5	B	15 %	A		5	D	33 %	C
Test 7	1	A	41 %	B	Test 16	1	D	58 %	A
	2	A	64 %	B / D		2	C	33 %	B
	3	D	3 %	C		3	C	16 %	A
	4	B	28 %	C		4	B	14 %	C
	5	B	66 %	C		5	A	66 %	C
Test 8	1	C	8 %	B / D	Test 17	1	D	26 %	B
	2	B	8 %	D		2	B	13 %	A
	3	C	2 %	D		3	D	22 %	A
	4	B	15 %	A		4	B	26 %	A
	5	D	3 %	B / C		5	C	38 %	D
Test 9	1	C	4 %	D	Test 18	1	D	47 %	B
	2	D	32 %	A		2	C	38 %	D
	3	B	9 %	D		3	A	49 %	C
	4	D	13 %	A		4	B	73 %	C
	5	B	48 %	C		5	C	43 %	D

測驗	題號	正確選項	錯誤率	最多人選的錯誤選項	測驗	題號	正確選項	錯誤率	最多人選的錯誤選項
Test 19	1	A	16 %	B	Test 30	1	B	48 %	C
	2	D	27 %	C		2	C	43 %	D
	3	B	49 %	A		3	D	58 %	A
	4	A	44 %	C		4	B	40 %	C
	5	C	28 %	B		5	A	48 %	B
Test 20	1	B	78 %	A	Test 31	1	C	47 %	A
	2	B	27 %	D		2	B	67 %	A
	3	D	28 %	C		3	B	35 %	C
	4	A	27 %	D		4	A	80 %	C
	5	A	30 %	B		5	B	71 %	C
Test 21	1	A	37 %	C	Test 32	1	B	56 %	C
	2	C	16 %	B		2	C	70 %	D
	3	B	43 %	C		3	D	72 %	B / C
	4	D	54 %	C		4	A	79 %	B
	5	A	55 %	C		5	B	46 %	C
Test 22	1	C	50 %	B	Test 33	1	A	27 %	D
	2	C	40 %	B		2	B	41 %	C
	3	B	49 %	C		3	C	38 %	B
	4	D	45 %	B		4	C	49 %	A
	5	B	48 %	C		5	C	46 %	B
Test 23	1	A	10 %	C	Test 34	1	B	50 %	C
	2	D	46 %	A		2	A	41 %	C
	3	D	40 %	C		3	A	55 %	C
	4	B	38 %	C		4	D	44 %	C
	5	D	44 %	A		5	B	44 %	C
Test 24	1	C	44 %	D	Test 35	1	B	33 %	D
	2	A	32 %	C		2	A	44 %	C
	3	D	45 %	B / C		3	D	76 %	C
	4	B	58 %	D		4	D	63 %	C
	5	B	45 %	C		5	C	52 %	B
Test 25	1	C	17 %	A	Test 36	1	B	61 %	C
	2	D	27 %	A		2	C	40 %	D
	3	A	32 %	C		3	D	65 %	B / C
	4	B	43 %	A		4	A	56 %	C / D
	5	D	42 %	C		5	C	37 %	B
Test 26	1	B	36 %	C	Test 37	1	A	51 %	C
	2	C	51 %	D		2	B	59 %	A
	3	D	55 %	B / C		3	B	73 %	C
	4	C	36 %	B		4	C	60 %	A / B
	5	D	62 %	C		5	B	66 %	C
Test 27	1	C	26 %	B	Test 38	1	D	64 %	C
	2	B	50 %	C		2	A	39 %	C
	3	D	44 %	B		3	B	63 %	C
	4	A	63 %	B / D		4	C	39 %	B
	5	D	33 %	A		5	A	78 %	C
Test 28	1	D	54 %	C	Test 39	1	A	54 %	B
	2	C	35 %	B		2	B	43 %	C
	3	C	46 %	B		3	D	57 %	C
	4	D	24 %	C		4	B	60 %	C
	5	B	45 %	C		5	C	64 %	A
Test 29	1	C	75 %	D	Test 40	1	A	58 %	C
	2	B	79 %	D		2	B	70 %	C / D
	3	C	32 %	B		3	D	76 %	C
	4	D	55 %	B		4	D	70 %	B / C
	5	A	51 %	C		5	C	59 %	B

心得筆記欄

劉毅英文家教班成績優異同學獎學金排行榜

姓　名	學　　校	總金額
賴宣佑	成淵高中	148050
王　千	中和高中	91400
翁一銘	中正高中	79350
呂芝瑩	內湖高中	52850
吳宥僉	縣中山國中	50300
楊玄詳	建國中學	41400
謝家綺	板橋高中	39000
趙啓鈞	松山高中	34450
丁哲沛	成功高中	34250
陳學脩	再興高中	34100
王芊蓁	北一女中	33650
袁好蓁	武陵高中	32750
吳書軒	成功高中	30600
蔡佳容	北一女中	30450
蔡佳恩	建國中學	28500
許晏魁	竹林高中	28350
徐柏庭	延平高中	28200
呂佾蓁	南湖高中	27850
何宇屏	輔仁大學	27400
王挺之	建國中學	27100
林祐瑋	耕莘護專	27050
黃宋覺	北一女中	26550
張祐寧	建國中學	26000
黃靖淳	師大附中	25450
蕭允惟	景美女中	25300
黃筱雅	北一女中	25000
趙祥安	新店高中	24600
許嘉容	北　市　商	24400
羅之勵	大直高中	23800
練冠霆	板橋高中	23400
王廷鎧	建國中學	23300
楊于萱	新莊高中	23200
盧　安	成淵高中	22300
李佳珈	新莊高中	22300
董澤元	再興高中	21800
許瑋峻	延平高中	21700
陳婕華	大理高中	21100
王裕琁	成淵高中	21100
張祐銘	延平高中	20950
蔡欣伶	新店高中	20500
陳冠揚	南湖高中	20400
林悅婷	北一女中	19400
吳灃晉	中正高中	18900
蘇芳萱	大同高中	18500
郭學豪	和平高中	18500
許瓊方	北一女中	18300
林侑緯	建國中學	17800
林述君	松山高中	17550
郭子瑄	新店高中	17200
陳柏諺	師大附中	17000

姓　名	學　　校	總金額
張宛茹	基隆女中	17000
林政瑋	板橋高中	16600
郭　權	建國中學	16600
林學典	格致高中	16500
張雅婷	海山高中	16250
蔡欣儒	百齡高中	16200
洪子晴	大同高中	16100
林怡廷	景美女中	15900
秦嘉欣	華僑高中	15800
潘羽薇	丹鳳高中	15600
邱瀞蕙	縣格致中學	15600
劉裕心	中和高中	15550
施衍廷	成功高中	15500
李品萱	松山家商	15500
陳品文	建國中學	15000
蘇柏中	師大附中	15000
許弘儒	成功高中	14700
季怡李	和平高中	14600
周欣穎	國三重高中	14400
劉詩玟	北一女中	14300
楊姿芳	成淵高中	14100
劉秀慧	進　修　生	14100
林姿妤	丹鳳高中	13900
林書卉	薇閣高中	13900
劉若盈	松山家商	13600
王雯琦	政大附中	13600
方冠予	北一女中	13500
曹　傑	松山高中	13250
陳瑾慧	北一女中	13200
林政穎	中崙高中	13100
黃小榕	中崙高中	13000
洪采媚	北一女中	12900
蔡瑄庭	南湖高中	12500
粘書耀	師大附中	12500
劉婷婷	板橋高中	12400
宋才聞	成功高中	12300
張馥雅	北一女中	12100
邱馨荷	市中山國中	12000
吳凱恩	復旦高中	12000
鄭　晴	北一女中	11700
陳　昕	麗山高中	11700
蔡承紜	復興高中	11650
范詠琪	中山女中	11600
何俊毅	師大附中	11600
盧昱瑋	格致高中	11550
陳書毅	成功高中	11400
林　佾	林口高中	11400
劉俐妤	中山女中	11300
黃鈺雯	永春高中	11200
劉仁誠	建國中學	11200

姓　名	學　　校	總金額
陳聖妮	中山女中	11100
呂濬瑋	成功高中	11100
劉苡琳	板橋高中	11100
陳瑾瑜	中平國中	11000
蔡岳峰	長安國中	11000
應奇穎	建國中學	10900
賴品臻	明倫高中	10700
謝承孝	大同高中	10600
柯博軒	成功高中	10500
黃浩銓	建國中學	10500
司徒皓平	建國中學	10300
吳思慧	景美女中	10300
呂家榮	陽明高中	10150
陳貞穎	中山女中	10000
李之琳	永春國小	10000
李欣蓉	格致高中	10000
孔爲亮	龍山國中	10000
李宸馨	北一女中	9700
陳怡靜	北一女中	9700
廖彥綸	師大附中	9700
羅映婷	內壢高中	9600
陳亭如	北一女中	9600
黃盟凱	國三重高中	9600
林瑞軒	基隆高中	9600
王簡群	華江高中	9550
簡士益	格致高中	9500
鄭涴心	板橋高中	9400
廖芃軒	武陵高中	9400
劉良逸	台中一中	9300
黃建發	永平高中	9300
黃靖儒	建國中學	9300
劉哲銘	建國中學	9250
陳冠儒	大同高中	9200
蘇倍陞	板橋高中	9200
吳柏諭	裕民國小	9150
林怡瑄	大同高中	9100
阮鎂儒	北一女中	9100
徐浩倫	成功高中	9100
劉禹廷	板橋高中	9100
徐健智	松山高中	9100
邱雅蘋	聖心女中	9100
曹家榕	大同高中	9000
藍珮瑜	北一女中	9000
胡家瑋	桃園國中	9000
陳宣蓉	中山女中	8800
潘育誠	成功高中	8800
黃新雅	松山高中	8600
何宜臻	板橋高中	8500
蔣詩媛	華僑高中	8400
劉妍君	新店高中	8400

姓名	學校	總金額	姓名	學校	總金額	姓名	學校	總金額
李宜蓁	中正高中	8300	胡勝彥	進修生	6700	鄭朵晴	大同高中	5600
李奕儒	成淵高中	8300	柯賢鴻	松山高中	6700	蔡承紜	景美女中	5600
施柏廷	明倫高中	8300	黃誼珊	華江高中	6700	林廷豫	台中一中	5500
吳冠穎	建國中學	8300	吳沛璉	靜修女中	6700	王子銘	縣三重高中	5500
林承慶	建國中學	8300	張君如	東山高中	6650	劉文心	中山女中	5400
許瓊中	北一女中	8200	鍾凡雅	中山女中	6600	林原道	和平高中	5400
徐子瑤	松山高中	8200	曹姿儀	南港高中	6600	洪子茜	明倫高中	5400
侯軒宇	建國中學	8200	羅友良	建國中學	6600	蔡佳原	松山高中	5400
王郁文	成功高中	8100	袁紹禾	陽明高中	6600	徐詩婷	松山高中	5400
王秉立	板橋高中	8000	俞雅文	市三重高中	6500	董芳秀	景美女中	5400
黃曉嵐	北一女中	7900	何允中	師大附中	6500	黃偉嘉	育成高中	5350
劉　怡	再興高中	7800	黃盛群	師大附中	6500	張育絹	大直高中	5300
朱微茵	松山高中	7800	李宛芸	北一女中	6400	李安晴	北一女中	5300
謝竣宇	建國中學	7800	張繼元	華江高中	6400	張家瑜	北一女中	5300
楊沐焓	師大附中	7750	林建宏	成功高中	6300	吳宇霖	海山高中	5300
韋　謙	北一女中	7700	宮宇辰	延平高中	6300	許家銘	大同高中	5200
蘇紀如	北一女中	7700	林冠宏	林口高中	6300	洪詩淵	中山女中	5200
吳念馨	永平高中	7700	吳鈞季	建國中學	6300	曾昱欣	中山女中	5200
李承祐	成功高中	7700	蕭宏任	桃園高中	6300	江　方	中山女中	5200
高維均	麗山高中	7700	陳杏仔	北一女中	6200	張瀚陽	成功高中	5200
俞欣妍	大直高中	7600	黃晟豪	建國中學	6200	楊承恩	東山高中	5200
鄭懿珊	北一女中	7600	洪坤志	建國中學	6200	陳庭偉	板橋高中	5200
蔡得仁	師大附中	7600	林鼎傑	建國中學	6200	謝岦錦	師大附中	5200
謝富承	內湖高中	7500	胡博恩	大同高中	6100	蘇瑢瑄	景美女中	5200
劉唯翎	台北商專	7500	江婉盈	中山女中	6100	王殊雅	育成高中	5150
鄒佳融	板橋高中	7500	林柳含	台中二中	6100	黃品臻	中山女中	5100
林好靜	格致高中	7500	蔡佳馨	南湖高中	6100	陳羿瑋	松山高中	5100
曾令棋	建國中學	7400	黃捷筠	華江高中	6100	胡郁唯	金陵女中	5100
張庭維	建國中學	7400	許芮寧	景美女中	6050	陳冠達	建國中學	5100
徐佑昀	中山女中	7300	李承芳	中山女中	6000	謝佳勳	師大附中	5100
廖彥筑	北一女中	7300	黃翊宣	北一女中	6000	王　婷	華僑高中	5100
樂語安	基隆女中	7300	陳　蓁	北一女中	6000	林姿妤	三民高中	5000
吳其錡	北一女中	7200	巫知毅	板橋高中	6000	盧姿妤	大安高中	5000
郭恒志	台中一中	7200	黃博揚	建國中學	6000	葉昭宏	大直高中	5000
楊唯駿	成功高中	7200	廖冠豪	建國中學	6000	張文怡	中和高中	5000
張馨馨	板橋高中	7200	廖鴻宇	建國中學	6000	林宣含	北一女中	5000
陳冠廷	薇閣國小	7150	邱婷君	新明國中	6000	許家毓	金陵女中	5000
林育妏	中山女中	7100	張祐誠	丹鳳國中	5900	李宗穎	長安國中	5000
黃恩慈	基隆女中	7100	施宛柔	木柵高工	5900	陳韋綸	建國中學	5000
司鴻軒	華江高中	7100	吳佩蓉	板橋高中	5900	陳忠鵬	建國中學	5000
任達偉	成功高中	7000	蔡湘芸	松山高中	5900	簡君恬	師大附中	5000
闕銘萱	南港國中	7000	陳得翰	祐德高中	5900	傅鈞澤	師大附中	5000
方奕中	建國中學	7000	張筑珺	中山女中	5800	施凱珉	松山工農	4900
潘威霖	建國中學	7000	黃　馨	中山女中	5800	李怡臻	格致高中	4900
陳志銘	麗山高中	7000	郭士榮	松山高中	5800	徐　偉	松山高中	4800
王辰嘉	北一女中	6800	沈　怡	金華國中	5800	鄭群耀	建國中學	4800
古宸魁	建國中學	6800	林承瀚	建國中學	5800	張長蓉	薇閣高中	4800
李卓穎	師大附中	6800	馬崇恩	成功高中	5700	謝怡彤	中山女中	4700
羅培勳	新店高中	6800	盧奕璇	松山高中	5700	許瑞庭	內湖高中	4700
許桓瑋	新莊高中	6800	邱弘裕	建國中學	5700	李柏霆	明倫高中	4700
何子鋐	台中一中	6700	廖崇鈞	大同高中	5600	林宇嫺	板橋高中	4700

※ 因版面有限，尚有領取高額獎學金同學，無法列出。

本書製作過程

　　本書之所以完成，是一個團隊的力量。全書由王淑平小姐擔任總指揮，由陳威如老師、謝靜芳老師、蔡琇瑩老師、林銀姿老師、張碧紋老師、陳子璇老師協助解題，美籍老師 Laura E. Stewart 校對，黃淑貞小姐負責排版，白雪嬌小姐設計封面，以及蔡宗勳先生協助校對音標，非常感謝他們辛苦的付出。

高三英文閱讀測驗

主　　　編 / 劉　毅

發　行　所 / 學習出版有限公司　　☎ (02) 2704-5525

郵　撥　帳　號 / 05127272 學習出版社帳戶

登　記　證 / 局版台業 2179 號

印　刷　所 / 裕強彩色印刷有限公司

台　北　門　市 / 台北市許昌街 10 號 2 F　　☎ (02) 2331-4060

台灣總經銷 / 紅螞蟻圖書有限公司　　☎ (02) 2795-3656

美國總經銷 / Evergreen Book Store　　☎ (818) 2813622

本公司網址　www.learnbook.com.tw

電　子　郵　件　learnbook@learnbook.com.tw

售價：新台幣一百八十元正

2014 年 11 月 1 日新修訂

ISBN 957-519-819-0